THE DILEMMA OF A DEAD SCHOLAR

GRAVESYDE PRIORY MYSTERY, #6

PATRICIA RICE

PLEASE JOIN MY READER LIST

Please consider joining my newsletter for exclusive content and news of upcoming releases. Be the first to know about special sales, freebies, stories from my writer life, and other fun information. You'll even receive a thank-you gift. Join me on my writing adventures!

To Join, Please Visit —
https://www.subscribepage.com/ricehr

AUTHOR'S NOTE

The Gravesyde Priory Mystery novels can stand on their own, but it's a little more fun to start at the beginning to see how the family comes together and grows and to watch the village and manor spring to life again over the length of the series.

For those who enjoy following the manor's growing family relationships, there is a partial of the earl's family tree on my website, https://patriciarice.com/wycliffe-family-tree-2/

For those of you who have difficulty remembering names (as I do), a character list follows, along with a brief history of Wycliffe Manor. A description of the manor is at the end of the book.

For the grammarians among you, I have chosen to modernize the spelling of "blond/blonde" because I can. Unfortunately, I cannot single-handedly eliminate the idiocy of lie/lay. I must hand that to future generations. . .

THE HISTORY OF WYCLIFFE MANOR

Wycliffe Manor is the ancestral home of the Earls of Wycliffe, built on the remains of Gravesyde Priory, for which the village is named. In the way of medieval fiefdoms, the earls resisted district boundary changes so the estate, in 1815, is an exclave of Shropshire, although south of Birmingham and surrounded by Worcestershire, creating legal havoc when it comes to crime.

The fourth earl, George Reid, lost his only son, and with no male heir apparent, arranged to distribute his wealth and all other estates to his female relations upon his death in 1781. His son's widow, Lady Gabrielle Reid, had a life interest in Wycliffe Manor and lived there until she died in 1801.

The fun begins when the trustees of the last earl's estate attempt to dispose of the manor after the viscountess's death. Since the earl left his worldly goods to ALL his relations, the manor now belongs in equal parts to every Reid descendant, including that of his siblings and a growing family he never knew.

Except this is the turn of the nineteenth century and the male trustees are reluctant to turn over a substantial estate to females, bless their feathery little heads. They insist on a male to accept the inheritance and the responsibility, and the only one they can find is an American Army officer, Captain Alastair Reid Huntley. Family legend says he is a descendant of Lady Reid's affair with a French count, but the marriage lines and birth are appropriately recorded.

By the time these legalities are decided, however, Captain Huntley is busy fighting the British, and it takes two more years of war and recuperation from serious injuries before he agrees to sail to England.

Amidst all the legal squabbling, the manor has been abandoned to a pair of elderly caretakers for nearly fifteen years. The earl left a legacy for maintaining the manor, so important repairs were made, but bats will play while the master's away.

And so our story begins in 1815, in *The Secrets of Wycliffe Manor*, with the arrival of Captain Huntley. As the heirs gradually return to their ancestral home, they discover unresolved mysteries and stir up new ones. Fortunately, the eccentric Reid family enjoys a good puzzle.

CHARACTERS

FAMILY and FRIENDS

George Reid, Fourth Earl of Wycliffe— *deceased*, last Reid earl

Captain Alistair (Hunt) Huntley— US Army engineer; great-grandson of earl

Clarissa (Clare) Huntley— wife of Hunt; great-granddaughter of earl

Oliver Knightley Owen— Clare's seven-year-old nephew

Arnaud Lavigne— Hunt's artist cousin, former French comte

Henri Lavigne— Arnaud's younger brother, tavern owner, peddler

Lady Elsa Villiers de Sackville— manor cook, great-granddaughter of earl

Honorable John (Jack) de Sackville— former soldier, son of Baron de Sackville

Benedict Bosworth Jr. — banker; the earl's illegitimate grandson

Lady Lavinia Marlowe— dowager baroness, earl's daughter

Lavender Marlowe— seamstress; illegitimate granddaughter of Lady Lavinia

Elaine, Lady Spalding— earl's granddaughter; Hunt's aunt

Marquess of Spalding— stepson of Lady Spalding

Dorothea (Thea) Reid Talbot— granddaughter of earl's brother

Davy Talbot— Thea's 8-year old brother

Frances Huntley— Hunt's mother; Lady Spalding's sister

Sofia Lavigne— cousin of Arnaud and Henri

Daniel Walker— Hunt's friend, steward; Meera's husband

Meera Abrams Walker— physician/apothecary; Clare's best friend

Paul Daniel Upton— curate

Henrietta (Nettie) Upton— curate's stepmother; housekeeper; Reid cousin
Patience Upton— Nettie's daughter and curate's stepsister; gardener
Minerva Peniston— great-granddaughter of earl's youngest sister

OTHERS

Arch, Reverend— vicar; Paul Upton's employer
Birdwhistle, Terrence — tutor
Boston, Professor Jeremiah— dead scholar
Cooper, Franklin— Jeremiah's eldest grandson; math teacher
Cooper, Timothy Boston— Jeremiah's grandson, steward
Eleanor— new maid
Ephraim, Abraham— magistrate
Finkley— Boston's drunken neighbor
Hanks, Herbert— new footman
Talbott, Neville— Dorothea's paternal cousin

ONE

ARNAUD: MONDAY MORNING

July 3, 1815

"You know they abandoned us on purpose."

Out of habit, Arnaud Lavigne ignored the inane mutterings of the dainty, fairy-blond heiress crouched at his feet, studying the ancient oil paintings he had taken down to clean.

Dorothea Talbot was as mad as the rest of her Reid family. Generally, she was *quietly* mad and hid with the elderly aunts. Today, for reasons unknown, she had chosen to work in this medieval, two-story foyer already crowded with two restless boys, their tutor, and Lavender, a seventeen-year-old Circe in the making.

Under the tutelage of their teacher, the boys measured the painting frames, matching them to squares of oak molding on the paneling in some ridiculous belief that they'd find hidden treasure. Unfortunately, the two-story walls held a sizable collection of ancient portraits and incredibly bad landscapes. Measuring would take time.

The small space also held Arnaud's ladder and his not-so-dainty self as he attempted to cover a hole in the arched transom above the massive, carved oak doors.

Perhaps Dotty Dottie lingered to chaperone Lavender and not just to annoy him. The heiress never smiled, but then, neither did he.

Although he couldn't help noticing that everyone except Miss Talbot was covered in cobwebs and centuries of filth from the ancient frames. Meticulously groomed, a single curl dangling on either side of her heart-shaped face, the lady hadn't allowed a speck of dust to besmirch her beribboned muslin. Heiresses apparently lived in protective bubbles.

Having spent the war years living in prison cells and poverty, Arnaud gave no consideration to keeping the remains of his wardrobe rags clean. He simply wore a painter's smock over his shabby linen and waistcoat. He never wore a coat under it. He needed room to move—and his old coats no longer fit properly.

Also an eccentric Reid, this one from the wrong side of the blanket, adolescent Lavender shrugged at the heiress's declaration of abandonment. "Cousin Clare is tired of being the responsible one. She thinks we all need to learn to be adults."

Arnaud was fairly certain that was not why both sets of newlyweds had run off to the city or wherever they'd taken themselves. Privacy was in hard supply at Wycliffe Manor—as the gathering in the vestibule proved.

Lavender and the tutor seemed to be taking advantage of the removed paintings to teach the boys how to graph the measurements onto paper. Arnaud had no idea why and refused to ask.

He had learned the painfully hard way to keep his lips shut and his opinions to himself. It wasn't as if his audience listened to him. As the descendants of the last earl of Wycliffe, the Reids blithely went their own way, seemingly without care to consequences. Frenchmen who sponged off their largesse deserved to be ignored.

"We *are* adults," the tutor said placidly. Barely out of university, Mr. Birdwhistle endured the oddities of his two young students with a great deal of patience for a young man in the presence of two rather extraordinarily lovely women.

And therein lay Arnaud's current difficulty. . . His mistress of the past year had decided to marry and move to the city. Deprivation apparently led to depravity, and he couldn't avoid awareness of feminine scents and soft curves. He was a painter. He observed.

In prison, he'd been deprived of food and women. After escaping to his great-aunt's abandoned manor, he'd survived in a state of insensibility, painting madly so he need not feel the loss of everything he once knew. But over these past months since the manor had filled with life, laughter—and food—he'd gradually emerged from his former state of semi-consciousness. Regrettably, returning to life meant suffering the pain of knowing he had decades ahead of him and no foreseeable means of carving out a future.

He'd just signed away his last claim to his estate and title—for good purpose, admittedly. Only now, without his home, his Parisian art world, or any goal, he felt like a dog trapped in a hole he'd dug.

Despite a manor filled with feminine resplendence, bedding the mad descendants of an earl was not an option. He'd learned the hard way that pragmatism was necessary for survival. So he puttered, mending what should have been left to crumble because he shared the manor with an aristocratic family who had as little purpose as he.

The ladder he stood on was precarious at best. If he fell, he'd crush women and children. Cautiously, he fit the arched oilcloth into the window frame. He could nail this end. The one in the middle of the window. . . He grimaced. He was large, but even his arms didn't extend that far.

"That won't work," Miss Talbot informed him. "You should ask the curate if he has a ladder. It will take two people to hold it in place."

He knew he wasn't a handyman, but he had wanted to be useful. Asking for help only created more work for others.

Arnaud rolled up the cloth. "I just wanted to see if it would fit. Perhaps when you're done playing in here, there will be room for two ladders."

"He speaks!" The heiress raised her golden arched eyebrows. "We are not playing. I am convinced each of these paintings fits a specific panel but they've been scrambled. There is no other reason for the irregularity of molding sizes. Oliver, show Mr. Lavigne your calculations."

The youngest boy silently held out a sheet of numbers.

Arnaud climbed down to study it. He was an artist, not a mathematician. But a seven-year-old's calculations were basic enough. "Each panel is a different size?"

He glanced up at the elaborate case moldings adorning the two-story oak paneled wall dividing the foyer from the main manor. The molding formed irregular blocks on the walls that, admittedly, resembled frames. "Are you measuring the portrait frames or the canvas inside the frames?"

Davy—Miss Talbot's eight-year-old brother—picked up one of the smaller oils and set it into one of the lower panels. It appeared to be an exact fit.

Enlightenment. One of the mad earl's letters had mentioned a lady's portrait in the vestibule as key to finding. . . whatever in hell he'd hidden. That had been the reason for removing the hideous paintings in the first place. No key had been found.

"You are hoping to prove that you are adults by finding *jewels*?" Arnaud couldn't conceal his incredulity.

He might not have been so skeptical if he hadn't been hungry. Since the manor's cook, Lady Elsa, the new Mrs. de Sackville, had departed on her delayed honeymoon, their meals had deteriorated, not improving Arnaud's mood.

"It's a theory," adolescent Lavender said proudly. "Thea says not all the paintings we took down belong in here. We are looking for the ones that fit."

"Tay-uh?" He'd worked it out before Lavender explained.

"Doro-*tay-uh*." Lavender glared a warning at him. "No one wishes to be called Dotty Dottie."

The delicate lady snorted. . . delicately.

He was French. She was English. He didn't think either language encompassed that pronunciation with that spelling, but what did he know? He was only an uneducated ex-comte and ex-artist. He regarded her warily. "You prefer Tay-uh? Not Thee-uh?"

"Not Dotty," she said curtly.

Fine then. Informality and eccentricity reigned in Wycliffe Manor.

He returned to studying the ancient oak paneling. As far as he was concerned, the vestibule had been an arcade of appalling English work that had only been improved by removing the paintings. He'd mostly ignored the pieces in here in favor of the more professional family portraits in the ballroom and loft, the ones concealing codes, presumably to hidden treasure. But after they'd discovered one of the mad earl's letters claiming a vestibule portrait held a clue, along with a cryptic message of diamonds in squares, Arnaud had been examining every painting in the manor. Given the centuries of bad art on the immense walls, that might take a lifetime.

So far, no more clues had been uncovered. He'd learned that one piece had been painted over, but removing the poor concealment had only revealed an equally bad original. He assumed some ancestor had taken up art and couldn't afford new canvas.

"You believe that wishful thinking is useful and proof that you are an adult?" Arnaud felt horribly old next to these naïfs. He was just on the fair side of thirty, but he'd seen more in his lifetime than people who lived to be a hundred.

That didn't mean he knew much. It wasn't as if war and revolution and prison taught more than how to survive.

Dotty—*Thea*—dusted her slender fingers on a lacy handkerchief and regarded him as if he'd just grown antlers. "You have a better suggestion? If we found the jewels, we could hire an adequate household staff and someone to actually glaze that glass you're covering."

"That is centuries-old leaded glass. Replacing it would require a master craftsman. The oilcloth will keep out bats until we find a buyer for the medieval manuscripts. We do not need jewels." He took down his ladder but couldn't easily maneuver it around the crowd.

They'd paid the manor's annual mortgage with the sale of rare books from the library, with money to spare. They might be living in decrepitude, but they were no longer desperate to keep the roof over their heads.

Fair-haired Oliver intelligently scrambled up on the backward-facing lion statue to get out of the ladder's way.

Arnaud thought the statue was probably a priceless Chinese antique and ought to be one of a pair, but the boy had no eye for art. Oliver was now studying the transom from his loftier position.

Leaning against the base of the lion, Davy pulled a sweet from his pocket and popped it into his mouth. He didn't speak any more than Oliver did, but the tutor apparently understood them. Mr. Birdwhistle didn't admonish them for neglecting the problem he'd set them but continued his measuring.

Arnaud feared he didn't belong at Wycliffe any longer. He'd had some incentive to stay when they'd desperately sought more codes for the apparently mythical jewels. But now that the library was providing extra funds, he needed to find his own path, not hang around, waiting for life to find him.

He might as well hunt imaginary jewels.

Before he could set down the ladder and open the front door—which none of the addle-pated Reids thought to do—the interior door swung open and his brother, Henri, popped through.

"Hunt and Clare have sent a cart and carriage full of fabrics and furniture," his brother crowed. "Play time, ladies!"

"Fabric?" Lavender stood and dusted herself off. "In the sewing room?"

"Unloading as we speak." Henri stepped aside.

She lifted her hem and dashed past him. Seventeen-year-old Lavender loved fashion, had learned to design her own clothes, and now designed for others. Even a child had more purpose than Arnaud.

"Carriage?" Arnaud asked warily. "Whose?"

"Ours, apparently." Henri beamed. "The auction of ancient tomes has made our newlyweds giddy, and they have acquired a carriage from Lady Spalding. The carriage is not new, by any means. I daresay parsimonious Hunt and the marchioness came to a mutually suitable arrangement. And I imagine Jack bought the horses for his breeding stable. They're fine specimens."

"If only they had sent more experienced maids and a footman or two. . ." Dotty Thea returned to sorting paintings by size.

Says the heiress who could have hired half the village with her fortune. . . Arnaud did not speak his bitter thought aloud. He'd once had estates and servants of his own. Wealth was not always the source of good sense.

"Are we to have a bonfire for the old furniture?" he asked, maneuvering the ladder through the doorway. "Or do we stack the new in the corridor until Clare directs its placement?"

"Don't you dare burn those old pieces!" the heiress cried. "They have stories to tell."

"And there she goes," Arnaud muttered.

His brother laughed at his disgust and took the other end of the ladder. "Do we sit by the fire tonight and listen to the faded sofas speak?"

"Laugh, if you must, but without the spirit of the late Lady Reid, you would not have caught those killers. You simply won't admit it." Dotty—Thea lifted the ruffled hem of her morning gown, revealing dainty slippers, and sailed past them.

The heiress's odd ability to find passages in the former viscountess's journals had allowed the manor inhabitant's to catch a demented killer, saving the book auction—with the help of a lot of other people.

"You read Lady Reid's journals and provided history." Arnaud followed, carrying his ladder toward the gallery. "The sofa does not speak."

"I read her agitation, and that *tower* speaks." Thea pointed at the front corner of the manor. "Has anyone ever found a way in? There could be catacombs or an ossuary in there, given the number of deaths this place attracts. The village is not called Gravesyde Priory for naught."

Arnaud winced. He had pondered the tower mystery for years. As a youth visiting his great-aunt's home, he'd been too busy to look into the one inaccessible, presumably empty, ornamental tower. Since his escape from France, he hadn't wanted to ever encounter another closed, dark prison.

He doubted he'd find jewels in the crumbling structure. But the manor contained many towers. Why had only one been sealed off?

TWO

THEA: MONDAY MORNING

T<small>HEA</small> <small>KNEW SHE REALLY SHOULDN'T HAVE MENTIONED THE GHOSTS HAUNTING HER.</small>
She hid behind decorum for a reason. Men exploited any sign of weakness.

But honestly, the scruffy Comte Arnaud Lavigne was entirely too toplofty. For
a man who resembled a disheveled vagrant, he was in no position to tell anyone
else what to do. Just because his stubbly, carved jaw, worldly air, broad chest and
shoulders, and. . . sigh. She shouldn't notice his physique—but he never
concealed it as a gentleman should.

Men weren't to be trusted for more than muscle power anyway. Dismissing
the distracting *former* count and his unjustified superiority, Thea turned her
admiration to the graceful curvature of the carved mahogany legs on the sofa
and loveseat that Cousin Clare had sent. Surely the bride intended it for the
parlor, the most used common room in the manor. Although really, the informal,
family withdrawing room would be far more comfortable in the evenings, and
more convenient for the staff, if only it weren't buried in cast-offs.

With Lt. de Sackville and Captain Huntley on their wedding trips, however,
she'd have to rely on the two Frenchmen for moving furniture about. Adam,
their one footman, might help, if he wasn't busy. Their butler was far too dignified, and old, to be pushing about chairs. She despised asking for help.

But clearly, it needed to be done. The manor begged to be refurbished, and
she had a talent for decoration. She had already conceived a plan for arranging
the public rooms for comfort and elegance. Did she dare be so presumptuous as

to act on it? Her parents never listened but the aunts who had taken refuge in the manor appreciated her suggestions.

If she was to prove herself useful. . . which she really should, if she didn't want to become a feeble-minded barnacle on the home that had welcomed her. . . she needed to act with a modicum of authority. After all, the manor belonged to her as much as anyone else.

The alternative might be to sit in boredom with the aunts. She might be an heiress, but until she married, she had only her meager allowance and couldn't afford rent. Since she never intended to marry, she needed another means of ensuring her little brother's safety. Her parents were too oblivious to provide it.

Quincy, their massive, balding butler approached her, no expression marring his stiff demeanor. Thea knew the aunts had their own homes and had abdicated any position of authority here. She supposed, without Clare or Lady Elsa present, that left her as the next best thing to mistress of the manor. Having always lived in her parents' homes, she'd never been mistress of anything. Perhaps this was what Clare had meant when she'd said they needed to learn to be adults. Thea tried to look intelligent, knowledgeable, and in charge.

"An applicant for the position of footman has arrived," Quincy intoned. "Mrs. Upton asks if you wish to interview him."

Oh, my. *Interview*? She'd never hired a servant. She had no notion if the manor had a budget for more. But they desperately needed another footman. Young Adam couldn't be everywhere at once.

And if she had an extra pair of hands. . . perhaps her allowance might stretch to cover a servant's pay, if Hunt objected to the expense? Or perhaps Clare and Hunt had sent him? That was a happy thought.

"Might Mrs. Upton bring him up and we can interview him together?" she asked, not sounding as authoritative as she would have liked.

Mrs. Upton was another member of the family, one who preferred the role of housekeeper since she'd been that for her adoptive father and husband all her life. Thea respected the widow's good sense. If she could have chosen her mother, she would have far preferred the plump, unfashionable Mrs. Upton to her own.

Quincy nodded, she hoped, in approval. "In the study?"

"Clare's office, please." It had windows, and chairs suited for ladies.

She stopped by the library to see if Minerva might be present. The latest addition to the manor family was generally buried in books or out visiting the village with the curate. Her cousin glanced up from repairing a book spine when Thea looked in.

"Mrs. Upton is to interview a new footman. Would you care to join us?"

Her dark blond hair pulled up in a nest of straggling pins, Minerva blinked from her work before registering the question. "A footman? As long as he has a strong back and shoulders, what more can we ask? It's not as if I have ever employed a footman."

Minerva had grown up with brothers and following the army and barely knew housekeeping. Thea conceded the point. "I shall measure his shoulders, shall I?"

She didn't think any servant would have shoulders as broad as Arnaud's, even though one could practically see his rib cage through his thin linen. She needed to quit looking.

A trifle anxious at finally being treated as more than an empty-headed doll, she continued down the central corridor to the small study at the rear of the manor, where her cousin Clare had established her own hideaway. Since Clare had been first of the family, besides Hunt, to gather the courage to live on the abandoned estate, she had taken over the sensible running of the household. More experienced in dealing with domestics, the new Mrs. Huntley had every right to establish her own domain.

Thea was fairly certain Clare would not mind sharing her office in the interest of employing servants.

Out of curiosity, she opened the desk drawer where Clare kept a locked box of papers she was always writing on. The box was empty and unlocked. Oh well.

Thea had cleared off the desk, returned books to shelves, and dusted the inkstand by the time Mrs. Upton bustled in, leading a sallow young man of average height—and shoulders. Footmen were normally hired for their looks and height. No wonder this poor man had been reduced to applying for a position in the decrepit, isolated manor.

"Herbert Hanks, Miss Talbot." Mrs. Upton took a chair near the bookcase, folded her hands in her lap, and left the talking to Thea.

Oh, my. Now what? She twisted Clare's pencil and tried not to study the servant's narrow face and bent nose. "Do you live nearby?" was all she knew to ask. Surrounded by empty fields and sheep-inhabited hills, rural Wycliffe Manor was in the middle of nothing, on the road to nowhere. Servants did not generally knock on their door.

Mr. Hanks nodded eagerly, his unattractive, reddish-brown brown hair falling into his face. "Me old mum's here. I thought to be closer, to help out now and again, y'know? She told me you be needing help."

"Commendable." Thea turned to Mrs. Upton. "Does he have references?"

The housekeeper removed a paper from her apron pocket. "I don't know the family."

9

Given her mother's sociable propensities, Thea at least knew *of* every family with any claim to society. She couldn't say she knew the Harrisons who signed the letter, but then, she could tell by his speech that Mr. Hanks didn't frequent the better homes. "And why did you choose to leave your last position?"

"Me old mum, as I told ye. Me dad died, and I 'ad to come 'ome. I'm strong. I can run fast. I'll be an asset to yer establishment." He looked puppy-dog eager.

Thea turned to Mrs. Upton. "Would you like to describe the position? Should we call in Mr. Quincy?"

"We've already discussed what we need," she replied with calm dignity. Formerly an impoverished curate's wife, she'd never hired servants either. "We need a strong young man, someone willing to fetch and carry, upstairs and down. We're too understaffed to consider any chore beneath us."

"I can do that, mum. I did that afore. Even carried the slops when the maids quit." He beamed happily.

Thea exchanged a look with Mrs. Upton, then tried to maintain a solemn air of authority as she turned back to the young man. Well, not so young. He might be slightly older than she. "Adam will show you to your room, Mr. Hanks. Report to Quincy when you've settled in. He'll give you the rules of the house and discuss your wages. Welcome to Wycliffe Manor."

Mrs. Upton winked at her and sailed out, leading their hapless new footman away.

Before Thea could depart to examine the cluttered withdrawing room, Quincy arrived with a packet of letters, delivering them just as if this were her office. She'd never particularly aspired to presiding over an office and desk, but being treated as more than a doll to move about at will was a new experience she could appreciate.

Ignoring the letters from family, she tore open the seal on the one from her solicitor. She was, after all, twenty-two and capable of taking care of her own affairs.

The solicitor's letter differed in opinion.

Scowling, she crumpled it and tossed it into a wastebasket to use for kindling. She ought to do the same with her family's letters, but a lifetime of habit was hard to break.

She read her father's command first. It hadn't changed.

"Davy is *not* a simpleton!" she shouted at the walls, shredding the letter and winging the pieces at the door—just missing the man entering.

The scruffy artist bowed, causing his overlong chestnut hair to fall across his broad brow. "I heard screams? Did you require rescue?"

She refused to cry. At times like this, when she was upset, spirits battered at her defenses, and she feared she'd succumb to the vapors, as she so often did. This right noble arse would probably let her fall and crack open her head.

Freezing her expression, she waved dismissively. "I apologize. I was indulging in a tantrum. If you'll excuse me, I shall go kick. . . I don't know. What does one kick in a tantrum?"

He wrinkled his brow as if actually considering the absurd question. "I have tried trees. I do not recommend it without sturdy boots."

"Of course." She stood and examined her cloth slippers, steadying her spinning head. "I shall find a cushion to kick. You are quite right."

Awkwardly, he gestured at her letter with his big hands. The left one was missing a pinkie finger. "I am not Hunt, but might the family help in some manner?"

Such an offer had to be difficult for the unsociable artist. She shouldn't be rude.

"Tearing out my father's throat, perhaps?" she suggested in her best airy manner, the one she used in ballrooms to disguise her desire to kill or be killed. "Best not to think that, I presume. Our ghosts might attempt to oblige."

He raised his thick dark eyebrows into points. "If he deserves killing, perhaps more legal means can be found?"

"No court in the world would stop him." The urge to sob caught in her throat. "No, I cannot concern you with our family drama. If you will let me pass, please."

Clutching her remaining letter, she waited for him to do as asked. A gentleman would.

Skeleton-man was no gentleman. He scooped up the fragments she'd flung and smoothed them enough to read her father's letterhead. "I am French, *vous comprenez*? I do not know your society so well as I should. But I did not think the English so rebellious as us. You defy your father's wishes?"

She choked on bile and sobs and had she been a man, she might have punched him. She'd probably fall on her face if she tried. "Let me by, please."

She wasn't a man, but she'd been raised as a proper lady, which was worse. She could not exhibit emotion in public—or to near strangers. She waited for him to move.

"I will just paste these together then." The obnoxious beast stepped inside and began picking up the strips. "Family helps family, do they not?"

"Not in my experience." Caught watching as he easily bent from the waist to scoop up her mess, she wished he'd at least don a coat. "Only a dunderheaded beast with the understanding of a brick would believe my parents ever help anyone."

He grunted and began laying the scraps out on a piece of stationery. "At one time or another, I may have been all that. So perhaps I shall comprehend your father better than you might?"

"He wants to put Davy in an institution for the insane and incompetent, *vous comprenez?*" she asked with a sarcasm he did not deserve.

THREE

ARNAUD: MONDAY

ABANDONING THE LADY'S LETTER SCRAPS, ARNAUD STRAIGHTENED SO QUICKLY HE almost threw his spine out. "Imprison a *boy*? For what?" He could not comprehend anyone imposing the horror of the bastille on a child.

He was not an empathetic man, but he could see tears brimming in the lady's eyes. Normally, he walked away from a woman's waterworks, but his lunatic rage at injustice roared to ugly life.

He'd spent years suppressing that rage, knowing it accomplished nothing but pain. Still, he could not walk away from a lady in distress, no matter how mad she might be. Or—perhaps madwomen made up drama? That served to calm his fury and force him to listen.

Thea gestured helplessly. "Davy is his heir. You've seen my brother. He is not like most boys. He must be watched at all times or he's a danger to himself and others. Physicians claim he is not right in his head—but he is! He's smarter than I am!"

Arnaud had not paid a great deal of attention to the boys. They weren't artists or food, just little boys. The world was full of them. Her brother was inclined to chunkiness and a bit on the clumsy side. He didn't seem to talk much. But no one had faulted Davy's mathematics when he'd been drawing graphs—a complicated task for an eight-year-old.

He ought to walk away from such nonsense, but if any part of the story was true, he couldn't. "He is a *child*. Boys are inherently dangerous unless watched. Why would your father wish to imprison his heir?"

Anger flashed in her eyes. "Because my cousin Neville is everything an heir should be—clever, good-looking, charming—all those useless things society prefers! He will make a brilliant marriage and produce a lot of little Nevilles to be sure the name carries on."

"Well, the name carries on in any event," Arnaud said dryly. "Even should Davy choose not to marry, your cousin will have a name to pass on. He must simply wait for the rest."

Her shoulders slumped. "Neville cannot wait. He needs the promise of inheritance to attract a wealthy heiress. He has no income other than what my father chooses to allow him."

More enlightenment. Isolation had truly turned him into a slow-top. "Your father wishes to control who inherits his title and fortune. He cannot control a child he cannot understand, but he can control an impoverished nephew. So he wishes to treat his unmanageable heir as one would a second son. And your mother?"

"Doesn't care. If she cannot show her son off like a new gown, then he is irrelevant. Neville flatters her, escorts her about town, and she sees no wrong in putting Davy away where he might be *educated*." She waved the letter she held. "I don't even have to open this to repeat her euphemisms."

She shoved the letter at him and stalked off, all flags flying.

Huh. Little Miss Heiress might have wits beneath the bland smile, along with a few thorns. It remained to be seen if she was sane.

Not much caring about propriety, Arnaud scraped the seal off the perfumed letter and scanned the loopy handwriting. She'd come pretty close to accuracy in predicting her mother's admonitions. Sane or not, the lady had reason to be outraged.

Years of survival urged him to back away from trouble and leave it alone.

Years of living with himself said he could not ignore injustice, even though the instinct plunged him into trouble broth time and again. It seemed to be bred into the Lavigne bones. His engineer cousin Hunt had the same ridiculous propensity. And look how that had turned out for him—leg-shackled to a crumbling mansion, a family that wasn't really his, and the thankless task of magistrate.

This was not Arnaud's home or his family. Any sensible man would walk away.

With a sigh of exasperation, he followed the heiress. From the crashing about across the hall, he gathered she'd decided to take out her anger on the rubbish room. Several moth-eaten cushions flew into the wide corridor. Stepping into the path of flying cushions wasn't the most dangerous thing he'd ever done. Placing his back against the jamb so as to make a smaller target, he eased into what must have once been a polite withdrawing room.

At the moment, it lacked draperies, organization, and a carpet.

He and Hunt had carried out the late viscount's fine new furniture, oddly thrown into the jumble. They'd returned most of it to the masculine-oriented west wing. Their assumption was that the viscountess had gone into a rage after her husband's death and cast all his new purchases into the withdrawing room she never used—because she had no money and no friends after he'd ruined her and bankrupted the estate, lavishing his wealth on himself. The east wing—the ladies' wing—held only ancient furnishings from the time the wings had originally been built.

A three-legged chair just missed Arnaud's knees as he eased into the room. Insanity or a well-concealed temper?

"The curate was to repair those," he admonished.

"Then put them in the stable until he does." She flung another wooden chair toward the hall. "The Lady agrees. It is time the women claimed a place of their own. I shall pile all this rubbish where you must stumble over it or carry it off."

The *Lady*? There it was. He had seen her have the vapors over this elusive *lady* she claimed was the viscountess speaking to her from the grave. It might possibly not be the best time to launch a logical discussion about the lawyer she needed to hire.

He had not had to think of anyone but himself for a very long time. He was a bit rusty at it. For the most part, he did what was told and went his own way. For now, it seemed wisest to avoid drama and haul off the broken furniture.

He grabbed the pieces most likely to be launched like cannon balls and set them more gently into the hall.

Before she could gather more ammunition, he carried out a ladies' desk that appeared to have had a hatchet taken to it, and almost ran into Paul Upton, the village's new curate and the housekeeper's adopted son.

"I thought I was to repair these chairs?" Paul separated out the tottering wooden chairs that might have suited a medieval banquet hall. He was not only a curate, but a carpenter.

"You are not moving them fast enough." Arnaud caught a flying cushion and settled it onto one of the sagging seats. "Does the inn stable have room to store them?" Like much of Gravesyde Priory, the ancient inn had been abandoned long ago.

Paul shrugged in disgust. "Everything in that place leaks."

Still looking as if ice wouldn't melt in her mouth, despite her hysterics, the golden lady arrived in the doorway carrying an enormous brass lantern. "Repair the inn roof. Start an inn. These pieces are seeped in history. They simply need refurbishing."

History? The history of a brawling end to a dynasty, perhaps.

Hips swaying, she stalked back to her plundering. Arnaud directed his unruly eyeballs back to the curate.

"I'll carry them to the east wing." He relieved the busy curate from having to deal with haunted, historical furniture. "Are you in search of someone?"

"Meera. We have a. . . situation. . . and I think we need her expertise." Welcomed as a family member, Paul had apparently let himself into the manor, avoiding Quincy, and keeping his hat, which he rubbed between his fingers.

Arnaud did not consider himself a student of human nature, but he wasn't a dolt. Meera Walker, their steward's wife, was the closest the village had to a physician. "Dead or injured?"

"Dead," Paul admitted reluctantly. "An older gent, lived alone outside of town. We don't know how long he's been there, but. . . he didn't die peacefully."

With nothing resembling law in this area for decades, maybe longer, crime had gone unchecked and unnoticed. Hunt was attempting to change that, but he wasn't here. Neither was the Honorable ex-Lieutenant, Jack de Sackville, who often acted as Hunt's right-hand man.

That left Arnaud, the useless artist, or Henri, the tavern keeper, neither of them English or an authority. Henri would lose patrons if he started accusing clientele of murder.

"You can't handle this alone," Arnaud said reluctantly. "I'll go with you."

The young, soft-hearted, curate looked relieved. "I never thought taking this position meant more funerals than baptisms." He followed Arnaud to the back hall and the infirmary where the manor's apothecary/physician resided.

Before Meera's new husband could present the usual argument over preventing his heavily pregnant wife from exertion, Arnaud reminded them, "We have the carriage now. You know Hunt has made certain it has the essential comforts. That is what engineers do."

Arnaud lacked his cousin's schooling and had no head for engineering in any event. He'd been raised to believe he would collect rents and indulge his artistic passions—until war came and life as he'd known it ended. Just one more example of his general uselessness.

Walker, Hunt's African friend and steward, preferred his office to dealing with people, but he was male and not immune to the novelty of traveling in a new vehicle.

By the time they had the horses harnessed, Minerva had joined them. Arnaud conceded his seat to the librarian. As daughter of a soldier, she knew far more about dead bodies than he had any desire to learn. But if murderers were about, they might need his strength. He'd never been a soldier but he could wield a sword.

Rather than ride with the driver, he chose to take one of Lady Elsa's restive horses for a run. He saddled it as the carriage rolled away. He'd not had the funds for horseflesh since he was a school boy, but these past months of adjusting to the saddle again had been no strain.

Lady Elsa's horses were young and well-trained, and he caught up with the carriage before it turned into the lane through town. The driver was being exceedingly cautious with their precious passenger. Clare's Jewish-Hindu friend might have been an outcast in London, but Meera was a blessing in these parts.

Arnaud pondered how the manor's diverse inhabitants were knitting themselves into this rural community. The village had been nearly abandoned when Clare and Hunt first arrived. As the manor inhabitants enlarged the staff, developed a small button and sewing business, and increased the demand for local crops and other products, the village had grown too.

And with the increase in population—had come crime?

Arnaud hadn't stretched himself to think in terms of what Wycliffe Manor meant to others. As his great-aunt's residence, it had provided a safe haven in his youth, but he owned no part of it. He'd need to leave eventually, find his own place in the world.

But remembering the empty shell the village had been just six months ago—he couldn't explain the economics, but he could see the result. Thatch had been replaced. Flowers bloomed over newly mended fences. A market of farm carts lined the narrow street, with weathered women knitting and gossiping as they awaited customers. He watched children heading for the chapel carrying bouquets, under the guidance of the curate's gardener sister.

Gravesyde Priory was coming to life, as he knew he must.

They both suffered growing pains.

When the carriage halted at the entrance to a rutted farm drive not meant for more than a donkey cart, Arnaud swung off his horse and helped the ladies descend. The carriage couples strolled ahead of him while he studied their surroundings.

Nearly hidden by an overgrown hedgerow, the cottage was built of a respectable stone and size for a farmer's abode. It had two floors, if the gabled window was any indication. It probably had two rooms up and down, to make the best of daylight and fresh air.

He hitched his horse to a post and circled the exterior while the others entered an apparently unlocked door. He wasn't a physician or curate. He couldn't help with the living or dead. He'd seen enough death for two lifetimes and wasn't inclined to embrace more.

A well-kept kitchen garden in the rear indicated one of the residents had a passing acquaintance with cooking. A nanny goat in need of milking cried in a fenced area. Where was the kid? A few chickens ran up, hoping for feed.

If the occupant hadn't lived alone, whoever lived with him had been gone for days. Arnaud rummaged in a shed and found feed for the chickens, but milking goats was beyond his limited husbandry experience.

He studied the cottage's neatly painted back door but saw no sign that anyone had broken in. The windows were open. The last few days had been warm, with no rain. He tried the door latch, and it swung in without trouble. This wasn't a man with enemies.

Inside, the kitchen appeared orderly, from what little he knew of kitchens. Scrubbed pans hung on hooks on the stone chimney. Pump and sink worked. Decent porcelain and mugs sat on a shelf. The inhabitant had been tidy and not poor.

The fire was cold, but the ashes had not been cleared out. Because the tidy person had died before the fire did?

The kitchen opened onto a large front room, with one wall unusually lined with books. The still figure lying face-down on the worn carpet could have been sleeping. He wore the tailcoat of a different era, old but well-mended breeches, and a decent pair of boots. Judging by the ring of white hair, he hadn't been young.

Studying the way he sprawled, Arnaud surmised someone had hit him from behind. Hard. The white hair on his collar was soaked in dried blood.

Gravesyde had another murder on its books.

FOUR

PAUL: MONDAY

"His name is Jeremiah Boston. My granddad asked after him." Holding his prayer book, Paul closed his eyes and said a few words so he didn't have to watch Meera poking at the corpse of a man he wished he'd had time to know. He'd been in Gravesyde little more than a month. Not owning a horse, he hadn't been able to meet all the people in his far-flung parish yet.

He commended the man's soul to God while attempting to block the stench. In the July heat, the odor of decaying flesh permeated the small cottage. He didn't know how Meera tolerated the proximity as she examined the wound.

"We need the communal casket." A man of few words, Arnaud entered from the kitchen, startling the distressed company.

Relieved to address more practical matters, Paul nodded. "I have a new one built. I've been using the old inn stable as a workshop." Which was how he knew it leaked. Thatching a roof that size in summer was a grueling project no one wished to undertake.

Walker lingered in the doorway, where the air was fresher. "Henri can bring the coffin on his cart. Are there neighbors who can help him with Mr. Boston?"

Practicalities diverted the horror, Paul knew. It was far better than retching up breakfast—as he'd done earlier upon discovering the scene. "If Henri will help, I can do it." He might not be as tall and broad as these men, but he'd done physical work all his life. It wasn't as if the position of curate paid anything.

Meera held out her hand, and surprisingly, Arnaud took it, gently helping her to her feet. Paul didn't know much of the reclusive artist. The unkempt man with the unruly thatch of dark hair kept to himself, unless asked to perform a task. Apparently, today, he thought he needed to stand in his cousin Hunt's place.

"The obvious cause of death is a blow to the head." Meera glanced around and nodded at a fireplace shovel. "With something broad and flat, like that."

Arnaud hefted the tool in his big fist, held the blade out for everyone to see. The blood had dried, gluing a few white hairs to the metal.

"I haven't met everyone in the area yet." Paul grimaced at his failing. "Mr. Boston didn't attend services. If he knew my grandfather, then he's quite likely Catholic."

From near the bookshelves, Minerva glanced up from the volume she perused. "If books make the man, he's a Theist, a former professor and scholar, a new farmer—books on animal husbandry are the most recent in his collection—and a student of codes and puzzles."

Codes.

Was Paul imagining it, or did a shiver of dread just pass through the room's occupants?

Meera took her husband's arm. "I cannot say for certain, but he appears to have been dead for at least two days. The heat. . ." She gestured rather than explain.

Flesh deteriorated faster in heat. Paul hid his wince.

"If he is a friend of your grandfather, you should take the horse and ride over to speak with him." Looking resigned, the tall Frenchman held up a hand to indicate they wait a moment while he returned to the kitchen.

He returned carrying a garden trug. "Before you leave, take the code books. Have Henri return with the cart and casket. I shall guard the house."

The artist was curiously uncurious about who might have killed a scholar. Arnaud seemed—inured?—to death and killing, as if it might be an everyday event, and he expected no retribution. Since the former French count had lived through a revolution, that was likely.

Paul thought he ought to pray for Arnaud as well as the deceased, but right now, they needed to verify there were no more bodies or any lurking killers.

"Perhaps the ladies ought to leave, if Walker will escort them back to the carriage?" Paul nodded at the stairs. "I'll take a look upstairs."

He apparently hadn't adequately conveyed the urgency of his suggestion. Neither Minerva or Meera even glanced at the exit. Minerva packed books into the trug. Meera jotted notes in Walker's notebook. Walker stoically leaned a shoulder against the door jamb, understanding his wife far better than Paul did.

Paul couldn't even blame this lack of fear on Reid madness. Minerva was the only Reid here. He didn't want to be the one to shout, *There could be a killer up there!*

Grimacing as if he understood, looking as if he'd rather cut off his right hand, Arnaud reluctantly agreed. "I will look upstairs. You must see to your grandfather. If you can, send someone who knows how to milk a goat."

"I can milk a goat. I'll stay. I need more time to go over these books." Minerva set a few more in the trug. "Really, Paul, you should be the one to search above. A man who likes puzzles is quite likely to have hidden compartments, and you know furniture best."

That was not an aspect he'd considered while wondering if a pistol-toting, knife-wielding villain might come rampaging out of the attic. In exasperation, Paul finally pointed out the more obvious concern. "The killer could be anywhere. Don't you think we need to clear the house before anyone goes up those stairs?"

"Why would anyone linger for days?" Walker asked. "I'd be gone simply to escape the stench."

Arnaud didn't join the argument but studied the entrance to the narrow, enclosed staircase with a haunted expression.

"It doesn't look as if the killer is hunting for anything." Meera gestured at the mostly untouched room. "He swung, got scared, and fled. He's probably in London by now."

Paul bowed to their greater wisdom on the matter of killers. "Then I'll stay and search." Arnaud's relief at his agreement made it apparent this was the right choice. "Leave the horse. Arnaud can go with you to fetch Henri and the cart. When they return with the casket, I can ride to my grandfather's."

Eventually, Meera was satisfied she'd done all she could do. As the carriage drove off carrying the Walkers and Arnaud, Paul realized he'd been left alone with the woman he wished to court—if only the perverse female would allow it. The Reids were very loose on observing propriety. Apparently, so was he, since he'd allowed it. "How did you know Arnaud has a weak stomach?"

Minerva slanted him one of those long-lashed, sapphire looks that shot straight to his groin. She trusted him more than he trusted himself, so he stifled inappropriate urges.

"It is not the smell that affects him so much as the prison-like qualities of a cottage: low ceilings, little light," she explained. "Arnaud lives at the manor for many reasons, but one of them is most likely because it is spacious, even if he doesn't recognize the instinct. I've seen too many prisoners emerge from confinement unable to sleep anywhere but under the stars. French prisons are medieval dungeons."

Paul glanced at the narrow, dark stairwell, suddenly understanding. The artist had been more afraid of the confined space than he was of a killer. "The garret is most likely worse. Do I search or milk first?"

"I can't search the furniture for hiding places, but I can milk a goat. Several of your parishioners could use any food we gather. We need to find the man's family. If he owns the land, it's a valuable property for someone."

They looked at each other as they realized what she'd said—the land may have been the motive for killing.

"I am hoping my grandfather can tell me more. In the meantime, I'll see what's upstairs." Paul ducked his head under a beam to climb up. He wasn't tall, but even he sensed the airless closeness of the walls.

Large-boned Arnaud belonged in a castle, like a knight of old. Paul suspected the French chateau Arnaud and Henri had grown up in was even larger than Wycliffe Manor.

Upstairs, the stench lessened but the heat intensified. No killer dashed from the shadows to knock him over the head, so he felt free to study the layout. The garret was divided into two small bedchambers under a low roof, with a window under each eave. He opened both casements to catch any breeze.

The front room held a substantial bed and wardrobe, a neat shaving stand, and a writing desk. A cursory search of the wardrobe revealed a few old-fashioned coats and long vests, linen shirts washed thin, a pair of polished shoes, and starched neckcloths. Paul wondered who did the laundry. Or had Mr. Boston once been a valet?

Not with that wall of books. They required education and funds.

He searched the ancient washstand and bed and found no hidden compartments.

The newer, more expensive desk contained decent stationery, ink, and pens, but no diary or journal, no letters with addresses. For a learned man, that was uncommon.

Paul examined the desk's structure, found the predictable space for concealment in the back corner, and maneuvered the side panel until it slid open. Thinking he'd make a good thief, he reached in and found only a book—the journal he'd expected.

And if he knew anything of human nature at all— He flipped it open. The pages were written in code.

Sliding the book into his pocket, he examined the other side of the desk, found another panel, and removed a packet of letters. Thin paper, tied in fading ribbon, written in a feminine hand. He glanced at the first—signed by *Emma, your loving daughter*. The address was a small town west of Birmingham, near the coast. The last letter was dated over a year ago.

The artwork on the walls didn't appear special. Paul wasn't an expert on frames and couldn't tell if anything had been hidden in them. He'd carry them down for Arnaud to inspect.

Someone had killed the old man for a reason. It could have just been an argument. But having recently dealt with the murder of his adoptive father, Paul had learned worldly cynicism. Mr. Boston's killer had been frightened by what he'd done, no doubt. But once the cottage was empty, he was likely to return for whatever they'd argued over.

Money was the usual motive. Would an elderly scholar have any?

Paul set the frames on the stairs and entered the next room.

This one didn't exhibit Mr. Boston's orderly personality. Two narrow beds indicated children might once have occupied the room or at least visited. A collection of balls, rackets, and sticks spilled from the wardrobe. The bowl in the washstand was cracked. No art hung on the walls. A couple of moth-eaten jumpers lay crumpled in a drawer, along with stained linen, and a few tattered schoolbooks.

None of this exhibited signs of an adult daughter. Grandsons, perhaps?

The furniture in here was of simple construction and not designed to conceal. He could check the walls, but that would wait until they knew more. He'd left Minerva alone too long while a killer potentially lurked in the vicinity. Just thinking that way had him hurrying down the stairs, carrying the artwork.

In the front room, the trug was now completely filled with books, with more stacked beside it. They'd have to return the books if an heir was located, but *codes. . .*

He glanced at the poor gentleman on the floor, and his stomach clenched with anger at this waste of human life. They needed to know more. It was obscene to kill a man and leave him like a worthless leaf on the ground.

Most of the population of Gravesyde Priory and Wycliffe Manor believed the last earl had hidden the family jewels. Had the killer been someone who had heard about the codes they'd found in paintings and thought Mr. Boston's books were a clue to treasure?

They needed to know more about Mr. Boston.

Escaping the airless stench of the front room, Paul left through the kitchen, locating Minerva in the garden.

"Eggs, milk, and a good crop of beans for your widow ladies," she called, hefting a straw basket. "Your grandfather's friend was a self-sufficient gent. I wish we'd known him."

"We've neither of us been here long. We will meet everyone in time." He wanted to ask if she meant to stay. Her father lived on a duke's estate and offered far more than the crumbling manor. But this did not seem the time or place to inquire.

"We should find a caretaker until family can be reached." Paul produced the coded journal and letters. "These were hidden in the desk. He might simply have had a secretive nature, or they might contain information someone will return to find."

Something worth killing for?

FIVE

THEA: MONDAY LUNCHEON

To Thea's relief, Mrs. Upton eventually tired of looking at the piles of worn and threadbare furniture, draperies, and rugs spilling into the corridor and set servants to carrying everything to the unused east wing, where they could start a new rubbish room.

Thea suspected the men of the household had absconded simply to avoid hauling furniture. They'd been gone for hours. Even the new footman had time to settle in and join young Adam in hauling off the larger pieces. That would teach the gentlemen not to help. If they had wanted anything in that pile, they would have to sort it out later.

She couldn't believe she had told the Skeleton Artist her story. Did she really think he had any means of helping? Or any inclination to do so? His immediate departure brought any such foolhardy notion crashing back to reality.

The Lavigne's adolescent cousin, Sofia, timidly peered into the nearly empty room. "May I help?"

The girl had stayed behind when her parents had set off for London, and eventually, to their lands in France, now that Napoleon had been defeated. Thea thought Sofia might be hoping her fiancé's spirit lingered in the lane where he'd been killed, but Thea had never sensed the recently deceased. Right now, she felt the viscountess hovering, but whether her ghost approved or disapproved, of this dismantling wasn't clear.

"Can you use that glassware?" Thea pointed at a carton of odd beakers and kettles.

Sofia crouched down to pull out the pieces. "Great-Aunt Gabrielle's *parfumerie*! In this place, you do not grow more than the roses for the oils, not even the lavender." She gestured at a window overlooking half-dead shrubbery and the muddy, gravel drive. "She did not have much fragrance to distill. Patience has planted my jasmine seeds, but your weather. . . a *conservatoire* is needed for growing."

"The manor may have had flower beds once. Patience remembers gardens around the chapel and has been uncovering them, but she didn't live at the manor. You know how to use these?" Concentrating on the task she'd set herself so she needn't think about her father's threats, Thea carried the box of glassware into the corridor.

"I observed my mother make the perfume, but mostly, I watch the pots boil and digged. . . dugged weeds." Sofia was still jousting with the difficulties of English. "Under Napoleon, we must earn our food by selling eau de Cologne. It is said he used two *quarts* a week and *sixty* bottles of jasmine a month. He must have bathed in them."

"We could earn money by making perfume?" Thea wasn't fond of heavy fragrance. It made her sneeze. But if they could earn funds. . .

"Maybe we make the rose water." Sofia screwed up her forehead in thought. "We may start there, to earn the alcohol to make the cologne? I do not like to waste effort and coin until we know we can make the essential oil."

Mrs. Upton returned to study the rubbish with exasperation. "You did not need to clean it all out in one day."

"You would rather leave Clare's new furniture sitting in the vestibule for Lavender's animals to jump on or the men to sit on to take off their muddy boots? Would it be possible to leave the east wing open so Sofia might set up a perfumery?" Helpfully, Thea carried the box in that direction.

"No, the captain says that wing is too accessible to intruders. It must stay locked until we have enough staff. Perhaps Miss Sofia could set up in the gallery with the sewing ladies?" Mrs. Upton declined to follow.

Thea stopped and frowned. "There is no place in any of the towers?"

"One of those in front is no more than stairs to a bell tower. The other has no door and is just for looks. The two old ones in the rear are occupied. The new ones only hold stairs and landings for the new wings. We might ask Meera if the glassware can be stored in her laboratory in the cellar since she is not currently using it." Mrs. Upton salvaged a few cushions from the wreckage.

"It does not matter," Sofia said shyly. "I probably cannot make it anyway."

The younger woman needed distraction and employment as much as Thea did.

"Not if you don't try." Pursing her lips, she contemplated the alternatives. The inaccessible tower teased at her—why would anyone build a tower that couldn't be used?—but they needed a room *now*. "The west wing is open. Do you think Clare and Hunt will mind dreadfully if one of the empty upper bedchambers are used for experimenting?"

The newlyweds had established their bridal suite in the large front rooms of that wing.

"I'm sure I cannot say." Mrs. Upton studied the boxes they held and sighed. "Perhaps if you use one at the far end? Then you can use the service stairs."

Sofia brightened. "The maids complain about the *parfum* bottles I am keeping. I will take those, too, *merci!*"

Thea had a notion that a bedchamber on a second floor would not prove satisfactory, but it at least removed more rubbish from her withdrawing room. She really needed to inspect the front tower, though. That seemed like the ideal place for smelly concoctions.

She had been too busy to notice the return of the carriage party, but word that there had been another death filtered down to her through the servants. Her father would not like to hear that, but unless the corpse was a member of society —highly unlikely in their rural isolation—he most likely wouldn't notice.

She was standing in the center of the now nearly empty withdrawing room, studying the flocked floral wall covering, probably 17th century, when the cart carrying a casket rolled past, completely visible through the windows. The draperies in this room had been removed long ago, leaving it open to sunshine and a view of the rutted drive. Honestly, the manor would turn into a funeral home at this rate. Although, she supposed, the crypt was much cooler in this weather than the tiny, thatched chapel.

Perhaps they could grow a trellis of roses outside the window so such grisly sights would not be seen.

A maid rushed down the corridor carrying a tea tray. Without Lady Elsa in the kitchen, their repasts were not what they had once been, but Thea's stomach reminded her that she had forgotten luncheon. She took the backstairs up to her room, washed her grimy fingers and face, shook out her hem, pinned her hair in place, and descended the marble stairs as the lady she'd been raised to be. She didn't have to settle into heathendom as the others had.

She would pretend she hadn't had a screaming tantrum earlier.

Apparently no one else had taken luncheon either. The kitchen had provided substantial sandwiches, cakes, and fresh berries in the breakfast room. The gentlemen hadn't bothered changing but carried stacked plates to the table, sprawling as if they were at a tavern. They looked weary, smelled worse, and she decided it might be wiser if she dined with the old ladies upstairs—but that would leave Minerva alone with the clodpolls. The other ladies seldom took tea in here. Clare would insist on chaperoning their cousin.

Thea didn't feel compelled to stand in Clare's place, but the moment Mr. Upton placed the letters and journal on the table, she sensed The Lady's presence, and she froze.

"I hope one of the code books you brought back will translate this." Mr. Upton shoved what appeared to be a leather-bound journal toward Minerva. "I asked my grandfather about his friend. The deceased is actually a *Professor* Boston, a scholar who retired from university to his family farm several years ago. They enjoyed a good game of chess upon occasion but he knows little more."

Thea couldn't easily concentrate on a ghost in the company of disbelievers, but she could observe what had the The Lady's attention. Taking a plate of smaller sandwiches and a teacake, she settled near Minerva.

"Did your grandfather know his family?" Arnaud asked. The tattered artist looked even more disheveled than usual. He could use a shave and a haircut, but Thea had to admit, his overlong, natural dark locks were far more appealing than the affected Brutus cut favored by London gentlemen.

Mr. Upton gestured at the bundle of letters. "Grandfather said there was a daughter who died a year or so ago, that Professor Boston hadn't been himself since. He couldn't tell me anything about the grandsons, but he apparently has family somewhere. The letters may tell us."

"Do we need to write Hunt?" Henri asked, piling cheese, onion, and ham on a roll. "Don't we need a magistrate to deal with murder?"

Arnaud looked up from his food for the first time and scowled. "You wish to disturb his wedding journey? Me, I would hack off your head."

Henri threw a piece of cheese at his brother.

Before a fight between could ensue, the curate stepped in. "I'll write to the vicar. The parish is his responsibility. He can notify proper authorities."

Thea waited but The Lady apparently had nothing she wished to add. The viscountess had held little authority over the estate in her lifetime. The English vicar in a distant parish had probably not offered the foreign Catholic lady much assistance.

"This is not the same code as the earl used," Minerva announced, flipping pages in the journal. "This may just be a basic alphanumeric code: hunt a common combination of letters like *the* or *and*. See, these three letters are used fairly regularly." She pushed the book across the table to Mr. Upton. "Write out the alphabet. Count if the number between these letters and between the ones in *the* or *and* are the same."

Henri leaped up, presumably to fetch pencil and paper. The skeletal artist continued plowing his way through his food, but he eyed the pages of the journal with interest. Thea could almost swear he was doing mental alphabet calculations.

He'd been the one to discover the codes in the paintings. Perhaps his mind worked similarly to Davy's? That would be an interesting development. She waited expectantly.

"No, if he is using that code, he is working with two separate alphabets." Arnaud swilled his ale without glancing at the book again.

"You can tell that just by looking?" Minerva asked in amazement. "And how do you know about the double alphabet?"

"The library, it has a book on codes. I've studied, hoping to decipher the earl's. It has not helped, but the book did mention your alphanumeric code. You start by assuming the *t* in *the* is in the second tier and the *he* is in the first tier. Dividing between *m* and *n* is common. Or if the word, it is *and*, the middle letter might or might not be in the second tier. He was not trying too hard, if that is the case."

"Not trying too hard?" Thea asked, unable to believe the selfish artist had more in his brainpan than turpentine. "He could write like that without having numbered alphabets pinned to his wall?"

Henri returned with enough writing equipment for all. "Start on the last pages. Was he expecting visitors? Look for capitalized letters that might be names."

Arnaud ripped his paper into three strips. "You need a sliding scale." He began laying out the alphabet on the first strip, then glanced up. "What is the chance that this Professor Boston knew the late earl?"

And had taught him the code hidden in the paintings—the one that might lead to hidden jewels? Even Thea felt the level of excitement rise.

SIX

ARNAUD: MONDAY BEFORE DINNER

Arnaud sat in the library with Professor Boston's journal and his sliding alphabet scale, decoding pages and jotting down notes of what he thought might be important. There weren't many. The man's last days consisted of how many eggs and pints of milk he collected. Earlier, in the spring, there'd been an altercation with a neighbor over the goats, but other than a derisive insult, nothing more was said of it.

They'd left the artwork in the cottage. Arnaud hadn't seen anything valuable in the old paintings or frames and didn't want to take them apart without permission.

The boys and Minerva were happily studying code books pilfered from the dead man's shelves. Copies of the earl's codes, maps, and letters littered the library table, but they didn't seem to be making any more progress than Arnaud was. The tutor must have the afternoon off, since he wasn't present as usual.

The mad heiress had departed earlier, uninterested in codes or mysteries. Arnaud would rather work with codes than her drama.

He had just deciphered the name of Boston's grandsons when the crazed lady swept in again, dressed for dinner. Unlike most of the manor's inhabitants, she actually possessed a fashionable wardrobe. His artist's eye noted that, tonight, she wore a shimmering sea-green silk with lace that foamed around her bosom. . .

Her eyebrows shot up in disapproval, marring the serene mermaid image.

"You think the absence of Captain and Mrs. Huntley is sufficient reason not to adhere to propriety?"

"The absence of food worth dressing for should be sufficient reason," Minerva muttered. The soldier's daughter had moved into the manor from her previous home on a duke's estate. Her trunks had been delivered, but she seldom wore more than plain clothes, dark for day, light for evening.

The heiress made them all look shabby. Arnaud scrubbed a hand over his whiskers, hiding a wince. "Having food to eat is worth whatever it takes." He had his priorities. He shoved away from the table. "We are supposed to be practicing to be adults."

"What?" Minerva looked at him as if he were the one crazed.

"You missed the discussion." The mermaid helped the boys gather their materials. "Lavender believes our newlyweds abandoned us so we'd learn to take care of ourselves."

"I've been doing that since I was born." As the librarian, Minerva didn't have to move her materials. She gestured at Arnaud. "Leave your notes out, if you like. We can all work through those boring pages when we have time to spare."

This petite whirlwind the curate fancied had followed her officer father and mother through war zones. Minerva was more capable than Arnaud would ever be. He'd *amused* his way through his youth. He liked to believe he'd made up for it since, but he still wasn't half as capable as the little librarian who commanded troops like a general.

Although he might have a bit more in the upper story than a mad heiress. He started for the door. "Do we have a chessboard, by any chance? I suspect when Professor Boston writes *Chess with W*, he means the earl. The dates match the time the earl lived."

"The diary dates back that far? The professor couldn't have been much more than out of university then." Thea glanced at the yellowed pages and faded ink and wrinkled her nose.

"His entries are sparse." Arnaud shrugged. "Mine would be, also, if I must write them in code."

"Why is he writing in code?" the lady asked, finally exhibiting some interest after sending the boys off for their own supper.

"That is why I looked at the opening pages. But there is no explanation." Arnaud shrugged and followed the boys out, letting them run ahead while he took the stairs at a more leisurely pace, pondering the poor man felled by a shovel. Why? What could an elderly scholar turned farmer have worth killing over?

He considered what he'd learned about Miss Talbot earlier and even the injustice she suffered wasn't worth killing anyone over. The law was there for a reason.

If the scholar had simply been killed in a fit of anger, that person needed to be caught before they reacted badly again.

As first occupants of the manor, Arnaud and Henri had claimed a couple of the larger bedchambers not far from the marble stairs. After his year in prison, Arnaud considered the worn linen sheets and faded counterpane of his new chamber the height of luxury. The high ceiling and tall windows allowed him to breathe.

The enormous mahogany wardrobe. . . was unnecessary. Henri had scrounged a dinner coat and trousers in the second-hand market that fit him well enough—tight through the shoulders but loose everywhere else. As a youth, he'd worn exquisitely tailored silk suits. Now he was happy with the simple wardrobe Lavender had made for him from secondhand garments.

He had a razor and could shave himself. He just wasn't inclined to do so most days, especially since Hunt had taken his valet with him, and there was no one to nag him.

Given his circumstances, a clean set of clothing was a luxury. The aging leather breeches and ancient wool morning coat he wore during the day needed airing after an afternoon spent with a corpse. He left the windows open and hung the clothes over the casement.

Finding jewels seemed the only means of his ever having funds again. He might make his way to London and attempt to earn a living with his art, but without Henri to sell his work, he'd starve. Art required salesmanship and connections, and he had neither.

The Reid jewels, should they exist, belonged to the earl's family, of course. He just hoped he'd be given a finder's fee of some sort. The earl's extended family, for the most part, wasn't poor. They could afford to reward him. Then he might start a small studio, build from the ground up, again.

He stepped out of his room just behind Patience and Henri, who had apparently met at the stairs. Arnaud tried not to be too envious as they chatted about events of the day. When had he last felt able to converse with such ease and abandon? Probably never. He wasn't like his younger brother. Charm and words escaped him.

Without half the family or guests in residence, the rest of the company had taken to gathering in the family parlor before dinner, instead of in the cavernous great hall. With plaster decorated high-ceilings, silk wall coverings, delicate Chippendale, and elegant glass lamp shades, the parlor had once been formal.

Decades of use and abuse had reduced it to a room of sagging, threadbare cushions where even Arnaud felt comfortable lounging.

The curate had joined them this evening. As had Meera and Walker, who usually dined in their own quarters. The limited kitchen staff, without Lady Elsa's instruction, had difficulty serving one meal, at one table. Arnaud wondered who was delivering meals to the aunts upstairs. The earl's sister and granddaughters preferred their own more sedate company and gossip to that of the younger generation.

Upton turned to greet his sister and Henri, and in consequence, Arnaud, who trailed in after them. The curate was young but had a sensible head on his shoulders. If nothing else, Arnaud was grateful to him for taking over the duty of searching the upper story of the cottage this morning.

"I have been speaking to members of my congregation," the curate reported. "Professor Boston did not mingle much, but he was deemed a fair employer and a genial gentlemen. He shared any excess from his small farm with anyone in need, although I'm not certain how he knew who that might be."

"Mrs. Smith." Patience took the small glass of sherry a maid handed her. "She cooks for the invalids and shut-ins. You met her, Paul. She prepared meals for your grandfather before Mrs. Brown took over his housekeeping. Her husband is a deacon for the church, so he knows who is in need."

"But Mrs. Smith didn't notice a corpse on the floor?" Arnaud asked dryly.

"That's just it. She cooks big batches in her own home for parishioners who are unable to fix their own dinner. Volunteers deliver the meals. Professor Boston wasn't on her regular list. He only occasionally requested meals. She thought he might do so when he had visitors, but she didn't know him well." Henri took a glass of brandy. "Deacon Smith is one of my regular patrons and a source of all gossip. He would have passed information to Professor Boston if he saw a family in need."

Arnaud half-listened while scanning the parlor for the heiress who had rousted them from the library and forced him into proper dress. Dotty Dottie suited her far better than *Thea*, however one pronounced it. The thorny bit of fluff was currently communing with a chess set.

A chess set. There hadn't been one in here before. Curious, he drifted away from his brother and the family Henri wanted to make his own. Now that he suspected the heiress wasn't quite as shallow as she appeared, he was interested in learning more, if only for little Davy's sake.

"Did you just magick that into existence?" he asked, studying the chess pieces. They were worn like everything else in the manor but didn't resemble any chess pieces with which he was familiar. He picked up one to examine it.

"It was buried in the rubbish room. I unearthed it earlier today and consigned it to the game room in the men's wing but brought it out again. It's a truly extraordinary set. I'd surmise late sixteenth century from the carvings. The rook as a tower and the knight as a horse's head might be more recent, but the bishop's miter and these pawns are not. And look at the material: ivory and ebony." She pointed at the chess board on top of the box the pieces must have been stored in. "The box and board are teak. I think this must once have graced the cabin of a wealthy ship's captain."

He quickly put the piece down again for fear he'd damage it. "How do you know this?"

"When my grandparents died, my parents sold off their possessions to collectors." She looked uncomfortable. "I was unnaturally attached to their belongings since their homes were the only ones I knew as a child."

"You thought their ghosts clung to their furnishings," he accused. Her pansy-blue eyes faded to crystal when she spoke of spirits. A sign of madness?

She scowled and nodded curtly. "I was only a child, mind you. No one paid attention to me. I listened to collectors and dealers talk about beloved pieces as if they were ripe oranges in the market. And then. . ." She sighed. "You will not believe me. No one else did. But my dead grandparents started speaking to me about the secrets hidden in a few pieces. When I produced one of Grandmother Diane's diamond bracelets from a hidden compartment. . . they quit chasing me away."

Logically, he assumed she'd watched her grandparents conceal their treasures. That did not mean the hurt child she'd been hadn't believed in phantoms.

He was not a sentimental man. He had barely noticed his Uncle Jules' departure for France, even though his uncle was the only family left besides Henri. He'd spent so many years just surviving, that he had no soul left for more.

Her story brushed against bits of him he'd rather leave dead. At least, he and Henri had a few happy family memories before war had ended them. Miss Talbot's family sounded colder and more soulless than he felt.

Quincy called them for dinner. Arnaud wasn't accustomed to acknowledging any of the ladies, but reluctantly, he offered his arm to escort this one. Just to avoid tears. She reacted like an automaton when offered formality.

SEVEN

PAUL: MONDAY DINNER

To Paul's surprise, the regal aunts joined them for dinner. The kitchen must have failed to deliver to their suite.

Or Mrs. Huntley, the captain's mother, wanted to learn more of the company. More genial than her titled relations, she wore her graying dark hair in a simple chignon, dressed in a modest maroon taffeta, and smiled affably as Paul seated her. Caught by surprise at their arrival, Henri and Arnaud hastened to help Lady Spalding and Lady Lavinia in their sweeping, old-fashioned silks.

The younger company set aside discussion of the day's gruesome events in favor of the older ladies' preferred discussion of fashion. Lavender listened avidly to the plans for the trousseau of Lady Spalding's daughter—a much more acceptable topic for a dinner table.

"And Dorothea." Lady Spalding turned to the pale heiress. "Why are you not seeking a suitor? Surely you have not assigned yourself to the shelf already?"

Miss Talbot was one of the newer additions to the manor. Paul had seen the prim lady spin in circles and collapse, heard her talk of spirits no one else could hear, and had rather assumed the unmarried state was her fate.

Apparently, he was not wrong.

At the nosy inquiry, the lady glanced up from cutting her chicken into tiny pieces. When quiet conversations continued elsewhere around the table, she laid down her fork and rapped her knife against her wine glass. Startled, the rest of the family turned in her direction.

"Our aunt wishes to know why I am not seeking a suitor. Does anyone know of a single male who might be interested in a woman who communes with ghosts and desires to decorate interiors with historical furnishings instead of Egyptian lunacy?"

Before the aunts could mention the fortune she stood to inherit, which was most likely unwise given the militant gleam in the lady's eyes, Arnaud actually replied. "Better question, what man would want a woman concerned only with her own whims?"

That set off a delightful explosion, interrupted by Quincy arriving in the open doorway, carrying the silver visitor's tray. A visitor at this hour never boded well.

When Quincy seemed uncertain who to address, Arnaud signaled for the card and read it aloud. "Neville Talbot?"

Her earlier militancy fled, the young heiress paled to the extent that Paul thought she might faint.

Then, unexpectedly, she responded furiously. *"Do not let him in.* Under no circumstances let that horrible man inside this house or anywhere near this property."

Now there was a dilemma difficult to address. No one spoke as the lady pushed from the table.

Fortunately, ever-facile Henri posed the problem. "It will be dark in an hour. There is nowhere else for him to stay."

"That is *not* our concern. He arrived without invitation or request. He may sleep on his horse for all I care." The proper Miss Talbot picked up her hem and stormed out.

Arnaud looked as if he might follow her, but he was left holding the card, so to speak. Someone had to tell Quincy what to do.

Paul understood the stunned shock around the table at this unusual tantrum. Except for Arnaud and Henri, they were all relatively new to Wycliffe Manor. None of them had more authority than the other. Did they allow one person to overrule the entire household, plus all propriety and hospitality?

From Arnaud's grim look, Paul thought he knew the answer. The gloomy artist wasn't much given to politeness on a good day, but he'd choose the devil he knew—the lady. The others would do the same. The family might be eccentric, but they respected one another.

Paul was the outsider here. "I will take him down to the parsonage," he offered. "I can sleep here this evening."

"He must be a terrible person," his sister said worriedly as Paul pushed back his chair. "Are you certain it's safe?"

"He is the gentleman Miss Talbot's parents wish to make heir instead of

Davy." Reluctantly returning to his seat, Arnaud reached for a wine glass. "She has reason to ban him from the manor, but he is unlikely to be a danger to Paul."

Ah, Arnaud knew what this was about. Interesting.

Minerva stood. "I will have the kitchen fix a basket for his dinner and have a servant follow you down."

Paul adored her sensibility, but she hadn't given him permission to hug her, as he'd like to do at her suggestion. She ducked her head at his smile of approval. He knew her family had never shown their appreciation for her diligence and hard work. He'd have to wear through her formidable defenses.

Walker headed for the door as well. "I'll warn the lads to keep watch. Jack and Hunt have trained them to report intruders. They're prepared if there is any threat to Davy."

Shaking his head in amazement at the odd tangents the manor inhabitants took over an unwanted guest, Paul followed the butler to the front door, where their guest had been left cooling his boot heels in the currently unadorned vestibule.

Leaning against the tall lion statue, the gentleman straightened at their entrance. "Apologize for the late arrival," he said genially, doffing his tall top hat. "Horse threw a shoe and I had to walk him for miles."

One of the many reasons casual travelers did not take this road to nowhere— no wayside inns to refresh and repair. The village had only recently acquired a blacksmith.

Paul bowed. "Mr. Neville Talbot? The family had no word of your visit. I'm afraid they cannot provide accommodations. I am Paul Upton, the local curate. I can offer you a bed in the parsonage. If you'll take the drive down to the village, I'll meet you there and show you the way." He wasn't about to ask the stable to saddle a horse for a distance he could walk in ten minutes, now that he knew the hidden path.

The gentleman stared at him in incredulity. "Is this a jest?" He gestured at the dramatically tall vestibule and formidable doors. "In a place this size, there is no room for a single guest? I am *family*, after all."

"As I understand it, you're not a Reid, sir. The earl's family wishes to be private. Surely you understand. Come along, it's regrettable that the village has no inn, but the parsonage is snug. The kitchen will send dinner down." Paul pushed past the gentleman to open the massive front entrance. Quincy shut the inner vestibule doors with a distinct click.

Of average height and the usual English fairness, Mr. Talbot took his time following Paul down the stairs. He studied the sprawling façade of the manor, the dark Gothic windows, and the untrimmed shrubbery amid a wilderness of

PATRICIA RICE

trees. Apparently deciding the fortress couldn't be easily stormed, Mr. Talbot reluctantly took the reins of his horse and walked beside Paul.

"Did my cousin not inform you of my arrival?" He tried again. "Perhaps my letter was lost in the post?"

"Unless you received an invitation, I do not believe the household would be prepared." And from the sounds of it, Miss Talbot would have burned any letter, if one had been sent, unopened. "The manor has been abandoned for decades. It takes time to restore it to habitation." Paul was trying very hard to be polite. He didn't know the story yet. "Master and Miss Talbot gave the household no reason to expect you."

"*Master?*" The visitor barely hid his scorn. "I doubt the cretin could even identify me. I do not call on *children*. Miss Talbot's parents are concerned for her welfare. I am sent to look after her interests."

Ah, Paul had a glimpse of the problem. "As I understand it, Miss Talbot is of an age to make her own decisions. As a Reid, she is part owner of the manor, as is Master David." Emphasizing respect for the boy, he then gestured at a newly trimmed hole in the overgrown shrubbery lining the drive. "If you are walking, there is a shorter lane to the parsonage."

The sun was setting on the far side of the manor, leaving this narrow, tree-lined walking path in shadow. Until recently, even the manor's inhabitants hadn't known it existed. A man—not much more than a boy—had died here. Paul said a prayer for his soul as they passed.

"If you have not noticed, Miss Talbot and her brother are slightly mad. They need caretakers. Her father cannot expect total strangers to look after them." The man managed to sound pompous and scornful while expressing supposed concern.

"You are obviously not familiar with the Reid family." As a curate, Paul had experience at speaking evenly in the face of ignorance and bigotry. It took extra effort in the presence of an educated gentleman who ought to be more broad-minded.

"Miss Talbot's father is a refined, intelligent gentleman. There is nothing mad about him," Talbot argued.

"Lord Talbot is not a Reid. As I understand it, *Lady* Talbot is the descendant of the earls of Wycliffe. The first Reid fought valiantly to win a title and these lands. Since then, Reids have sailed the world, conquered jungles, mined in India and Africa, experimented on steam engines. . . the history is extensive. You would do well not to disparage any member of the family." Paul led him across the brook to the field behind the vicarage.

"All families have their weak shoots. Nevertheless, it is my responsibility to look after my cousins. How am I to do so from a parsonage?" Mr. Talbot attempted to stride across the brook and missed, soaking his fancy, cuffed boots.

"That is not for me to say. I merely offer my humble home so you need not risk the perils of the road in the dark. There has been very little law in these parts for a long time. We've had no reports of highway robberies, but then, we seldom have visitors who venture out at this hour. These are desperate times." Paul led him around the chapel to the parsonage.

Patience had spent these last weeks returning the grounds to the welcome haven they'd once been in their childhood. The first flush of spring was past, and the newly leafed-out hedges brimmed with wildlife. Rustling followed them along the drive.

"I have no stable." Paul opened the gate to let the visitor pass, then shut it behind them, testing the posts he'd recently replaced. They stood solid now. "The yard is safe, there is a trough by the pump, and there should be sufficient grass to feed your animal. He'll come to no harm."

"I've heard Lady Elsa Villiers has rebuilt the manor's stables. I could have left my mount there." In the gathering gloom, the gentleman's expression was not visible but his voice held petulancy.

"You can be on your way more easily from here." Paul wanted to say Talbot's lady cousin had made it clear he was unwelcome, but that would only lead to further argument. "Women from the parish keep up the cottage, so you should find everything to your comfort. I daresay dinner will arrive shortly. I'll leave you to settle in and wish you well of your journey on the morrow."

He didn't wait to hear protests but let himself out again, leaving the unwanted gentleman staring in perplexity at the tiny, shabby parsonage when he'd evidently meant to spend the night in luxury.

Not that Wycliffe Manor would have provided that either.

Paul met Deacon Smith out for his evening constitutional. The older man usually aimed for the tavern after dinner, but Henri had taken to closing it on Sundays and Mondays.

Paul had forgotten to grab his cap and had to nod in greeting. "I just installed a gentleman visitor in the parsonage. He's not wanted at the manor."

Smith pulled on his pipe and squinted at the parsonage's low, thatched roof barely visible above the hedge. "Aye, we'll keep a watch. Anything to do with poor Boston?"

"I shouldn't think so. This visitor is related to Lord Talbot. But ask around about the whereabouts of Boston's grandsons, if you will. The family needs to be notified. Do we have someone to look after his animals?"

"Aye, there's always someone willing to work for food. Believe there's a lad out there old enough to be helping his ma and the youngers. I'll stop by on the way home." He tipped his hat and sauntered on.

Paul thought that should alert the entire village to be on the lookout for the unwanted visitor as well as the grandsons. Gravesyde might not have many inhabitants, but they communicated by means he'd rather not investigate, since he had reason not to approve of gossip.

Pondering the need for a steady stream of coffins in a village this small, Paul took the longer drive up. By the time he reached the manor, dinner was over. The company waited for him in the parlor—except for Miss Talbot. She had not returned.

"Did you learn anything of interest from our banned guest?" Minerva whispered, offering him a plate of cold meats and bread.

"Only that he's rude and believes Miss Talbot and her brother are mad. I encouraged him to ride on in the morning." Paul enjoyed the fragrance that encompassed them as he assisted the lady into her seat. Was that the jasmine the others spoke of, the perfume the late viscountess wore? It was a heady aroma.

"Well, we are all mad in our separate ways. It could be the reason we gather here—the company is congenial." She laughed as he took the seat beside her.

Paul glanced around the room. Their numbers were larger than usual. Did they linger to be certain Talbot did not disturb their peace? The steward and his apothecary wife generally preferred their own apartment, but Paul was glad of their presence. After finding Professor Boston dead, Talbot's arrival agitated his uneasiness.

"Are the soldiers on alert?" he asked. "Our Mr. Talbot seems insulted that we did not allow him to leave his horse with us and is more than peeved at being turned away."

The captain had given employment to former soldiers sent home penniless after the war. Many of them camped on the grounds rather than sleep in cramped quarters.

"They're training the hounds to patrol the hill and alert us of intruders. I don't expect him to bother returning, though." Walker shrugged.

"He will," Arnaud said gloomily from the large wing chair he'd appropriated. He was another one who did not often grace the parlor. The absence of Hunt and Jack may have obligated him to take their places. "He wants the Talbot fortune, and Miss Talbot and her brother are the keys to the treasure chest."

The new footman approached with a tray of cordials. He didn't seem adept at carrying trays. A glass tilted as he lowered the tray to Patience. The liquid splashed, and she hastily brushed at her one dinner gown.

The man apologized and hurriedly returned to the buffet to polish glasses.

Was Paul imagining things or did the new servant seem to be surreptitiously studying the company? Or the room? Concluding the day had simply left him out of sorts, Paul gestured at the bowl of cheese and berries meant for late nibbling. He'd missed his pudding. "Herbert, is it? Would you mind carrying around the cheese?"

Herbert wasn't a large man, but he was certainly large enough to carry a glass bowl. Presumably, he just tripped over his feet when he nearly dumped the bowl in Paul's lap.

"You can't serve cheese without plates." Minerva indicated that he leave the bowl on a table where the company could reach it.

Old enough to sport a reddish fuzz on his jaw, the footman wasn't too young to know his job, but he appeared confused and continued to hold the bowl. "Shall I ask in the kitchen for plates?"

"Please do." Arnaud snatched the fruit from the footman's hands before he could run off with it. Setting it down, he helped himself to the cheese without benefit of plate.

Paul chuckled. Arnaud lent new meaning to the term *starving artist*. Helping himself in the same manner , he waited until Herbert had departed before asking, "Should we write the solicitors and the banker and ask if they might know of Professor Boston or his family?"

"I'll do that," Walker volunteered. "They'll think the inquiry is from Hunt. I'll also write to the direction on those letters you found. The sons may have inherited their mother's home."

"We'll need to bury him soon," Henri warned. "I'll call in the gravediggers. I'm not sure how much space is left in the cemetery. We're likely to be digging up bones."

"Hunt found posts and foundations he believes were once the wall around the cemetery." Walker helped himself to a handful of berries. "He drew a survey map. Judging by the location of the markers, there appears to be room in the northwest corner. It's rockier there, unfortunately."

"I should probably work on finding gravestones," Paul said in resignation. "But several centuries of graves. . . We cannot expect to find even a small portion."

"If we could open the front tower, we might start stacking bodies in there like a crypt instead of using the cellar," Arnaud said cynically. "Or there may already be bones piled high, for all we know."

"Just what we need, more empty rooms." Minerva wrinkled her small nose in distaste.

"Didn't Sofia express a desire to make perfume?" Paul asked. "I believe Miss

Talbot mentioned that. Should we cut back the shrubbery and see if there's a door?"

"Sleeping Beauty's tower, covered in thorns," Patience cried in delight. "I can do that. I've been wanting an excuse to work on the landscaping."

Paul grimaced. He'd seen the ossuary in Rothwell with thousands of skulls lined up on shelves. He supposed it was better that no one fell through a window and landed on the bones as legend said they had in Rothwell, but he wasn't looking forward to whatever they found.

EIGHT

THEA: TUESDAY MORNING

HAVING WARNED THE TUTOR NOT TO LEAVE DAVY UNGUARDED FOR ANY REASON, AND after spending a fretful night in fear Neville would somehow insinuate himself into the household, Thea vowed not to let the vile beast overset her safe haven.

She steadied her rattled nerves by examining the ancient covering on the withdrawing room walls."It is historic. I hate to destroy it. We will never see the like again."

"Thank goodness," Mrs. Upton said dryly. "The wool flocking is filthy and flaking off. The pattern may be interesting, but the chimney smoke has ruined it, and the inks have faded into indistinction."

Thea accepted that a housekeeper looked at the walls in terms of cleaning. But her heart ached at the thought of ripping off hand-printed paper that had cost fortunes at the time it had been installed. It had once been the pride and joy of some previous countess. Or mistress, she conceded. All but the first countess had had far more luxurious homes elsewhere.

Meera waddled in. The apothecary was short and round to start with. The child she carried was nearly as large as she was—as was the ledger she carried, open to a page of accounts. "Walker found the entry! It's nearly impossible to read. *Parlor walls Jan 1676. . .* The cost appears to be seven pounds and some pence but the numbers are cramped and faded."

"Nearly a hundred and fifty years," Mrs. Upton said with a scoff. "I think it is time for a change."

As Meera read the entry, Arnaud appeared in the doorway. Last night's clean jaw was now stubbled with whiskers, and he wore his abominable smock over his vest and shirt. Examining the wall covering critically, he tested the flocking, then stepped back to scan the walls in the sunlight. "I can cut out an undamaged square from behind the artwork. Paul could frame it. That would preserve the history."

Thea glared at him in horror. "Cut hand-printed and flocked paper?"

"It preserves a piece of history." The artist shrugged his dismissal.

"Walker wants to put these ancient ledgers in the attic. Should we remove this page and add it to the frame?" Meera suggested. "Historians might be interested."

Thea hated the idea, but the Lady's spirit didn't seem to object. The late viscountess hadn't possessed the funds to decorate, so the walls were nothing to her. "Is there any budget for removing the paper?" Accustomed to her opinions being ignored, she resisted in the only way she knew how, with pence and shillings.

"Hunt is trying to have the trust maintenance budget increased, claiming rising costs from the war." Meera set the book down on the only table Thea had left in the room. "I'll ask Walker what he thinks." She waddled out, leaving Arnaud tugging at a torn corner of paper.

"Paint it," Mrs. Upton said emphatically. "Paint is much easier to clean." She sailed off, leaving Thea most improperly with the tall gentleman.

To her horror, he yanked off a strip of paper as if it had personally injured him. Before she could cry a protest, he said, "Your cousin is making the inquiries about renting. I do not believe he means to leave."

Thea's heart froze. Wall covering didn't matter in the overall scheme of things. Davy did. She didn't want to drag Davy from this home where he was accepted and comfortable. "Can we keep him out?"

"We may keep him from the manor, but we cannot control the village property, not until the suit is settled with the bank. It is complicated." He viciously ripped off almost an entire strip.

"He will grow bored where there is no wenching and gambling." She hoped. "Do not believe for a minute that he actually cares about our welfare."

"He has no income of his own?" Arnaud picked at the next piece of paper.

So very few cared about her position, that she readily spilled her fears rather than ask why he bothered. "Only the allowance my father gives him. He considers himself a gentleman above the need to earn a living. But his father's property is small and already encumbered with debt, so he has nothing to fall back on. He could stay home and help his father, but they don't get along."

With a sigh of mourning, Thea stood in the way of his plundering to block off a clean square of paper. "Don't tear more until you preserve this!"

"Lavender and Sofia are taking apart the wall in the gallery," he offered, irrelevantly, applying his knife to cut the square's edges. "We should limit our repairs to one room at a time."

Ah, the young ones were disturbing his studio. If she weren't so cranky, Thea might have laughed. Skeleton Man wasn't here to listen to her complaint. He needed help and didn't like asking for it.

"Taking the wall apart?" She wiped her dusty hands on a cloth she'd brought for the purpose. "May I watch?"

He didn't even have the courtesy to look relieved. He laid out the clean square on the table and set out down the long corridor as if he were doing her a favor. Really, he was no gentleman. But then, the gentlemen she met in ballrooms were all polish and no substance. She rather thought the Comte Lavigne was the opposite, although his substance was thick-headed and insensitive.

He had all but called her *self-centered* last night, in front of all the company.

Still, he had listened to her plaint without dismissing her. She could show she wasn't selfish and see what his problem was about—although curiosity provided equal incentive.

In the long walking gallery, they found his adolescent cousin, dark-haired Sofia, timidly attempting to chisel a hole in the southeast corner wall, while the young, fair-haired goddess Lavender brutally stabbed at the plaster with a knife.

The tutor and the boys had joined them and were attacking the wall with various instruments. Well, at least she knew Davy was well-guarded.

The sewing and button ladies gawked, although their fingers flew at the same time.

"Are you hoping to find a place in the wall that isn't stone?" Thea asked, crossing the enormous room to study the holes. Interesting that someone had bothered to plaster over the original stone—probably to beautify the ballroom. "Do you even know if a door exists?"

"We are working from an old architectural drawing that shows the tower but no entrance." Mr. Birdwhistle sounded apologetic. "I believe the tower may be purely ornamental, similar to the bell tower."

From outside the murky bubbles of the two-story gallery windows, Patience waved. She carried a scythe and a saw and led a couple of the orchard workers. Thea had never really looked out these windows. The front hill was naught but trees, and carriages seldom pulled up the weedy drive to the front steps. She admired the aging glass, but the imperfections distorted the view.

"Should we go outside and see what they are doing?" she suggested, hoping to draw the young ones from the work area. It was a lovely summer day. They should be having picnics and playing quoits or battledore. Defiantly, she refused to let Neville ruin their lives. "The boys need fresh air."

To her surprise, the artist followed them out. She had thought he would be relieved to have his studio cleared out so he could return to doing whatever it was he did. Perhaps he needed fresh air too.

Or did he guard Davy? Admittedly, the mild-mannered tutor wasn't exactly the sort who might successfully stand up to large bullies.

Tramping down the grassy drive, they studied the manor's foundation. Decades of dying boxwood, volunteer pines, vines, and just plain weeds hid the thick stone walls of the original priory. Various attempts had been made over the years to keep the greenery from reaching the windows, but that appeared to be the extent of any haphazard landscaping effort.

Thea wasn't an outdoor sort of person but she did like things to be neat. This. . . might as well be wild forest.

Tow-headed Oliver, her cousin's seven-year-old nephew, pushed between bushes nearly engulfing him. "Here," he yelled. "Tower."

Patience signaled for her men to start chopping a path to the foundation at the point Oliver indicated. Arnaud continued around the circular foundation, examining the empty windows. There weren't many on this level. Interestingly, Davy followed him. So Thea did the same.

The Wycliffe history books indicated the monastery's Gothic facade had been preserved when the first Reid destroyed the priory and drove out the poor monks. Well, probably wealthy monks, given the era and the size of their church. Had the tower been saved as well?

Arnaud shoved through the shrubbery underneath a pane well above his head. He gripped the ledge and pulled himself up with brute strength, shoulders bulging beneath his shirtsleeves. Thea thought she ought to look away, but she was too fascinated—with the windows, of course.

"Leaded glass," he called down. "Old." He dropped back into the shrubs.

"Not exactly a guard post. Do any of the windows look like one that might be above a door?" Thea studied the distance from the gallery's tall, pointed windows to the ground. . . The tower foundation was on a slanted hillside and much lower.

Arnaud continued circling toward the east side, near the drive. Due to the slope, the side stairs into the manor were not as high as the grandiose ones in front. Not finding anything, he circled back, still studying the foundation.

Davy popped a piece of candy into his mouth and took a seat on a mounting block. "Stairs," he commented with his mouth full.

Her brother was capable of complete sentences but seemed to be imitating Oliver, who was even less communicative than Skeleton Man.

Thea thought her brother was referring to the lack of stairs leading to a door, but Arnaud dropped back to where Davy sat and studied the tower. "He's right. Except at the top, the windows don't line up. There are no windows level with the ballroom, properly so if one wanted a guard tower. But see. . ." He pointed at the lowest window. "That one is about the height of the family floor." He walked around to the side. "That one spirals up to about level with the attic. And then there, behind the chimney stack, is one above the rooftop. There seems to be proper windows at the top, possibly a watch tower?"

"Attic," Davy said, poking his candy through the gap left by his missing front teeth.

"Roof," Oliver. . . argued?

Standing back, not touching anything, Lavender and Sofia followed their gestures with disappointment.

"We can't use a door on the *roof*." Wrinkling her delicate nose in disgust, Lavender sailed off, flounces flying.

Sofia lingered to examine the rose thorns Patience was uncovering with her shears.

Mr. Birdwhistle's gaze followed flamboyant Lavender, but the tutor remained with the boys, commending them for their perspicacity and asking them to gather leaves from the shrubbery so they might identify which plants might be valuable.

Thea scanned the wooded hillside to be certain she saw no sign of Neville. Now that the boys were outside, she was having second thoughts about leaving Davy visible to visitors.

Just like her father, Neville lacked compassion. If the two of them decided Davy presented an obstacle to their wishes, they'd pick him up and haul him off to the nearest asylum without a second thought. She should have married a duke and moved her brother to a remote castle, preferably in Scotland. Her father might have been satisfied by marriage settlements with a duke.

She had been selfish in holding out for some girlish notion of love or respect. Arnaud was right, in his own way. She'd been thinking of her needs, not Davy's, by fleeing marriage to come here. But *someone* had to consider her needs too. Her parents never had. She couldn't expect a husband to do so.

Besides, she could better look after Davy if she was free to use her own money. She simply needed to persuade the trustees that she did not intend to marry and have them release a portion of her funds.

Oliver gathered a handful of leaves and proceeded toward the front stairs, obviously uninterested in shrubbery or roses. Even though he was older, Davy ambled after his cousin, not even bothering with the leaves. He'd never had a friend before.

Mr. Birdwhistle murmured in passing as he followed, "They'll be heading for the attic or the roof." She could almost hear the *cunning little brats* in his voice. At least he said it in amusement.

Thea didn't want to explore a filthy attic and certainly not a roof. But curiosity seized her as Arnaud loped around to the side door.

The service stairwell used for carrying luggage was there. It went to the attic. Perhaps there were pieces stored in the vast wilderness of the upper story that she could use for the withdrawing room.

Really, the untouched canvas of Wycliffe Manor was far more entertaining than the staid museum of a duke's palace.

She hurried after Arnaud.

NINE

ARNAUD: TUESDAY MORNING

Arnaud cursed himself for being three kinds of fool for leading a parade into the attic to explore an obviously useless tower, one of several, he reminded himself. They were fake towers, built for an illusion of grandeur. One found fairy tale castles all over the Loire Valley, although those towers usually housed chambers of some sort. The first Reid of Wycliffe had simply wanted to impress and had an entire mountain of stone to quarry.

They had a dead body in the cellar, a grieving family and a killer to find, and he needed to be finishing a painting, or at the very least, working on the code books. Climbing into the manor's filthy attic with two boys, a tutor, and a mad heiress. . . Perhaps madness was contagious.

He hadn't expected Thea to even listen earlier and certainly hadn't anticipated that she'd follow him. That had been a foolish notion, he realized now, as he opened the door into one of the attic's many storage rooms. The heiress loved old bits, and he'd opened the path to rubbish heaven.

Every bit of ancient detritus discarded over the centuries had gravitated upstairs. The Reids never threw out anything as far as he could determine, and they had a *lot* of possessions. Before he'd given away his more elegant estates to his daughters, the earl had presumably hauled his favorite furnishings to his ancestral home. His predecessors had quite possibly done the same. Deteriorating books, hideous paintings, furniture that might make a good fire, moth-eaten clothing from centuries past. . .

Arnaud had amused himself during his isolation poking around, hoping to find clothes just to stay warm. Satin breeches weren't warm, and they'd all been too small. The earls hadn't been large men. But there had been moth-eaten blankets and counterpanes and old cushions, so he'd stayed warmer than he had in a prison cell.

Thea, the boys, and the tutor swept past him after he lit an oil lamp. This front attic had windows and wasn't as bad as some toward the center of the manor. It might even have made a good schoolroom, only the earls hadn't raised children here. Arnaud assumed the detritus had been gathering for centuries.

Thea lifted her delicate muslin hem and turned about, examining the chaos. "Had this space been on the floor below, it could have been the solar of a medieval castle. What a shame to waste it on an attic!"

If he'd given it any thought, he'd have to agree.

Like little monkeys, the boys scrambled over trunks and discarded furniture. The tutor ambled over to the windows to look out. Thea studied the attic's grimy contents with the narrowed eyes of an experienced hunter. Arnaud almost admired her single-mindedness.

But for reasons beyond his comprehension, he was supposed to be looking for an entrance into an ornamental tower. He held up the lamp so he could discern the squared-off front corners of the room—no sign of a round tower here. He shoved aside crumbling old trunks with his battered boots, forcing a path to the leaded glass windows overlooking the front. . . *not* a lawn. Mostly, he could see a sea of evergreens and treetops. This storage room seemed to be directly above the gallery.

The boys knocked on the dark panels on the tower side. No door was immediately visible.

Thea exclaimed over what appeared to be an extremely delicate writing desk. He'd crush anything like that if he so much as leaned against it.

His eye caught on a massive wardrobe next to where the boys worked. The doors hung on one hinge and a gash marred the darkened wood. As he approached, Arnaud expected to find a skeleton inside. Life in Gravesyde Priory led to morbid imaginings, especially after studying the knife marks. Had someone used the door for target practice?

He expected the piece to molder to sawdust when he put a shoulder to the back corner in an effort to shove it from the wall.

"Jacobean," a soft feminine voice wafted over the loud scratch of wood against wood. "Centuries old. Perhaps belonging to the first earl? I need to study the histories more instead of the lady's journals."

Picturing a black-wigged pirate in billowing sleeves and a feathered cap slashing at the wardrobe with a cutlass, Arnaud shoved harder. Maybe the fellow had hidden his jewels in here and someone had smashed the wardrobe in search of them. He had no illusions about the Wycliffe fortune. The men had been ruthless soldiers and pirates—privateers, if they had the king's approval—plundering monasteries and Spanish ships for treasure.

One did not accumulate Wycliffe's riches by politely painting portraits or scribbling novels. Even Henri, with his brilliant business acumen, would never become as wealthy as the Reids, because he enjoyed people and shared his good fortune instead of using his cleverness to rob his customers or his competitors.

Behind the wardrobe was the same cracked paneling the boys pounded on. They peered behind the wardrobe and grunted in disappointment.

Forcing his shoulders into the narrow aperture, Arnaud took out his knife and pried at one of the longer cracks in the wood. The knife slid in to the hilt. He pounded his fist against the wall and got a hollow echo instead of a thud.

"Door," Davy said, retreating. A moment later, he returned with what appeared to be a rusted kitchen utensil.

Arnaud wished the Wycliffes were given to storing useful tools in the attics, not cake servers or whatever this was, but it had an edge he could use. He jammed it into the crack and levered it, not daring to pull hard or he'd crack the handle. He cracked it anyway.

The boys scampered through the attic, hunting for more levers.

"Mr. Birdwhistle, if you will," Thea called, "Ask Quincy if there are any keys to the attic and if he has anything to pry open a door. I will keep an eye on the boys."

Keys? While the tutor obediently trotted out, Arnaud stepped back and considered a locked door. . . behind the panel? He shoved the sagging wardrobe further out of his way and applied his boot to the wood.

It cracked more.

"Don't," Thea warned. "We don't know what's on the other side. It's best to keep a door that can be locked in case it is dangerous."

The chances of finding centuries-old keys. . . Rather than bark at her, Arnaud made room in the cluttered chaos to reposition the wardrobe, leaving access to what they had to assume was a hidden door. He began poking around, looking for hinges or lock or anything that might be pried open.

"No lock, no door," he concluded by the time Quincy ran up with his ring of keys and several small tools.

Quincy was not an old family retainer with all the secrets to the manor. The prior caretakers were both dead. Arnaud's engineer cousin might have worked out the best way of accessing a fake tower, but Arnaud had only brute force. He took a chisel and pried at a panel.

"Why am I doing this?" he asked as the wood cracked and chipped.

"I am not entirely certain." Ignoring his efforts, Thea sorted through the rubble, moving small pieces that she apparently meant to rescue toward the entrance. She used a ragged garment from one of the trunks to dust off the worst of the filth on her treasures.

"Perfume," Davy explained.

Right. He wanted Lavender and Sofia out of the gallery if they were intent on setting up smelly perfumeries.

They wouldn't want to set up shop in the attic.

He was as mad as the rest of Hunt's family. Perhaps madness was a result of being dead inside. Would that apply to an heiress raised in opulence?

While Quincy returned to his duties, Arnaud continued working on the cracked wood. The panel finally popped loose. With a bit more eager prying from the boys, they pulled it off in splintered pieces.

A solid door blocked their way, one with a latch and a keyhole—neither of which matched Quincy's more modern keys.

"I can probably hammer it out," Arnaud suggested, not eager to do so after Thea's warning. The boys lived up here, and they would want to explore.

Mr. Birdwhistle examined the ancient brass lock. "A locksmith might open and replace it. If you don't mind, I'd prefer that."

The boys had found a trunk of puppets and didn't protest.

Their new footman trotted up, gasping for breath from the climb. "Quincy says as we have a visitor, and he ain't trotting back up here." He strained to see what they were doing.

"You could have carried the calling card," Thea reminded him.

"No card, miss. He's calling at the side door, askin' for the master of the house." The sallow Hanks straightened his narrow shoulders. "I told him to go 'round to the kitchen, but he says he won't."

Arnaud gathered up his tools. "I'll heave him out on his ear, pretend I'm useful, shall I?" He stomped for the door, forcing the nosy footman backward.

TEN

PAUL: TUESDAY MORNING

WEARING HIS TOOLBELT, PAUL MADE THE ROUNDS OF HIS PARISHIONERS. HE KNEW the vicar frowned upon his lowly occupation, but he found helping with small repairs encouraged people to talk so he had a better idea of the village's needs. He thought he heard more hope now than when he'd arrived, but that could just be because the sun was out.

As he mended a fence post in a front yard, he noticed a stranger riding toward the manor. His slouch hat and loose coat didn't appear to be the attire of a wealthy gentleman, but not many poor men owned horses.

"That's one of poor Mr. Boston's grandsons." Mrs. Oswald, wife of the village postmaster, watched the stranger trot past. "They haven't visited in ever so long, but I'd recognize that long, sharp nose anywhere. His great-granddad had the same."

"Thank heavens one of the family has shown up." In relief, Paul thumped the post in a little tighter and shook it to be certain it would hold. "I'd better return to the parsonage to see if he's headed there."

He'd been avoiding his home to avoid the presence of Thea's obnoxious cousin, who had apparently not left this morning. Paul had sent a warning up to the house when he heard the rumors that Mr. Talbot meant to find lodgings in the area. He couldn't in all conscience warn the villagers against taking rent from a man who might bring them a little extra income.

Following the stranger, he noted him turning up the Wycliffe drive instead of continuing to the parsonage. Given that the chapel had been abandoned for fifteen years, he could understand that. He hurried up the walking path, arriving at the manor about the same time as the rider who had to take the more circular drive.

The walking path approached the front door. The formal drive offered a choice between front and side. The stranger hesitated, then turned his mount toward the portico. Paul dashed up the crumbling front stairs, confident that Quincy had seen him and would open the door.

He was disappointed. He had to ring and knock before the new footman arrived. Paul handed him his hat. "Where's Quincy?"

"In the attic, and how I'm to answer two doors at once is beyond me," Hanks grumbled.

"One at a time." Paul headed for the library, knowing Minerva would be there.

She glanced up from the code books she'd spread around her. "If our dead scholar read all these books, then he'd have been able to crack the earl's feeble code. I wish we'd known him."

"His grandson is riding up to the side door. Do you think he's studied codes?"

"The side door? Does he look like a scholar, one hopes? Do you need to take him to the study? I'll have tea brought up." She reached for the bellpull.

"I have no right to the captain's study. . ." But the captain wasn't here, the formal parlor was too large, and a curate was best to break the news to the man. Although, the fact that the grandson was here might indicate he'd heard the sad tidings.

Minerva ignored his protest and ordered up tea. By the time the maid had come and gone, voices could be heard at the side door. They were not exactly quiet.

"Keep the connecting door ajar," Paul advised Minerva. "You might understand our visitor in terms I won't."

Straightening his shabby coat and waistcoat, adjusting his neckcloth, Paul hurried toward the side door. By the time he arrived, Quincy had allowed the visitor in but Arnaud blocked his entrance into the manor. The side door really was only for guests and family since there was no vestibule to leave them in. Quincy had better things to do than stand guard on visitors.

"The earl is long dead," Arnaud was saying brusquely as Paul arrived. "State your business, and we will determine who might help you."

"Who is in charge then? My grandfather is dead, and I was told the manor might tell me how. Has he been buried?" The stranger sounded more frantic and angry than anguished. About the same height as Paul, but less broad, he didn't fill out his loose coat, and his waistcoat and neckcloth didn't appear quite clean. If he'd ridden from the city, then there might be reason for that.

Paul eased past the massive boxer of a butler and giant Arnaud to hold out his hand. "I'm Paul Upton, the curate. And you are?"

"Timothy Cooper, Jeremiah Boston was my grandfather. He was a friend of the earl's. I want to know what happened!" The man looked agitated, twisting his hat between large-knuckled fingers.

Paul nodded toward the main corridor. "Let us go somewhere quiet. Mr. Lavigne, would you care to join us?"

"You know as much as I. I shall be in the gallery if you need me." The surly artist stomped off to his studio, leaving Paul to lead their guest to Hunt's study.

A maid hurried in with tea as Mr. Cooper took the seat Paul indicated. She set the tray down and fled on the way to her many tasks. The manor truly did need more help. They couldn't complain too much about incompetent footmen who might learn as they worked.

"I regret the circumstances under which we meet, Mr. Cooper. Do you live nearby?" Paul tried to relax the gentleman, but he twitched and grimaced and glanced around at the oak-paneled study and book-filled shelves with discomfort.

"Outside Birmingham a way. I got word from a fellow I oncet knew. I hadn't heard my grandfather was ill. Can you tell me what happened?" His speech wasn't polished, but it wasn't uneducated either.

"Did your grandfather usually lock his doors? Was he likely to take in strangers?" Paul would prefer to console, but someone had to act in Hunt's place if Arnaud refused.

Mr. Cooper looked confused and even more anxious. "I don't know, now, do I? I haven't lived with him since I was a lad. What's this got to do with his death?"

"It appears an intruder may have hit him." Paul didn't want to reveal more. As he understood it, this man or a sibling stood to inherit a nice piece of property. He had to be suspicious, even if it went against the grain. "We were hoping you could tell us more. Did he have valuables a thief might have stolen?"

The man's eyes widened in fright. "I didn't do it! I don't know nothing about it! All I know is he's got books and goats and the like. Mayhap he just fell? He was old."

"Not that old and apparently in good health, according to our apothecary. He didn't have the smell of alcohol about him. Do you know if anyone had any reason to wish him harm?"

"I don't know nothing, I tell ya! I ain't been to see him in years. My ma came down ever oncet in a while. But she died a year back or so. Saw him at her funeral, but that wasn't in this godforsaken place. You think someone *killed* him?" His terror seemed genuine.

"It appears that way, to the best of our ability to tell. If we have a killer on the loose, we need to find him, which is why we need to know anything you can tell us about your grandfather's habits. Did he have frequent visitors? Invite in strangers? Own anything valuable?" Paul was growing a trifle impatient with a man who didn't show an ounce of sorrow for a man who, from all reports, was an exceptionally civilized, respectable scholar.

Mr. Cooper shook his head vehemently and pushed back his chair. "I don't know nothing. Where's he buried at? I'll pay my respects, but I got to get back to work."

"We've been waiting for family to tell us how you would like to have him buried. Is there a family plot? More family we should notify?" Paul stood when the other man did. How the devil did he hold him here?

"He ain't buried?" Now Mr. Cooper looked panicked. "I ain't got coins to pay. You do what you have to but I have to get to work."

Paul blocked the door. "Family, sir? To whom do we write?"

"My brother, that's all. Don't know where he's at. He went to university, may still be there. Ain't seen him since our mother's funeral. You ask for Francis Cooper, maybe at that place in Cambridge. Doubt you'll hear from him, though. He fancies himself a nob." The man put his cap back on and waited for Paul to let him pass.

Before Paul could respond, Minerva slipped through the connecting door. "Mr. Cooper? I am so sorry to hear of your grandfather. I understand the earl enjoyed Professor Boston's extensive library and a good game of chess. Do you know who is now responsible for his property? We wish to show his memory the respect he deserves."

Paul bit back a desire to laugh. She'd just slapped their guest's lack of compassion with words.

Mr. Cooper pulled off his hat again and made a hasty bow. "Ma'am. Yes, reckon he was a good man. I'm not the bookish sort. My brother might know what to do with all them books and things."

"He's the eldest then? He inherits?" Petite Minerva was all blue-eyed innocence from beneath her haystack of hair. Paul thought a pencil might be holding the tresses back.

Mr. Cooper nodded hastily. "Now that Ma's dead, I reckon he does. Never asked."

"I don't suppose you could take a little more time from your position to go over to the cottage and notice if anything is missing or disarranged? As it is, anyone could ride up and claim to be your brother, and we would not know the difference. Perhaps you could stay for the funeral?"

"I can't pay for it," he repeated frantically. "I've got responsibilities."

"Finding the person who may have harmed your grandfather is a little more important than paying for a funeral," Paul said soothingly.

He would never earn a fortune making caskets, he knew already. The manor's maintenance fund reimbursed his costs, labor, and the gravediggers. At some point, the village might have enough people for a government and a tax to cover the indigent but not any time soon.

"If someone doesn't look after the cottage, vagrants will move in," Minerva added, sounding sorrowful. "You may wish to choose some cherished mementoes before that happens."

Paul was fairly certain she was being manipulative, which is why he adored her. His natural inclination was straightforward. She'd learned to hide behind any disguise that suited the situation. Any clue to a killer might help, even if it necessitated playing on emotions.

Mr. Cooper relaxed his tense shoulders a fraction as he glanced at her. Minerva was petite, not exactly delicate but not formidable either. She was wearing a simple blue morning gown, topped by a modest fichu, and her fingers were stained with ink. No one could possibly see any harm in her. Fortunately, they couldn't see into her inventive, devious mind.

Their guest crumpled his hat in his gnarled fingers, then nodded, once. "Aye, then mayhap I should stay until you put the old gent in the ground. He was good to us."

"Thank you, sir." Paul bowed his gratitude. "The gravediggers are at work. Would you like to see him before you go over to the cottage?"

He considered this. "Will there be a service?"

"I'd planned to hold one in the chapel this afternoon, but we have no means of laying out a coffin. He'll go directly from the crypt to the graveyard." Paul opened the door to escort him out while Minerva slid quietly back into the library.

"Then I'll attend the service," Mr. Cooper decided. "It ain't right to see the old gent when he's not at his best. He liked to be proper, he did."

"That's good to know, thank you. If you'll allow me to have a horse saddled, I'll accompany you to the cottage to be certain no one has attempted to enter overnight. My deacon has been looking after the animals, but word goes around. You know how it is." Paul directed their guest down the side hall where he could pick up his hat and gloves. He'd taken to leaving spares at the manor, never knowing where he'd be from one hour to the next.

"What animals has he got now?" Mr. Cooper looked more interested than he had since arriving.

"Goats and chickens, I believe. Do you work with animals?" Paul collected his belongings from the new footman and peered into the gallery, signaling Arnaud that he was departing.

Arnaud noticed and nodded. Paul hoped that meant he'd be following shortly. Neither of them qualified as a magistrate, but they could act as Hunt's witnesses.

"Aye. I'm steward for a working estate up north of the city. Nothing fancy, but he's got good farm land, a few head of cattle." He cast a glance at the orchard down the hill. "Used to sneak up here and steal apples when I was a lad. Didn't no one take care of the place."

"Yes, it's been in the hands of solicitors for a while, but the family is trying to take it back. If you'll wait here. . ." Paul left him feeding a handful of grain to his own mount and ran back to the stable to borrow one of Elsa's mares and warn them to have one ready for Arnaud.

Wycliffe Manor might be a dead end, impoverished and likely to stay that way, but the inhabitants were generous and congenial. For a first parish, Paul couldn't have asked for better. Anywhere else, he would have had to cover miles on foot and probably starved.

Mr. Cooper surprisingly took a different direction than they'd taken yesterday, a footpath through a fallow field instead of straight through the village. The path led to a nearly overgrown hole in a hedgerow and directly into Boston's back pasture, bypassing the village and its gossips.

"I'm new here. I hadn't realized that path was there," Paul admitted, climbing down to tie his horse to the fence, where it could nibble grass.

"Granddad didn't like to be seen heading up to the manor, I reckon." He tied up his horse and followed Paul to the back door. "I wasn't around then, but he told us stories. From his tales, I always thought the manor was a palace."

"To a booklover, I daresay it was a treasure trove." Paul glanced around. The goats were gone. So were the chickens. He held up a hand to stop his companion. "The neighbors were supposed to look out for the animals, but they seem to have taken them home."

Mr. Cooper frowned. "Might make chores easier, I reckon. I don't know if Frank will ever visit. Seems sad to let the property run to ruin."

"I don't know if there are buyers, but he might try to sell it. Perhaps we can find his direction inside." Paul didn't carry weapons, but he still wore his toolbelt. Not liking the missing animals, he kept his hand on his chisel as he approached the cottage. Arnaud and Henri had found keys and locked up after they'd removed the body. There shouldn't be anyone in there, but he erred on the side of caution.

Before he could reach behind the shrubbery under the window for the peg Henri said he'd hung them on, Mr. Cooper brushed the bush aside, indicating he remembered its placement. The peg was empty. He shrugged and waited for Paul to produce the keys.

"Did everyone know those keys hung on that peg?" Paul asked, testing the latch. It was unlocked.

"More'n likely." The weathered farmer frowned. "You think someone's been inside?"

"I fear so. We left the cottage locked." Paul gave the door a shove but stayed outside. He'd prefer any intruder to rush out the front door.

He'd be running into Arnaud's arms, if so. Paul could hear a horse coming up the lane at a gallop. The former French count liked his horses fast.

Hearing no disturbance inside, he held his chisel and eased inside.

Someone had torn through the tidy kitchen like a cyclone.

ELEVEN

ARNAUD: TUESDAY MORNING

After helping the curate search the scholar's cottage, unable to determine if anything had gone missing, Arnaud left the dead man's grandson with Upton. Chickens and goats did not vanish on their own. Neither were they easily transported unless one had a cart and cages. But someone living nearby. . .

He followed the lane to a broken place in the hedgerow, beyond which he could see a badly rutted path. Careful of his borrowed mount, he eased into an overgrown pasture, wary of cattle of any sort. He didn't see fresh manure.

The path led to a falling down fence and a badly tended vegetable garden. Wondering about land ownership and rents in this district where the manor and the bank fought over ancient, misdrawn deeds and maps, Arnaud swung down and proceeded cautiously toward a low stone cottage nearly hidden behind overgrown hedges.

He heard the goat before he saw it. Following the bleating, he located it tied to a fence post, chopping unmown weeds around the garden. A hen squawked and half leapt/flew past a stump to peck at a bare patch among what Arnaud assumed were potato vines. He couldn't tell one goat or chicken from another and didn't recognize these as a certainty.

Before he could hunt for a door on the thatched cottage, a lanky farmer in torn trousers and ragged linen, sporting an unshaven, gaunt jaw, emerged carrying an ancient blunderbuss.

"Who you?" the scarecrow demanded.

Excellent question, not one Arnaud could easily answer. "Professor Boston's grandson has arrived. I have come to return the goat and hens. It was kind of you to look after them." Always go for the simple answer when faced with a weapon was his policy.

"Ain't his. They's mine now. Et a hole right through my turnips." He gestured loosely at the weedy garden. "Old bastard owes me."

"I believe you have to take that up with the magistrate—or his grandson will call it theft." Wondering if turnips were worth killing a man over, Arnaud pondered how to question an armed man. "Has Mr. Boston caused you harm?"

"Aye, he cut down my hedgerow and blackberries! And he refused to pay for the damage. Told the bastard he'd pay, one way or 'nuther. I reckon the goat will do." The farmer staggered slightly and lowered his weapon. "His spawn ain't got the sense to look arter them. They'll be gone tomorrow."

The man was drunk and just disgruntled and big enough to swing a heavy shovel to release his animosity. But how the devil did one prove he was the killer? "Have you seen the grandsons recently? Do you have reason to believe they have caused you harm?"

To keep his balance, the farmer held the blunderbuss barrel and planted the stock in the dirt. "Useless lot. Ain't seen nothin' of them since they was tads. Nah, it was the old bastard who did in my vines. Liked things tidy, he does, except for his tart. That one's a sight. She'd be worth a hen or two."

Gathering that the neighbor didn't know Boston was dead, Arnaud led him a little more. "Tart? I didn't know we had any such around here." Well, he'd had a lonely widow lady who couldn't support herself and didn't mind his occasional company, but no one could call her a *tart*. She even attended church on Sundays.

"Don't. She comes in a little gig. Saw her all tricked out in frills, prancing up to his door like she's the queen 'erself. Guess he likes his women tidy too."

"Could she have been his daughter?" Arnaud tried to ask casually.

Apparently not casually enough. The drunk frowned. "Why you askin? I ain't givin' back them animals."

He was really bad at this. Until recently, he'd had no interest in farmers or goats or frilly tarts. But Arnaud knew how hard his cousin struggled to play the part of magistrate and bring justice to a district that had gone lawless for too long. Any little bit of information might be helpful. Could women swing shovels?

Reluctantly, he offered, "My name is Lavigne, a cousin of the new magistrate. And yours?"

The farmer staggered slightly in attempting to hold the blunderbuss and tug his cap. "Finkley, pleasure. Magistrate?"

Assuming Finkley had no wife to attend church and gather gossip, Arnaud nodded. "Captain Huntley at Wycliffe Manor is the new magistrate. He will be pleased to hear your grievances. I fear Boston's grandsons are likely to complain of the loss of livestock if you do not come to terms with them."

Finkley snorted. "Them two ain't likely to do nothin'. Me and Boston will fight it out."

One more try. "Have you noticed anyone else visiting with Mr. Boston lately?"

Finkley shrugged. "Only notice if I'm down by the lane. Ain't down there now there's no berries. Why you askin'?"

Not seeing any means of learning more, Arnaud finally explained, "I fear Boston is no longer with us. They are burying him today, I believe, now that one of his grandsons has arrived. You will need to take up the matter of the berries and the goat with him."

Finkley staggered again, this time in surprise. "What? I just 'eard 'im over there, t'other day, choppin' wood. What'd he do, chop his foot off? Foolish old bugger."

Did the farmer look nervous? Arnaud wasn't inclined to notice such things, so couldn't really read anxious tics. "No, I fear it must have been a thief. Do you know if he had anything valuable anyone might want to steal?"

Finkley blinked as if attempting to process too many ideas at once. "I got his goat, didn't I? What's that got to do with him dyin'?"

He should have sent the curate over to do the questioning. Arnaud surrendered. "I do not believe the thief wanted a goat. He tore the house apart. Did you hear that, perhaps?"

Finkley finally frowned, possibly figuring out the reason for the questions. "I think you better go now. I ain't got nothin' to do with that old bastard except his goat. And it's mine now."

Arnaud tipped his hat and mounted his steed. "Your new neighbor may question the loss of Professor Boston's animals. It might be neighborly to take them back, tell them you were tending them. Perhaps they won't cut down your blackberries next time."

He rode off, praying the drunken old goat didn't decide to take aim at his back.

TWELVE

THEA: TUESDAY LUNCHEON

After Quincy and his son carted Cousin Clare's new furniture into the newly-empty withdrawing room, Mrs. Upton protected the new pieces with stiff, unbleached Holland linen. Clare had chosen silver-blue and gold damask for the sofa and loveseat. The fabric square Arnaud had cut out for framing was predominantly gold, accented with vividly colored blue-green peacocks. Thea thought she could work with those colors. She'd love to do wallpaper, but it was not only expensive, it was not easily cleaned. Maybe someday. . .

If she stayed. She tried not to think of all the reasons she might have to flee this haven. She had felt safe here, until Neville arrived on the doorstep. She didn't know if she could trust the manor residents to protect Davy, as her parents never had. She didn't trust her own judgment in this.

To her utter amazement, the aunts actually descended from their suite to peruse the new furnishings, removing the covers to peer under them.

"My mother's portrait would work well in here," Great-aunt Lavinia decided. Tall, thin, wearing a mobcap over her gray hair, the earl's seventy-five-year-old daughter held precedence, if anyone did. "Her gown uses that blue with the Reid diamond pendant."

Thea had definite opinions about how this room should look, and it didn't include bewigged old ladies glaring down at them from the walls. If society had taught her nothing else, it had taught her to dissemble, however. "I'd hate to disturb the portrait gallery. The earl hung the paintings in a particular order and removing one would leave an odd empty space. I thought pastoral scenes might be soothing."

The captain's mother, newly arrived from the Americas, twirled to study the dirty, tattered walls. Mrs. Huntley had slipped into the family as if she'd always been there, although it was Thea's understanding that the late viscountess's daughters had previously been estranged. Perhaps the death of their mother had repaired their relations. Thea couldn't sense what The Lady thought about having both her daughters here, in what had never really been their home.

"Cozier than the formal parlor," Mrs. Huntley concluded. "Perhaps sweet paintings of children and pets? Most of the landscapes I've seen here have been dark and stormy."

"Horses, for the gentlemen," her sister, plump, amiable Lady Spalding exclaimed. "I know they'll sit and drink their brandies in the dining room, but if we wish to have them join us afterward, they need to feel they're not invading a feminine nest."

"Very astute, my ladies. We may need to find sturdier chairs as well. I will start a search after luncheon, thank you!" Thea intended to return the vestibule paintings to their proper places in hopes that might help find the key mentioned in one of the earl's odd letters. But the manor walls and attics were filled with artwork. There was even some in the mostly empty east wing. . .

"A sturdy writing desk," Lady Lavinia suggested. "And a small card table, of course. This will be delightful come winter! I hope Huntley has commissioned chimney sweeps. Ours smokes dreadfully."

Thea left the ladies to their decorating. This was their house, too, even if they seldom emerged from their quarters to enjoy it. She'd spent enough time with the aunts to know they would make a thousand suggestions and forget them all by day's end. She wasn't worried about her occupation being usurped. She might not deal well with people, but she knew furniture.

She heard the men clattering in the side door, but she was hungry and didn't wait. She could pick up a few nibbles and retreat to somewhere comfortable if they stormed the breakfast room, as they were wont to do.

She'd forgotten that half the male inhabitants had gone to Birmingham. Even Henri was on one of his peddling trips.

The only men to intrude upon her luncheon were Arnaud and Paul, and black clouds of gloom practically hovered over their heads. Minerva followed, her brow wrinkled quizzically. Despite her reservations about male company, Thea lingered.

"Was someone else murdered?" Minerva demanded, filling her plate. Death apparently didn't unnerve a colonel's daughter.

Thea hadn't followed the story of some old man's death, since it didn't involve her or Davy. She took a seat and nibbled at her cheese while jotting notes of things she must do next.

"The professor's cottage has been ransacked." Paul answered. "We left Mr. Cooper sorting through the debris, but he says he hasn't visited his grandfather in years. He'll have no idea what was there. We should have left a guard."

"We do not have enough people to leave a guard. We should not need a dam. . . an army. What sort of place is this if scurrilous scoundrels rob dead men?" Arnaud slapped a stack of meat between thick slices of bread and bit into it angrily.

Startled by his outburst, Thea couldn't help watching in fascination. She was so accustomed to sophisticated gentlemen bowing and scraping in her presence, that she couldn't quite comprehend a man who behaved as if she didn't exist.

"You both saw the cottage yesterday. Could you not tell if anything large went missing?" She couldn't resist speaking just to see if she had turned invisible.

Instead of sitting, Arnaud paced like an angry bull, gnawing at his sandwich.

The curate was the one to answer. "I don't believe they were stealing furniture. His books were strewn all over the floor, his kitchen cabinets emptied. One assumes they were after the items we found hidden in Boston's desk, which means we need to study them more carefully."

"The books?" Minerva paled. "Did they harm them?"

Mr. Upton took the time to pat her shoulder. "I don't think so. We'll fetch them later, if Mr. Cooper allows."

"Did you tell this Mr. Cooper that you had some of his grandfather's effects?" Out of spite, Thea rose to refill her plate and step in the path of Arnaud's furious pacing.

He almost walked into her, frowned, turned around, and stalked to the other side of the table.

Well, she wasn't invisible.

"I didn't know if it was wise," Paul responded apologetically. "He didn't seem upset about his grandfather's death or care much about the books. And I have only Mrs. Oswald's identification that he is actually the grandson, and she based that on his nose. Perhaps after this afternoon's service, if others recognize him. . ."

Minerva shook her head. "No, don't tell him about the journal or the letters. For all we know, this Timothy Cooper might have done it. We have no other way of hunting for a killer. The professor evidently possessed *something* that someone wants."

Arnaud snorted. "His goat. His neighbor stole that and the hens. He claims Boston chopped down his blackberries, and it is fair trade. He did not look the sort to read."

"Two thieves?" Minerva asked. "One to steal animals and the other to steal books?"

Arnaud shrugged. Paul shook his head and filled his plate. Both were more interested in eating than explaining.

Thea made a moue of distaste. "I had hoped to work on rehanging the artwork in the vestibule this afternoon. The boys have calculated where each piece goes and numbered them accordingly. But it sounds as if we must first read the letters of the deceased's daughter, if only to find the rest of the family. I can help you with that, I suppose. His journal, however, might be beyond me."

Arnaud finally stopped pacing. "I shall help hang the oils. Paul and Minerva are better at paperwork."

Now, he looked at her. The man truly was single-minded. "There are some discrepancies," she warned. "Not all the art fits into the spaces allotted."

"Seeing the haphazard way the paintings were hung, I do not doubt that." Now that he was on ground he understood, he quit pacing to examine the buffet again.

"Will Mr. Cooper have enough to eat?" Minerva asked. "Do we need to send a lunch basket?"

"The cottage's pantry still had supplies, and he wanted to visit the neighbors he remembered from childhood." Paul filled his plate but politely waited for Thea to return to her seat.

Thea had been so fascinated with Arnaud, she'd forgotten her own manners. Hastily filling her plate, she sat so the men could. "Does this mean we ought to attend the funeral service to watch for anyone suspicious?"

Arnaud slapped his plate down at the end of the oval table. "I thought we are to hang paintings."

He actually wanted her help? "I assume the service won't last long?" She gazed questioningly at Paul.

"Just a few words and allowing others to speak of him. It would be thoughtful if some of the family attended, since he was a friend of the earl's." Paul poured watered cider into his glass.

"I'll go and take Lavender, since she knows the village ladies better. Her workers might want to attend. I'll work on the letters after." Propping a book in front of her, Minerva nibbled at her potato salad.

That was a relief. Thea hadn't brought her few blacks. Of course, that left her helping Arnaud in the vestibule, since he wasn't part of the earl's family and didn't need to attend.

Since no one mentioned Neville, she had to assume he'd hied off to complain to her father. Excellent.

After luncheon, Thea aimed for the schoolroom in the attic to involve the boys in the art-hanging project. She ran into Lady Lavinia, who'd apparently been lying in wait. Her great-aunt had helped her to escape to the manor, so she stopped to listen.

"It is Lavender's eighteenth birthday tomorrow. I have a gift, but a birthday like that should have a bit of celebration, should it not?" The overbearing *grande dame* appeared almost hesitant.

"Oh, very definitely," Thea assured her. This was a task she could manage. "I'll have the boys draw birthday greetings to put on the table in the morning. And ask the kitchen for a cake. I don't believe we have any more Champagne but perhaps music after dinner?"

"No, no, it should be quiet, given the circumstances of her birth. Perhaps ask her grandmother in the kitchen to join us?" Lady Lavinia grimaced as she asked.

Ah, the grandmother who'd been a kitchen maid. . ."I'll have Mrs. Upton do that for you. That's an excellent thought. If you think of anything else, let us know. Lavender is such a lovely girl, she deserves a little acknowledgment!"

She deserved a *lot* of acknowledgment, but as a baseborn child, Lavender had been ostracized most of her life. Not until she'd come to the manor had her talents been recognized. Thea understood how lonely it could be to be ignored. She would make certain the girl had the best celebration ever.

Lady Lavinia nodded grandly and swept on.

Thea ran up to the schoolroom to speak with Mr. Birdwhistle. Minerva had hinted the tutor wasn't who he was said to be, but she found him harmless enough. He did seem vaguely familiar, but a tutor would never have been allowed in any social setting she had attended before she ran away.

"The boys aren't very artistic," Mr. Birdwhistle warned when she asked for cards. "But they like Miss Lavender. They will think of something. Shall we bring our vestibule charts down now?"

"Yes, please. Arnaud is lining up the artwork. He's cleaned it all and not found anything significant, I fear." Departing the schoolroom, she glanced in the storage area, wondering if Walker had called a locksmith to open the tower door yet.

Inside, Herbert, the new footman, was poking furtively about in a trunk. He glanced up guiltily when Thea stopped in the doorway.

"We was hoping to find more uniforms." He straightened and bowed. He was wearing a coat designed for a taller man, presumably one of Henri's second-hand purchases.

"I doubt seriously that the late earl bothered with uniformed servants, and Lady Reid couldn't afford them. Henri will bring back something Lavender can tailor for you." She would have swept on, forgetting him, but she was aware that she and Minerva now served as the only mistresses of the house at the moment. "Is your room satisfactory? Was there anything else you needed?"

"No, ma'am. I'm very happy to be here, ma'am." He bowed again.

That's when she experienced a panicky fear of a stranger having access to the upstairs where Davy slept. She gestured for him to precede her, then instead of following, rushed back to the schoolroom.

Mr. Birdwhistle raised his eyebrows questioningly.

"The new footman was up here, poking around," she whispered, so as not to alert Davy. "You will need to be very vigilant until we know we can trust him."

He widened his eyes. "That tower. . . it could very well be an escape route, out of sight of the household. Is there a lock for the storage door?"

"I'll ask. I think he'd have to make a lot of noise breaking in the tower's lock, though, and I don't believe anyone has found an exit at the bottom." Thea tried not to look for trouble. Neville wasn't likely to get himself dirty, but if he had a partner in evil deeds—

Mr. Birdwhistle pointed at the schoolroom window overlooking the side yard. Both boys were watching. . . what?

"The gardeners have almost cleared the shrubbery at the bottom of the tower," the tutor informed her. "The men have been working in one location, so I assume they've found an entrance. I've been wondering if I should let the boys outside to watch. If we join you in the vestibule, they might not be paying as much attention as you could wish."

So much for working mathematics and learning Latin. But it was summer, and the boys should be allowed a little freedom. They ought to be out riding horses and playing hoops, but neither seemed much inclined toward sports.

"Very well. Set them free for a bit. If the tower has a door, surely, it will be locked, but curiosity will be satisfied." Besides, the notion of working in that small vestibule, shoulder to shoulder with Arnaud. . . left her believing the outdoors was a far safer idea.

She heard the boys shouting with glee as she fled downstairs again. She had thought living a life of morning calls and soirees and ballrooms was hectic. Wycliffe Manor presented a whole different assortment of tasks. As soon as she became comfortable with one, three more took its place.

Minerva and Paul, dressed in black, were just donning their church hats as she reached the side hall.

Thea took her bonnet and shawl from the closet under the stairs. Quincy must be outside. "Patience has apparently uncovered the tower base. Where is Arnaud? He probably ought to be there if there's a door."

"Arnaud is helping to transport the coffin to the cemetery. I'll warn Patience not to get carried away until we return!" Paul hurried Minerva out.

That warning apparently came too late. When Thea stepped into the side yard, the gardeners were already setting aside their shovels. Standing on her toes, she peered over their shoulders. They'd cleared the shrubbery from the place where the boys had indicated the bottom of the tower stairs might be. A newly dug hole revealed a muddy wooden door in the foundation.

THIRTEEN

ARNAUD: TUESDAY AFTERNOON

ARNAUD WATCHED THE COFFIN CART ROLL OFF BEARING THE DECEASED AND BRUSHED the grime off his hands. He would have run up the front steps to see if they'd started work in the vestibule, until he noticed Paul and Minerva gesturing from near the tower.

He trotted down the rutted gravel that passed for a carriage drive. He was still in his filthy linen, neckcloth askew with the heat of exertion, waistcoat unbuttoned over ancient buckskin breeches. He didn't think the curate and soldier's daughter minded, but once he reached the tower, he saw the heiress posing over a muddy hole. As if she were Zephyr summoning a breeze, her gauzy gown wafted in a draft, conforming to her delicate figure. He should have gone in for his coat, at the very least.

She glanced up at his arrival, then hastily looked away at his indecent attire. *Merde.* One of these days he would return to being a gentleman. This wasn't one of those days.

"Minerva and I have to be at the chapel for the funeral service." Upton nodded at the workmen waiting for orders. "You, Patience, and Miss Talbot will need to decide what to do about that door." He sounded worried.

As he should be. Arnaud understood at once that a hidden door in the tower could lead to the hidden door in the attic—and no one inside the manor would be able to detect intruders entering or exiting. No wonder the damned thing had been sealed.

Looking for a tower entrance had not been a brilliant idea—probably why

THE DILEMMA OF A DEAD SCHOLAR

Hunt hadn't done it. As an officer and an engineer, he knew how to establish perimeters.

The curate's sister nervously twisted the strings of the leather gardening apron she wore while working in the orchards. "I don't think that door will lead us to a room suitable for a perfumery."

By this time, Lavender and Sofia had joined the gathering. They studied the muddy hole with dismay. Rightfully so. There were no stairs.

Arnaud didn't dare look back at the heiress, who held herself distant, presumably keeping an eye on the boys sprawled on the trampled grass, peering over the edge. Like the rest of the crowd, she waited expectantly for some intrepid explorer to open the door.

He was no explorer. He knew there would be nothing pleasant behind that rotted panel. It would be dark and stink. The low ceilings and dripping walls would shut out any breath of air. . . .

It had taken over a year of practice, but he'd almost learned to block out the memory. He was no longer in prison. These good people wouldn't lock him up to rot.

He couldn't be a coward and send in a workman if he wouldn't go in himself.

Hunt would no doubt kill them all when he returned. Arnaud had to take the responsibility. With resignation, knowing the lady watched, he gritted his teeth and swung into the hole. If he concentrated on the logistics and not the relentless devils shrieking in his brainpan. . .

Logistical: It would be simple enough to dig steps, should the tower be usable. It appeared dirt and debris had simply washed down and built up over the. . . centuries?

Relentless devil: There were no windows and that door was underground.

"The top arch of the door was hidden by the shrubbery," Patience called down. "That's how we knew to dig there."

He tested the ancient wood. Water-soaked and rotted, the timber crumbled under his push. So much for locking it. Not wanting to break knuckles punching holes, he ran his fingers over the edges, finding rotten leather hinges that buckled when he tugged. There had once probably been a leather latch as well, but that was long gone.

"A shovel, *s'il vous plait*." He held out his hand for a tool.

"Are you sure?" Thea called from a distance. "We can't possibly use it for a perfumery. Perhaps it should just be buried again?"

Leave it to the neat and tidy heiress who liked her walls papered and her colors matching. He'd have to show her that—contrary to the pastel bubble she inhabited—the real world was a black and ugly place.

71

As much as he would love to bury what could easily be a dungeon, Arnaud knew his duty. "Now that there is the hole, animals will burrow in," he argued. "We shall need to replace the opening with brick or stone to keep them out."

Besides, curiosity would kill them all.

He took the pickax a workman handed him and slammed it into the rotting wood. The entire door caved, ripping off one of the rotting leather hinges. Another few blows, and an entrance opened. A musty, fetid stench wafted out. He shuddered and edged backward, heaving himself back to level ground, taking deep breaths. No bars, he reminded himself.

A bat flew out the opening.

The women screamed and scattered. The boys hooted in excitement.

Arnaud thought a few dozen curses, and surrendering to the inevitable, ordered a lantern. How the devil had bats got in? The same way they entered the manor? Broken windows, gaps in the roof. . . He grabbed the pickax again and swatted at a few more startled flying rodents.

"Don't!" Davy cried. "They eat bugs."

"Well, they should be fat and healthy." In disgust, Arnaud took the lantern a stable boy handed him. Nothing would be done for the rest of the day if he didn't go in and see what was there. If there were skulls. . . He'd seal it up and let Hunt deal with it.

Bracing himself, shutting down his vivid imagination, he took a gulp of clean air and stepped inside the tower cellar. The walls immediately closed in on him. The grim monsters he'd bled onto canvas when he first arrived raised their hideous maws, and he had to battle past the shroud of memories tearing at his soul.

Clenching his fist around the lantern handle, he fought to beat back his nightmares. He was in control here. No chains bound him. No guards threatened to shoot him. He had food and escape was only a step away. . .

He forced his boot inside, lantern first. The light illuminated cobwebbed rows of shelves and bins—not rows of skulls. He took a deep breath and examined the walls more closely. The structures seemed sturdy enough, protected in the shelter of solid stone and earth. Stalls and unidentifiable constructions covered the walls, but there was enough room in the center to store cattle—which may have been done at some point, given the width of the door. The pirate earl hadn't destroyed the cellars when he'd taken down the priory walls.

Releasing his pent-up breath, fighting morbid associations, Arnaud scuffled through rotted remains he didn't wish to examine until he reached the high-ceilinged center. He gathered his frayed nerves and circled the stone floor, snorting at the stink of long-rotted potatoes and straw, shaking a wooden stall.

Above his head, on the side wall, he could see chinks of light through holes nearly filled with the mud that had settled over them over the years. Bat holes. But judging by the mortar nests below them. . . He grunted in recognition.

He located stone stairs in a narrow stairwell but didn't follow them up.

"Are you all right down there?" a feminine voice called worriedly—Thea? "Do we need to send anyone down with you?"

The heiress was concerned about his welfare? That was about as likely as a root cellar and dovecote under an ornamental tower. He returned to the doorway, handed up the lantern, and swung back to solid ground. He surreptitiously took a few deep breaths to settle angry black memories as he rested on the edge.

Now that he knew where to look. . . He gestured at the few mud-chinked holes uncovered by the digging. "In France, we might call this a *columbier*. Some ancestor liked pigeon pie. Or perhaps they raised homing pigeons."

"May we see?" Oliver cried in excitement.

Arnaud lowered the boys so they could peer inside.

"Root cellar," Davy said in disappointment.

"How does he know about root cellars?" Arnaud couldn't resist leaning back to watch the boy's sister. She'd wrinkled her nose in consternation.

"My parents farmed him out with some tenants last year." The heiress kept a worried eye on him. "Don't go inside, Davy. We don't know if it's safe."

"It has been there for centuries. It will not go anywhere. Someone fetch Walker. He needs to know about this." Arnaud slid back down to test the height of the doorway. He had to duck, but the stone framing was solid. He took a stick and poked at the mud chinking the dovecote openings so there'd be more light inside. "We will have to dig a trench to uncover the rest of these holes. And then we must cover them with wire to keep out bats and rats and. . ." Bats must have found the higher openings.

"But might it be used for a perfumery?" Lavender asked.

"I am no architect," he said. "I cannot say. But it will take a great deal of work before you will wish to set foot in there."

Mr. Birdwhistle kept a worried eye on the boys. "It will need a door."

Hunt, the engineer, might not be back for a week. Arnaud could do nothing more constructive than stretch canvas. He lifted the boys back up to solid ground. "When Paul returns, he can nail something together."

He really needed to take the stairs to see where they led—without the boys.

From the heiress's troubled expression, she'd had the same thought.

Walker trotted around the rear corner of the manor just as Mr. Cooper rode his horse up the drive. The funeral service at the chapel must have ended.

Arnaud had forgotten all about the casket and the cart waiting at the stable for the mourners. Or the one mourner.

Mr. Cooper dismounted and handed his horse to a stable lad before wandering over to see what they were doing. "Byre?" he asked, tilting his head to examine the width of the opening. At the puzzled expressions around him, he added, "Barn? In the old days, they used to keep cattle in the house."

"Root cellar and dovecote, at least, possibly a barn." Arnaud stepped back so the other man could peer in.

The man was wearing fresh linen, presumably from his grandfather's wardrobe, and didn't leap down to look closer. "Store grain, too, I bet. Or mayhap in that other one." He nodded at the faux tower on the far end of the manor.

That would be a good, practical use for the cellars. The monastery's land had once encompassed most of the fields around the manor. There would have been grain and animals. Except the other front structure had been used by the priory as entrance to a crypt and bell tower. No storing grain there.

Arnaud studied the windows above. Did *columbiers* have stairs? He'd seen dovecotes in Brittany attached to the house. "Hired hands lived above?"

Cooper shrugged and studied the thick walls. "Ain't never seen nothin' that size before." The man's speech veered between dialect and educated.

Thea continued to study the façade with a troubled expression. "The monks may have had some structure here, and the first Reid built on to it. Most of the stone work above ground resembles the manor more than the monastery's Gothic wall."

Fastidious Walker refused to climb into the dirt to look in. He consulted with one of the workmen, then waited as Paul and Minerva strolled up the drive from the chapel. No other mourners followed them.

They stopped to investigate.

"Can you build a door to block that hole?" Walker asked their curate/carpenter.

"I can build a door. But I'll have to climb down and take a look to see if we can hang one. That will have to wait until I change clothes." Paul Upton gestured toward the cart and gravediggers. "I'll say a prayer over the grave, if anyone wishes to accompany us. Then I'll come back and take a look."

Arnaud glanced down at his filthy attire. Some day, he'd remember to change clothing, too, once he had more to change into.

Women didn't generally attend burials, so there would be no one else at the graveside. The murdered scholar deserved more respect than that. "Give me a moment and I will join you." Arnaud trotted off to grab his hat and coat.

Which is why all the gentlemen in the household were in the graveyard when a fancy nob on an expensive thoroughbred belatedly trotted up to join them.

Mr. Cooper cursed under his breath as Paul finished his prayer and tossed a handful of dirt on the coffin.

Arnaud studied the newcomer dismounting. Not a speck of road dust dared cling to his immaculate linen. His coat was tailored to conform to his slender form. Padding filled out the shoulders. Arnaud assumed the turned-down boots were the latest fashion.

The sharp nose and narrow eyes very much resembled that of the farmer standing beside him. "Your brother, I assume?"

"Come to make certain the old man is dead," Cooper agreed in disgruntlement.

FOURTEEN

PAUL: TUESDAY EVENING

A DILATORY BAT FLAPPED AGAINST THE TRANSOM BEFORE FINDING THE BROKEN PANE and escaping into the evening. Paul eyed the arched window but didn't think he was competent enough to replace it.

"Clare would have invited Mr. Cooper to stay." Thea gestured at the next painting in the stack and pointed at an empty inset on the vestibule wall. The newly polished oak molding gleamed in the lamplight.

"Hunt would have objected," Arnaud countered, climbing the ladder to hang the ugly portrait of an old man wearing a pointed cap falling over his wrinkled brow.

The garishly carved and gilded frame fit perfectly into the molding designed for it. Paul finally grasped what they had been doing in here. When finished, the vestibule would hold each individual painting framed in its own oak molding, instead of haphazardly hanging practically on top of each other. The entire vestibule would be filled with sparkling gold frames—and ugly paintings.

"Neither of the Coopers expressed a desire to stay. The elder wished to return order to his grandfather's home. Or inspect his inheritance." Paul settled the bickering while studying the numbered list the boys had made indicating which oil went where.

The ways of the wealthy were beyond fathoming. Building an entire wall to house an art collection that couldn't be moved around? *Shouldn't be*, he corrected. The artwork had definitely shifted over the centuries. He'd had to pull nails out of molding so they could rehang inside the bevels instead of on top—after Arnaud had inspected every panel to be certain it hid no hoard of jewels.

No treasures had been uncovered. The disappointment hadn't been as great as it would have earlier in the year, before they learned the library was a treasure trove worth more than jewels.

"I believe Mr. Timothy had intended to stay at the cottage after the funeral, but the brothers seem to be at odds," Paul added.

A cloud settled over the entry occupants. They had no notion of how to go about finding Professor Boston's killer. Minerva was in the library, still working through the victim's coded journal one page at a time. She'd skimmed the daughter's letters without discovering anything of value. They simply did not know enough to understand why anyone would wish to kill an innocent scholar —other than his knowledge of codes and berry-hacking desire for tidiness.

"Did you determine how the older brother learned of his grandfather's death?" Arnaud asked, standing back to examine their work.

Paul pointed out the next frame on the chart the boys had drawn up. "He did not say, and I did not ask. The gossip network would be my assumption."

He'd not had *time* for questioning. He'd spent the hours after the funeral pounding together any lumber that could be found to create a barrier over the newly-uncovered tower entrance. The result was ugly and unwieldy but would keep out animals. Walker had set a patrol with hounds on the drive to guard against curiosity-seekers. At some point, the rest of the tower should be explored, but it would be better done in daylight.

Paul had been surprised to hear that Arnaud had entered that dark cellar. If the Frenchman truly had a fear of narrow, dark places. . . Perhaps the tower wasn't as bad as a French prison. It was hard to say with Arnaud. He didn't talk much at the best of times.

"Henri spreads gossip when he goes into the city," Arnaud explained. "I assume that means Cooper does not live far from Birmingham?"

Henri led a busy life, peddling in the city several times a week, returning in time to run his own tavern in the evenings most nights. That the new arrival had heard Henri's chatter might make sense, if he lived near Birmingham.

Gossip had killed Paul's adoptive father, but he supposed news, in any fashion, could be useful—if it didn't bring killers and thieves to the doorstep. "We can ask Mr. Timothy who broke the news of his grandfather's death when he returns from the tavern."

Walker entered from the corridor, turned, and studied their progress. "Why is there a blank space between that landscape and the fancy buccaneer?"

"None of the artwork we found fits there." Arnaud climbed down from hanging a military battle over the doors and studied the empty molding. "We must go about the house to search for a frame to fit that spot."

"The boys have already measured it and started in the attic, but we've locked up a lot of the rooms to keep them out of trouble." Thea wrinkled her nose at the wall. "Personally, I'd hide most of them in a closet."

Paul laughed. "Minerva and Clare claim the paintings are historical."

"Historically bad. The lady has a point." Arnaud studied them in the lamplight. "I suppose, though, they may have significance of some type. I am not familiar with the earl's family or English history."

That might be more than the taciturn artist had said all evening. Obviously, art was a subject on which he could converse.

"Minerva is studying the Wycliffe histories when she has time," Paul offered. "But they are written by the earl's family and aren't always. . . accurate." Minerva's disgust at bigotry and hubris had been vociferous.

"History is in the eye of the beholder," Walker said dismissively. "I have come to ask if we are interested in hiring Timothy Cooper."

Everyone put down their respective tasks to stare.

"Mr. Timothy wishes to stay in Gravesyde?" Thea asked. "I thought he was in a hurry to return to wherever he came from."

"He talked to Henri at the tavern this evening, then rode over to ask about positions. He and his brother have come to an agreement over their grandfather's property. If he can find a situation at the manor, he will oversee his grandfather's property and use any profit to buy it from his brother. Apparently, Mr. Timothy wishes to marry and needs a home and better income for his bride." Walker seldom expressed an opinion, but his tone seemed to approve.

"We don't think either of the Coopers are killers?" Thea asked uncertainly.

"Without any evidence otherwise, it's not for us to judge, is it?" Paul asked. "Is that property worth murdering over? And if so, why now? Mr. Timothy seemed more than eager to return to his current post until his brother arrived."

Paul wasn't family and didn't have to live in the manor, but his mother and sister were here—as was Minerva. He didn't wish to expose anyone to a potential killer, but the manor needed help. "For what position is he applying?"

"He's currently steward for a small estate." Walker waited for the backward clock in the corridor to quit chiming. "The question is, can he work with Patience and the orchard?"

"That's easy. Patience will work with a two-headed ape if he can deal with the orchard workers. She would much rather be growing than managing." Paul knew his stepsister wasn't precisely shy, but she'd been sheltered in a parsonage all her life. She had been blessed—or cursed—with lush curves, and men were. . . crude.

"Henri is trying to raise funds to build a conservatory for growing the delicate plants," Arnaud said. "I assume that is her preference."

"In other words, none of us know how to interview a steward?" Thea wrinkled her nose. "Will Captain Huntley be offended if you hire him on your own?"

Walker emitted a grunt surprisingly similar to Arnaud's. "He doesn't know any more about hiring than we do. Miss Patience and I will be the ones working with him. I'll wait for her opinion."

"That's the best idea. He won't mind riding from the cottage to the manor every day?" Paul asked. "In winter, it could be unpleasant."

"Haven't asked. If he's willing to do it, it's one less mouth to feed. It's not as if we have anything resembling suitable housing for hired help, other than the attics. Most stewards expect accommodations."

As household steward, Walker had accommodations. He and Meera were considered family and friends as well as valuable staff. They had taken up residence in a suite of offices at the rear of the manor, as Mrs. Upton had taken the housekeeper's apartment off the kitchen in the new wing.

A land steward probably ought to have his own cottage on the grounds, but all the manor had was Elsa's magnificent stable and empty chambers in the new wings.

Arnaud carried another painting up the ladder. "Fellow seemed decent enough. If he knows how to manage workers, I have no objection."

Paul smothered his amazement. In the captain's absence, his cousin seemed comfortable asserting his natural authority. Paul wondered if Arnaud was even aware that he was stepping into Hunt's role.

With Walker holding the door open, they could hear voices approaching from the side hall.

"That's them now." Walker propped the vestibule door open and stood in the corridor to direct the new arrivals into their impromptu meeting.

Patience sparkled with a laughter and confidence she'd never exhibited prior to their arrival in Gravesyde, and Paul was certain Arnaud's brother was the reason. The younger Frenchman was charming and hardworking. Paul could only pray Henri was as honorable as the other men in the manor.

They entered the vestibule to examine the newly arranged artwork.

"Much better," Patience declared. "The colors are so much brighter! I can't wait to see them in daylight. But why the empty space?"

While Thea explained the search for the missing painting, Walker quickly outlined their concerns about hiring Timothy Cooper.

Henri nodded his head to indicate they step into the hall, away from the chattering women. "Thea's cousin, Neville, was in the tavern this evening, asking the Coopers if he might rent their cottage. If Tim has decided to occupy it, then I assume they won't be renting it to the cockroach?"

"Not if he's bringing a new bride. There are only two rooms upstairs. I doubt a newlywed would want a stranger living with them." Paul thought about it and added, "I doubt the toplofty Mr. Talbot wishes to share a garret."

"Then let's ask Patience. She spoke with Tim a few times this evening." Henri led them back into the vestibule. "What do you think of Tim Cooper?"

Patience blinked in surprise. "Me? He seemed a pleasant fellow. We talked about apples. He didn't think they were a useful crop, but I may have convinced him otherwise."

Paul had thought all his sister did was sing to collect coins for the chapel and keep Henri's customers buying. He hadn't realized she'd actually learned to converse with strangers. He should probably disapprove, but she looked too happy for him to rebuke.

"Do you think he might manage your workers?" Walker asked. "I know you enjoyed having Sofia's father helping while he was here."

"Monsieur Lavigne knew nothing of apples, but he was a lovely gentleman who knew how to give orders." Patience grinned in excitement. "Does that mean Mr. Timothy might take his place? That would be wonderful! Then I could work on the landscaping and setting up a nursery for the new trees."

"Cooper will be here in the morning," Walker explained. "We can discuss it then."

That decided that. Did that mean Thea's unwelcome cousin might move on? Paul hadn't tried to throw him out of the parsonage. Yet.

FIFTEEN

THEA: WEDNESDAY MORNING

"Hurry," Thea urged the boys. "Lavender breaks her fast early. You'll want to wish her felicitations on her birthday in person."

No, they wouldn't, but someone needed to encourage the pair to socialize, if only a tiny bit. They liked Lavender, so this shouldn't be too difficult.

Mr. Birdwhistle was the one who held back. "It would be presumptuous of me."

Thea almost rolled her eyes at the tutor's recalcitrance. "Setting the boys loose on the household would be *negligent* of you. Your presence is perfectly acceptable."

Although come to think of it, he seldom ate with the family, if ever. He ate in the schoolroom with the boys most days.

Davy and Oliver raced past her, willing for any excuse to slide down the banister.

"You want me to stop them?" Thea asked pointedly as the pair disappeared from sight.

Grudgingly, he hurried after his students. Thea followed at a more leisurely pace, hoping to hear voices from the blue salon on the family floor that would indicate the aunts were awake. She was uncertain as to when Lady Lavinia wished to deliver Lavender's birthday gift.

Since she saw no sign that the aunts had broken their habit of rising late, she assumed the gift would wait until dinner. Lavender would think her paternal grandmother had forgotten her. The pair did not understand each other at all.

Well, they came from opposite worlds. It was only to be expected.

She hurried down the marble stairs in time to hear Lavender exclaiming excitedly from the breakfast room. Thea had a notion the girl had never had a birthday celebration, tucked away out of sight in a boarding school as she had been.

The linen-covered oval breakfast table was littered with colorful ribbons, packages, and even a heart-shaped cake with pink frosting. Mrs. Ingraham, the stout, garrulous presence who normally occupied the kitchen, had lumbered above stairs to beam in delight at her granddaughter's excitement. Several of the maids had joined her but quickly dispersed upon Thea's entrance.

Mr. Birdwhistle all but hid in a corner on the far side of the buffet from the door, hands behind his back, keeping an eye on his charges. The boys leaned excitedly over the table to point out their contributions.

Lavender had tears in her eyes as she hugged her maternal grandmother. "Thank you! I didn't think anyone remembered."

"Didn't," Mrs. Ingraham admitted. "Miss Thea asked for the cake."

Lavender glanced at Thea in surprise. "How did you know?"

Grateful for a way to let her know that her haughty paternal grandmother wasn't as uncaring as she appeared, Thea explained, "I didn't. Lady Lavinia asked me to arrange a celebration. And everyone else took it from there."

Lavender stiffened, but the boys' eager demand that she look at their offering distracted her. She picked up the messily-wrapped package and carefully pressed its ribbon with her fingers as she opened the paper. "A book, how lovely of you!" Her tone held a degree of puzzlement.

Ouch. Clare had explained Lavender's reading difficulty. Thea hadn't understood, but she bit her lip now, fearing the boys may have offended.

The book was obviously handmade, with cardboard covers glued with bits of fabric and lace they must have scavenged from the sewing room floor. Inside the covers, the paper was stiff, possibly stationery. Or drawing papers?

Lavender cried out in delight when she opened it. "Bird! You've drawn a bird." Her finger followed the letters written below the illustration, then flipped to the next page and the next. "Guinevere!" she cried in excitement. "It looks exactly like Guinevere."

Guinevere was Lavender's fluffy, white dog and a difficult word to read. Thea leaned over to study the page Lavender held up for everyone to see.

The boys had very definitely not drawn that delicate pencil sketch of a fetching snout, pointed ears, and big eyes almost buried beneath a fringe of fur. They may have printed the careful letters and smeared the background with watercolors, but as Mr. Birdwhistle had said, his students were not in the least artistic.

She glanced questioningly at Mr. Birdwhistle. His cheeks turned rosy. "Mr. Lavigne helped. We did not have much time."

Oliver shouted, "Mr. B did the birds! There's a bluebird and a robin."

Clare's nephew liked birds and often studied ornithology books in the library.

Lavender carefully read the words beneath each picture, then hugged the book to her bosom. "Thank you, thank you! I will read this every night before I go to bed."

The boys cheered and ran to smear toast with jam while Lavender finished opening her other packages: a knitted shawl and new ribbons from Mrs. Ingraham and the button ladies. She opened Thea's handkerchief-wrapped gift last, lifting out a hairpin glittering with tiny stones.

Lavender gasped and glanced instantly to Thea. "Yours? I cannot. . ."

Thea shook her head. "Emeralds and diamonds aren't my stones, they're yours, if you'll study the gallery portraits."

She had no understanding of how or why the earls of Wycliffe had distributed their jewels, but each branch of the family displayed particular pendants. Lady Lavinia's portrait showed emeralds and diamonds. Thea's grandmother had worn sapphires and pearls, like Clare's grandmother.

Lavender gazed at the tiny hair ornament in awe. "I've never had jewels before."

Thea had worn her mother's sapphires at her presentation. She'd been given trinkets like this for years. The Reid jewels had been meaningless baubles until now. "You weren't an adult until today. Now you are entitled to dress like a lady."

Lavender's expressive face brightened, and she beamed as her grandmother took the hair pin and tucked it above a dangling blond curl. "If this is what it is like to be a lady, I like it, thank you!"

Davy frowned and cast Thea a puzzled look. "Do we get birthdays?"

Never. They'd never had birthday celebrations unless a nanny asked and remembered the dates. They had gone through a lot of nannies over the years. Thea tugged him back into his chair and tousled his hair. "We will now," she promised. "Your birthday is in September. You should make a calendar."

When she looked up, Arnaud leaned against the door frame, arms crossed over his waistcoat—he had actually shaved and was wearing proper attire, presumably in honor of Lavender's birthday. "And yours?" he asked, looking at Thea.

"My birthday? I'm too old to have them. I should don a cap with the next one." She returned to settling the boys into chairs and eating their breakfasts without smearing jam over any cloth in their vicinity.

This was the reason she meant to stay in Wycliffe Manor, given any choice. She'd shoot Neville before she allowed him to drag Davy away from a chance to be normal.

She had reason to recall that threat when Davy disappeared later that morning.

～

THEA JOINED THE FAMILY GATHERED IN THE LIBRARY WHERE ARNAUD HANDED OUT newssheets cut to the dimensions of the empty panel in the vestibule.

"This is the size of the missing painting."

When he didn't explain further, Thea added with a hint of exasperation at his taciturnity, "If everyone carries these patterns about and checks the size of any artwork you run into, we might find the missing oil. We're hoping it's a portrait, so take particular notice of those." The earl's odd letters had mentioned a portrait as a clue to the jewels.

Thea folded up her pattern. "I'll be working in the east wing, looking for furniture suitable for the new withdrawing room. I'll start searching there."

Herbert stopped in the doorway. "Mr. Walker, a gentleman to see you."

Someone had found the new footman an ill-fitting, black frockcoat and starched linen so he looked a little more proper today. He studied the gathering with an undeferential impudence. Thea feared no one in this household would teach him otherwise.

"That will be Mr. Cooper." Walker folded up his pattern and shoved it into his pocket. "Meera and I will go through all the rooms in the back hall. Patience, are you ready?"

"I'll go through the east cellars later," Patience said, taking her paper. Looking as nervous as the potential new steward probably felt, she followed Walker out, taking the nosy footman with them.

Minerva scribbled notes of who was searching where so they didn't duplicate their efforts.

Quincy arrived to call Arnaud away. Thea raised her eyebrows that the butler had decided on the ungentlemanly artist as head of household in the captain's absence. Size apparently mattered.

Minerva set down her pen and grabbed a pattern sheet. "I'll go upstairs to the front guest hall since we have no guests to disturb."

"Several of us will probably have to do the attics at once," Thea suggested.

"Or we'll all be wandering lost and missing some rooms while duplicating others."

"Excellent idea. I wonder if there are any portraits in the servants' quarters?" Minerva followed her out.

Arnaud's angry voice carried through the closed vestibule doors at the front. Quincy stood guard on this side of the doors, so Thea didn't worry. . . too much. The moody artist probably had a temper, but it wasn't her place to intervene.

Militant Minerva lacked Thea's qualms. "I'll see what that's about."

Relieved, Thea set off for the east wing where the more delicate ladies' furniture had been left to decay. The pieces might be ancient, but a few repairs and some new upholstery. . .

An hour later, she had only found a shabby loveseat and a sturdy walnut game table for the new room and was holding her newssheet pattern up to a portrait of a bewigged lady in a shockingly low-cut gown when a maid hunted her down.

She bobbed a curtsy. "They needs you up front, miss."

"Why?" She panicked at just the possibility of Neville showing up again. "I have said I don't want to see—"

The maid shook her bobbed curls."Missure Lavigne took care of the caller. But Master Davy has gone missing."

Oh, no, not again! Not here. She thought he liked it here. Panicking, Thea picked up her hem and raced back to the main manor, entering through the back hall where Meera waited. "How long has he been missing?"

Meera shook her head. "A while now, we think. Mr. Birdwhistle and Arnaud have organized a search."

"What is this about a caller?" Remembering Arnaud shouting at someone— an hour ago?—her panic escalated. "Was that Neville at the door? Did he *dare* to come here? Is there any way he saw Davy?"

"Yes, it was your cousin, but Arnaud wouldn't allow him in." The mother-to-be followed Thea into the main corridor but couldn't easily keep up with her, forcing Thea to moderate her terrified pace. "Everyone has been hunting for the missing portrait, so events after that are unclear."

Madness, utter madness, hunting for a portrait just because it might be a key to treasure. *People* were treasures, not lumps of rock. Forcing herself to go slower gave her time to quell some of her panic and *think*.

"Did Arnaud make certain Neville left?" Thea glanced up at voices above stairs. Apparently, even the aunts were out and searching. If the bedchambers were locked, surely Davy couldn't enter them. . .

"Arnaud told your cousin to leave and not return. They argued." Meera grimaced as they arrived at the bottom of the marble stairs. "Arnaud does not have Hunt's patience."

Thea gritted her teeth at that obviousness and waited for her to continue.

"Arnaud threw your cousin down the front stairs," the apothecary said with a sigh. "I can't imagine he lingered."

Another day, Thea would have laughed at the image of the shabby painter grabbing handsome Neville by his thick neckcloth and garish waistcoat and heaving him down the stairs. Right now, though, all she could think about was Davy. Davy hated Neville. Neville despised Davy.

"Where was Davy seen last? Do we know?" Thea tried to recall the kind of places her brother liked to hide, but the manor was enormous. He could be anywhere, inside or out.

That's what he was doing, she told herself. He was hiding. He'd heard Neville and had. . . run away. He'd done it before. She fought panicky thoughts of kidnapping.

Had she endangered Davy by insisting that he live as other boys? Were her parents *right* to lock him away?

Not if Neville was allowed near him.

Minerva emerged from the library with a paper in her hand. "We've assigned searchers to every level and every wing. Walker has the men outside searching the grounds. The new steward is learning our eccentricities the hard way. They're dividing the men up and assigning them directions. Your brother can't have gone far."

Meera patted Thea on the shoulder. "He's a smart boy. He'll be fine. Minerva can tell you more. I'll finish searching the back hall. He sometimes likes to study my laboratory, but I've not seen him since breakfast." Colorful shawl swinging, their *enceinte* apothecary waddled back down the hall they'd just traversed.

"Where was he last seen? When?" Thea demanded of the manor's new librarian.

"The boys decided to conduct their own search for the portrait in the attic storerooms. They're more organized than most of us, so Mr. Birdwhistle let them explore. He could hear them and thought it safe to conduct his own search. When he couldn't hear them anymore, he went looking. He found Oliver but apparently all Oliver could tell him was which rooms Davy had chosen." Minerva looked fierce. "Quincy didn't see him come down. They'll be upstairs somewhere."

Thea prayed it was so. The manor had multiple stairs. *Think.* Where had Davy hidden before?

He'd never had reason to hide in the manor. No one ever knew exactly what set him off, but he always hid from his cousin. Davy was not dumb.

"Is there any chance he may have heard Neville? Davy runs whenever he shows up. The last time, he hid in the stable, fell asleep, and we didn't find him until dinner." Thea recalled all the other times her brother had disappeared, only to be found by smoke or screams or. . . Davy wasn't good at sitting idle, unless he fell asleep. And he was growing a little old to need naps.

"We have no way of knowing," Minerva admitted. "I can't see how he heard anyone, if he was in the attic. Paul and I have been searching the rooms on the ground floor. There are concealed entrances all over, but I think we know most of them. Mrs. Upton and the maids are scouring the cellar and following along behind us to be certain we don't miss anything."

Thea had been in the normally locked east wing, but. . . "I didn't lock the east wing while I was working. Surely I would have heard him. . ."

"With so little furniture, I should think there are few hiding places in the wings, although I believe the window seats can be opened." Minerva marked her list. "I'll have Herbert search those next. Adam is tearing apart the ground floor west wing. The men have been leaving that unlocked since we moved in furniture. The attic is hardest to search. With all those interlocking spaces, we'd really need to station someone in every doorway so he didn't slip from room to room."

"I don't think he's that devious." Thea glanced up the stairs. She needed to be up there. "He finds a space he feels is safe and then he. . . I don't know. Explores? Investigates?"

Sets fire to haystacks by experimenting with glass. . .

They had the same thought at once and grimaced, glancing in the direction of the tower.

"He can't remove that panel Paul installed," Thea protested. "He's only a little boy."

"Besides, one of the men would have noticed if it was removed," Minerva said reassuringly. "Arnaud has Lavender and the sewing ladies turning the gallery and great hall upside-down. Will you feel better if we send him to follow Neville?"

"If he is willing, please send Henri after Neville. My cousin would avoid Arnaud if they've already come to blows. Henri might persuade bees from trees." Thea worried at her bottom lip. Was it even possible for Neville to carry off a little boy? How? "Who is searching the servants' quarters?"

"Just about everyone has by now because they started in the attic. But if he's exploring. . ." Minerva let the thought trail off.

"Exploring and not hiding? They could just be missing him if he's moving about." Thea started up the stairs. "If no one saw him come down, then he must be up there." She hoped and prayed. Small boys could be so slippery. . . and there were enclosed stairs in the back towers as well as the servant stairs in the manor. "Do we have enough people for Quincy to station someone on all the staircases?"

Minerva grimaced. "Not really. We'll have to hope the aunts know how to be thorough. I don't dare tell them what to do."

"I'm so sorry he's causing such trouble," Thea said as they ran up the stairs to the attic floor. "I had hoped he would stop running away once he felt safe."

"Boys are horrible creatures who never think of anyone or anything but themselves," Minerva insisted vehemently. "I grew up with brothers. I know."

"Not all boys," Thea protested, although she had very limited experience. "I cannot imagine a gentleman like Mr. Upton causing anyone concern." She could, however, imagine an arrogant one like Arnaud doing whatever he pleased—like flinging a gentleman off the steps.

"Oh, I daresay even our good curate caused his share of trouble as a child. He just grew out of it. Some men don't. Well, I suppose, to be fair, some women don't either."

They reached the top floor. Voices carried from the vast, windowless interior. As Minerva had said, many of these attic chambers were interconnected. It would be impossible to station someone at each doorway plus the stairs.

At a sound behind her, Thea swung around, remembering Herbert searching trunks in the old storage room. The door had always been closed until the other day. Surely it was kept locked?

Apparently not. She pushed it open to find Arnaud opening trunks, then stacking them neatly to one side, before moving on to the next. He'd cleared half the floor.

Minerva entered with her. "Mr. Birdwhistle said this room was locked, didn't he?"

Arnaud tossed the contents of another trunk about, then consigned it to the stack. "The door is warped. It was locked, but I shoved it open without a key."

And Davy knew about the tower.

Thea's gaze went straight to the wardrobe concealing the tower door. The wardrobe sat on fat clawed legs. Davy could crawl under it, but he couldn't move it. She had to look anyway. The tower was just exactly the kind of place Davy would like to explore—dark, hidden, overlooked by the adults he feared.

As they had yesterday, the broken wardrobe doors easily swung open. Davy wasn't inside. She peered around behind it to the concealed door. He couldn't possibly move a piece of furniture this heavy. The door was just as Arnaud had left it.

"This is the armoire that hides the door?" Minerva asked, peering inside. "And there's no other entrance into the tower?"

Thea began hunting behind all the discarded items leaning against the wall. "Why would there be two doors?"

"Why would there be three doors into the library, two of them hidden?" Arnaud asked, heaving a leather portmanteau aside and striding across the space to join them.

Thea spotted the opening first, between a headless dress form and a cracked marble washstand. She shoved the form aside to reveal a crawlway door, still open.

Arnaud dropped to a crouch beside her, yanking the door wide and holding his lantern to the dark opening. "Crawl space." He swung the lantern. "Davy? It's safe to come out now."

"I can't," came the weak cry. "I'm stuck."

SIXTEEN

ARNAUD: WEDNESDAY MORNING

THE CHILD'S PLAINTIVE CRY AND SIGHT OF THAT NARROW PASSAGE SHATTERED Arnaud's icy indifference, rousing vivid nightmares.

He froze, attempting to block the wails as he had once blocked screams of anguish and terror no normal human should experience. But these past months of peace had weakened the mental barriers he'd erected, and his gut churned.

He willed the icy barricade in place, shutting out the lady's terrified expression, the child's cries, and his own fear. "Sledgehammer, hatchet, saw," he commanded. He couldn't fit even one shoulder into that opening.

Minerva obediently ran off.

"You could hurt him!" Brushing Arnaud aside as if he were no more than dandelion fluff, the lady got down on hands and knees, ripping her gauzy muslin on old nails and dirtying her fair hands in the grime of centuries. "Davy, can you wiggle toward me?"

No response but a frustrated thumping.

Having a fragile lady in this pit of hell. . . hammered at the ice barricading his fury and fear. Arnaud slammed his boot heel into the wall above the crawlspace, but as elsewhere, it was solid stone on the other side of the plaster and wood.

He couldn't do this with a female in his way. Bodily lifting the lady—his crude hands encompassed her waist—Arnaud shoved her aside so he could reach the crawlspace frame. He gripped the aged wood with both hands and tugged, loosening nails and mortar.

Despite his manhandling, the fearless idiot swung a lantern past him. "Can you see our light, Davy?"

Still no response except the sound of a small boy kicking walls. What the devil was the purpose of a crawl space?

Arnaud could sense people gathering on the other side of the attic doorway. Someone intelligently held them back. He was barely responsible for himself. He didn't want to be responsible for anyone else.

The ancient frame finally worked free, revealing unevenly stacked stones and crumbling mortar. With his bare hands, Arnaud began shoving and tugging the edges loose. Thea returned with the broken-handled kitchen implement they'd used the day before. If he'd had that in his prison cell. . . He pried the mortar loose one dig at a time.

Paul pushed his way through the crowd, wearing his ubiquitous tool belt. He handed over a chisel, then persuaded the hysterical lady to move away so he could squeeze in beside Arnaud and work on the other side of the opening with his hammer.

The curate's calm presence thawed the ice slicing Arnaud's soul, allowing him to think beyond the frantic need to punch walls and escape. Taking deep breaths, he chose stones carefully, prying them loose in a pattern to prevent the entire wall from tumbling, pointing to the ones Paul needed to remove.

The space still wasn't large enough for his shoulders to push through. He gestured for the lantern and beamed it into the dark opening. He couldn't see the lad. "Davy, can you see the light?"

He thought that might be a whimpering *yes.*

Paul removed a brick jammed between stones on his side of the opening, then eyed the lintel. "I don't think we can take that piece out. Want me to see if I can squeeze through?"

Paul might be smaller, but his shoulders were thick with muscle from his carpentry.

A few months back, Arnaud might have been able to wedge into the opening. Only he'd been eating well and exercising since his cousin's arrival at the manor, and he'd never been a small man. And as much as he wanted to help that little boy, he did *not* want to attempt that narrow space.

"I do not want to have to rescue the two of you," he said gruffly. "Where is a long pole? Let us see if we can learn how far he is in there."

The crowd of onlookers scattered in search of a pole. Paul and Arnaud continued chipping at the sides of the hole, propping the upper wall with bricks they'd loosened as they worked.

He thought the heiress was praying, but when he stopped chipping to test a pole Walker handed him, he realized she madly sang a child's song. He let the calming tune mollify his icy rage as he eased the stick into the opening. Paul held the lantern.

"Davy, can you feel the pole?" Arnaud gritted his teeth to keep his voice low and soothing, while crushing the need to curse and rant. "Can you pull it up beside you?"

In reply, the rod rattled in his grip.

"*Et voila*! Can you wrap both hands and maybe your legs around the stick?" Shutting out everything except the tension in the rod as the boy grasped it, Arnaud pulled slowly. "Are you hanging on? Can you wiggle?"

After emitting that ridiculous word, he realized he'd repeated the phrase from the lady's soothing song. What the devil was she singing? *Wiggle, wriggle, squirm. . .* He rolled his eyes. Caterpillars. She was singing about *les chenilles*.

Thea sang louder. Others heard the tune and joined in. The English had ridiculous songs. Beside him, even the curate was singing about wriggling worms. Arnaud fishtailed the pole to accompany the tune, while dragging it slowly toward him with its heavy weight clinging—and wriggling—on the other end.

Echoes of *wiggle, wriggle, squirm about* continued even as Arnaud saw small shoes in the lamplight and reached in to grab the lad's ankles. Behind him, the lady openly wept. Paul clutched one small foot, and, with Arnaud holding the other, they had the boy squirming sufficiently so they could yank him out.

With a final tug, Davy popped free from the hole. Arnaud sat back so the lady might hug her brother. Their tears melted his frost too quickly, and he returned to examining the crawl space they'd opened. The lamplight revealed little more than a wood structure stretching into the darkness. He still couldn't see the tower interior.

"We need to open the tower," Paul murmured, studying the situation. "It's a death trap without access."

"Could be a death trap *with* access. We need someone who knows mortar and stone to examine the walls to be certain they won't come tumbling down." Arnaud sat up—only to nearly be knocked over again by the feather-light lady flinging her arms around his neck.

"Thank you, thank you. I don't know how to repay you, but. . ." She broke into tears again, sat back, and hugged her filthy brother.

After being struck by that hot bolt of femininity, Arnaud could think of a dozen ways she could thank him, none of them appropriate.

Shattering ice was dashed uncomfortable, as the English might say.

Arnaud stood, leaving the curate to deal with weeping women and children.

He escaped to hunt down the terrified tutor in the hall, clinging to the hand of Clare's nephew.

"I understand I have failed in my duty," The tutor hastily admitted. "There aren't enough apologies in the world to cover my failure. I will pack and leave as soon as I can arrange transportation."

"Clare would hang and gut me if I allowed that." Arnaud retorted grumpily. "Tell me instead that you can teach the boy not to wander off."

"Davy was afraid." Oliver piped up, wide-eyed. "He hides when he's afraid."

Arnaud thought that a bit of a mouthful from a child who rarely noticed the existence of others. Realizing he was not only towering over the scrawny tutor, but must be an intimidating wall for a seven-year-old, he crouched down. "Do you know why he was afraid?"

Oliver shrugged and wrinkled his freckled nose. "Loud voices."

Arnaud glanced up at the tutor.

Mr. Birdwhistle shook his head. "Neither of them deal well with unexpected noise or anger or any upheaval. I am trying to introduce them gradually to everyday activity, but the attic is their safe place. Generally, it is quiet. The servants use the stairs on the far end unless they're carrying luggage or we have guests."

"So, someone was up here? Or on the stairs?" Arnaud studied Oliver's reaction.

"Stairs," the boy said succinctly.

"I see. Next time Davy is scared, can you take him to Mr. Birdwhistle or me? We won't yell." Arnaud waited until Oliver nodded before returning to his feet and facing the tutor.

"There is a possibility that Davy has been mistreated in the past. He does not trust adults. Can we fix that?" Arnaud had seen enough animals and people treated with cruelty to grasp the need to flee—especially if one is too small to fight.

"Boxing," Oliver said solemnly before the tutor could reply.

Even Mr. Birdwhistle seemed startled. "Boxing?"

Oliver nodded. "He likes punching."

The boy might not speak much or exhibit emotion, but he paid attention to others, possibly more so than Arnaud had lately.

But he most definitely noticed the arrival of the intrepid Miss Talbot holding her brother's hand. Her tear-stained cheeks and dust-smeared gown tugged at his missing heart strings. The prim and proper heiress had been pushed to an emotional brink that should release all the madness she'd exhibited in the past.

With her pale curls tumbling from their pins, she appeared vaporish, yet her anger conveyed her message clearly. *"Punch?* With a fist? Who?"

Arnaud wasn't taking on that battle. There was more here than met the eye, and he had to control his temper to find out what. Tearing his gaze from the lady, he turned to Davy, who sucked his free thumb. "You like to box, Davy?"

The boy removed his thumb to nod. "Beat up bad men." His gap-toothed smile of satisfaction appeared as if he'd lost the fight.

Arnaud's gut ground.

Thea—he had to quit thinking of her as some mad goddess—reacted with shocked confusion. "Bad men?"

Davy nodded and kicked with his scratched and damaged boot. "I kick them, and they let me go."

Arnaud swore to teach him how to kick in areas causing the most damage.

Appalled, his sister crouched down to hug him. "Do you know who the bad men are?"

He shrugged his chubby shoulders. "Anyone."

"And you heard these bad men today?" Arnaud asked. Simmering fury had melted any remaining ice.

"Don't know. They were angry."

With a grim set to her jaw, Thea stood up again. "Mr. Birdwhistle, do not let him out of your sight. I have never known Davy to lie."

The tutor bowed. "Neither have I, Miss Talbot. The boys are not natural story-tellers."

Arnaud endured a ripple of ridiculous jealousy when Thea nodded her approval at the milksop tutor. So, he wasn't a noble courtier anymore. War had made him a beast. He might as well accept that.

"We can have the blacksmith secure the doors in the attic, but fire is always a problem with locked doors. Let us give it some thought." Nodding a curt farewell, Arnaud left them to whatever one does when a child nearly loses his life.

He was coming unglued by a pretty face and a gap-toothed grin. He was pretty certain he needed to punch someone. Until the war, he'd never felt the urge to take up arms and kill. What he'd done to survive. . . Couldn't be thought about. He'd never wanted to do more than paint. But right now. . .

Every nerve and muscle ached to throttle anyone who hurt children. His anger and his strength may as well be put to good use. It wouldn't make up for the past, but it might relieve some of the pent-up anguish released by melting ice.

The rest of the household had scattered. Paul was removing the storage room door to adjust the hinges so it would close properly. He didn't even look up as Arnaud stomped past.

He couldn't box. He'd never been in a fistfight. The village boys knew better than to tackle the privileged heir of a comte. And then he grew too big for anyone to dare attack him. He'd once stopped a knife-wielding drunkard by grabbing his hair and yanking him off his feet. But boxing? No. It didn't interest him. He needed his hands to paint.

Quincy now—was an ex-prize fighter. He was probably in his fifties and not swift on his feet any longer. Could he teach a boy?

At the bottom of the stairs, he went in search of the butler, who usually stationed himself between both doors as if guarding against unruly company. Given this household, he probably was. Today, he must be needed elsewhere.

Had someone attempted to kidnap Davy in the past? Was that the reason he'd developed the habit of running away? And *kicking*. Surely, though, the boy would be able to identify his cousin Neville. Hired thugs, perhaps?

Arnaud found Quincy and half the household in the main corridor with a furious Minerva. The colonel's daughter didn't do hysterics, but she appeared ready to scalp someone with her letter opener.

"It's gone," she shouted emphatically at Quincy's question. "Unless one of you has it, someone has stolen the code journal!"

SEVENTEEN

PAUL: WEDNESDAY LUNCHEON

NEEDING A NEW HINGE FOR THE ATTIC STORAGE DOOR, PAUL YANKED THE PANEL closed as tight as he could, tested the lock, and took the service stairs down, thinking to take the walking path to his workshop.

Minerva's wails shocked him so badly, that he disregarded his improper attire and dashed toward the main corridor. Under the light of the gas lamps, all of the protesting, arguing occupants of the manor appeared distressed, including the usually implacable butler.

Minerva waved a letter opener like a sword, but Paul could tell she was near tears. He caught her small shoulders and led her toward the breakfast room, where luncheon should be laid out at this hour. "Tea," he commanded. "Then one person at a time, please."

He'd been reluctant to order the noble Reid lords and ladies about when he first arrived, but nothing was accomplished by weeping and arguing. Hunt or Clare normally took charge and brought order, but they weren't here. Even hermit Arnaud appeared ready to pull off heads, which wasn't helpful.

Refined Thea slapped plates on the table. Young Sofia and Lavender drifted aimlessly, until Arnaud pointed at the plate of sandwiches and directed it to the table. Lavender wore her bejeweled birthday pin in her hair. Paul realized he should have brought her a bouquet as a token gift.

A maid arrived with tea and ale, and gradually, the table filled while Minerva recited her tale of woe to anyone who had missed it.

She'd spent hours translating that code. Paul adored the petite librarian above all else but he had no right to hug her. "Your notes?" he asked, taking his tea and plate to the seat beside her. "Weren't you taking notes of what you found in the journal?"

"I haven't worked all the way through the journal," she cried. "I only jotted notes of days when he had visitors, things out of the ordinary. The notes are still in their drawer but what good are they without the book?"

Her teacup rattled as she returned it to the saucer. She was seriously shaken, as she had every right to be. Her library had been violated.

"And no one else has borrowed it?" Paul had to ask, but he knew the answer. No one took a book from the library without telling Minerva. They were too valuable. As expected, everyone shook their heads negatively.

"Notes, like altercations with the neighbors?" Arnaud asked, taking a different tack than theft.

Minerva nodded, visibly calming herself with this practical question. "Professor Boston's codes are mere abbreviations, so they translate like *F usual berries*, *bb* which is positively indecipherable, except he presses on the nib and the ink flows thicker, and I assume he's irritated, so I take note, although I have no idea what *bb* means."

"Blunderbuss," Arnaud suggested. "His neighbor's name is Finkley, thus the F. He aimed a blunderbuss at me when I approached. I expect Finkley is a drunkard, and the argument was over Boston cutting back the blackberry vines in the hedgerow. This is not material worth stealing, unless Finkley killed Boston and is trying to hide it. I find it unlikely that he has sufficient coherent thought to know about the journal."

"Did the manor have visitors today?" Paul asked. He didn't want to believe anyone in the household had stolen Boston's journal. Outsiders were more likely.

"Tim Cooper started work today," Walker said. "He's wanting to fix up the cottage before bringing his bride home. I talked with Mrs. Upton about housing him in the east wing, near the stable, until then. He's been out walking the grounds all day."

"Boston's grandson is staying in the manor?" Arnaud asked, frowning.

"If we trust him as steward, we have to trust him in the house," Meera said firmly, supporting her husband's decision.

"Besides, he'd have no reason to ransack his grandfather's cottage if he knew he could do it at leisure later." Minerva scowled at her sandwich as if it offended her.

"Neville Talbot was here, however briefly," Arnaud added. "He was not allowed inside." He hesitated, then reached for his ale. "Except Oliver reports there were loud voices in the stairwell that frightened Davy. Perhaps he came to the side door?"

Lavender glanced up from poking at the contents of her plate. "There was an altercation earlier. I heard it too. I don't think it was Quincy. He never lifts his voice. I believe Herbert spoke with someone at the door, and there was a disagreement."

"Neville, trying to talk his way in." Thea glared at Paul. "Mr. Upton, you must remove him from the parsonage, at once."

Before he could reply, Patience and Henri swept in, apparently having gone to their separate rooms to wash and dress properly, as Paul obviously hadn't. He winced but reminded himself he wasn't gentry.

"Are we talking about the Talbot *imbécile*?" Henri loaded up Patience's plate before starting on his own, with what remained of the buffet. "He absconded from the parsonage this morning, although I understand he has let a room elsewhere."

Paul frowned. The village didn't have a great many vacant cottages that weren't in severe disrepair. If Neville Talbot was letting a room. . . And Cooper had an empty cottage and needed blunt. . .

Everyone simultaneously reached the same conclusion.

The gentlemen cursed under their breaths. Thea jumped up and fled. Patience looked puzzled until Meera leaned over to whisper an explanation.

Talbot may have moved out of the parsonage, but he was still in town. He may have argued with a servant and Davy heard him. Had he found some way to steal the journal?

The gentleman had no reason to even know of its existence.

Minerva set down her cup with a distinct thud. "How many new servants do we have in the house?"

Was she suggesting Neville might have bribed one for entrance? Or stolen the book?

Even Patience saw the deeper implications of this question. She wrinkled her brow worriedly. "Mother has hired several new maids and the footman. . . But she was told to do so. Surely you don't think one of the new hires let Mr. Talbot in?"

"The boys could have taken the journal to work on the code," Lavender suggested, diverting any anger toward their most excellent housekeeper. "I have several new ladies in the sewing room, but I cannot see how they'd be able to sneak into the library or answer the side door to let anyone in."

"Given the value of the books in the library. . ." Paul looked to Minerva, who nodded, while still scowling. He rather adored her scowl. At least he always knew where he stood. He hadn't taken her question as an insult to his step-mother, just as a fact-finding mission.

"I should have been locking the doors all along. We'll need to remove the library keys from the downstairs key rings. I'll do the dusting and such, hence-forth." Taking her remaining sandwich with her, Minerva slipped out of the room before any of the gentlemen had the presence of mind to stand.

Paul immediately missed her company and her ability to ask the right questions. He simply wasn't cynical enough to believe the staff was guilty of theft. Or anyone else.

In his usual surly mood, Arnaud set down his mug. "One other thing Boston's drunken neighbor mentioned, and I apologize to the ladies. . ." He waited a moment for the women to object, but Patience and Lavender had utterly no idea what he might say and simply waited. Meera and Sofia shrugged. "Mr. Finkley said his neighbor occasionally received visits from a. . . he did not use the word lady. . . who drove a gig. Does anyone around here own a gig?"

Paul caught his meaning immediately. "You think one of our new maids might be this. . . person? I shouldn't think maids could afford gigs."

"Or know how to drive one," Meera added. "I wouldn't."

Arnaud scraped his chair back. "We are coming to meaningless conclusions. We cannot accuse the entire staff of stealing a book half of them cannot read and the rest cannot decipher. Let us concern ourselves foremost with protecting Davy and Miss Talbot from their cousin. I am not familiar with the outside staff. Henri?"

His brother nodded. "Walker, shall I round up some of our ex-soldiers and station them at the doors?"

Leaving Henri and Walker to discuss guards, Paul tackled the gig question. "Let me talk to my parishioners. They're in a position to note who is coming and going. They'd certainly notice a gig. And as we've done before, Mother and Patience can listen to the staff. They likely know more than we do."

"Quincy knows everything. Anyone interested in boxing lessons? I am to ask him to teach Davy how to fight back." Arnaud strode off, leaving everyone to gawk in astonishment.

Even Henri looked startled. "My brother, he does not fight, except with his art. He does not even carry weapons."

"His fists are effective weapons." Paul glanced at the empty seat where Thea had been sitting. "I think, perhaps, he doesn't like to see anyone bullied."

"Do I need to write Hunt and warn him that we have another killer plus a bully and a thief in the village?" Walker looked resigned as he shoved back his chair.

"Not yet," Paul suggested. "I gather our newlyweds are not far away and could arrive quickly? Let us see how we fare with guards and gossip."

"Should we arm the guards?" Henri asked, also rising.

Hunt had an armory. Some of the soldiers had their own weapons. Paul was a curate, not a soldier. He stayed while Henri and Walker departed, discussing weaponry.

Patience toyed with her food. "Henri keeps guns and knives. I hate that we must use them."

"We will use our thinking caps." Meera stood to follow her husband out. "We have protected ourselves before. We can do so again. Are we burying the tower door or does that need to be guarded as well?"

Paul grimaced. "Someone should probably explore the tower before we close it up again. I am working to secure the locks. I'll take a look in the lower part this afternoon, if I can find someone to accompany me. I don't think anyone should go in there without a partner to run for aid, if needed."

"I had hoped to speak with Mr. Cooper about the orchard, but if we're busy setting up an army, perhaps I should go with you instead." Patience finished her tea. "I will talk to Mother about the new servants, then change for playing in mud."

"Unless there's a door into the tower from the manor, I'm not interested. We have that new shipment of fabric to sort." Lavender rose and, taking Sofia with her, sailed out of the room.

"Maybe I should ask the aunts to join us," Paul said dryly, rising. "I'll meet you outside in half an hour, shall I?"

The backward clock struck seven, and Patience laughed. "Does it even keep the hour? How will I know when half is gone?"

"I'll wait until you're ready." If he were a rich man, Paul would buy all the occupants of the manor timepieces. Of course, half of them wouldn't wear one.

Paul assumed he had time to run down to his shop and find the hinge he needed. He was beginning to understand the captain's need to build a fortress around the manor, but really, it wouldn't do much good if the danger was inside.

EIGHTEEN

THEA: WEDNESDAY AFTERNOON

On her way back to her room after luncheon, Thea tried to cool her temper and fear by debating where she might run away with Davy on her meager allowance. Lavender's grandmother calling to her from the blue salon diverted her path and thoughts.

"Yes, my lady?" She stepped inside to see all three of the aunts sitting around a lovely Chippendale table that had probably once adorned the withdrawing room. She really would like to finish decorating. . .

"I have thought about it, and I think perhaps a little music would not be amiss this evening. I cannot think how to present my gift without a little ceremony." The mole on Lady Lavinia's lip bobbled when she pulled her lips into a frown.

Thea had to think twice before she remembered—Lavender's birthday. "Just gracing us with your presence for dinner is sufficient ceremony, my lady," Thea assured her. "You may present your gift when the cake is served."

"We all have a little something for the gal." Hunt's aunt, Lady Spalding, gestured at their perpetual needlework. "It is not too early to start her trousseau."

Impatient to be gone, Thea did not argue, although a trousseau was the last thing Lavender needed or wanted. "Perhaps, after dinner, I could play a little for you in the great hall? Would that suit?" She'd have to warn Mrs. Upton of the change in routine so she'd have the sconces lighted.

"Yes, I think that will do. A music room would be pleasant. We should see to that." In a gesture of dismissal, Lady Lavinia returned to her luncheon.

A music room, of course, in a household where they had only one badly tuned instrument and at most, three people with a passing acquaintance with sheet music. And she would be leaving shortly, if only she could think to where.

Thea hated that Neville was driving them from still another home, but she saw no alternative. Perhaps a cottage she could guard with vicious dogs and a shotgun— She'd need to learn how to load one.

Heading for her chamber with the notion of writing acquaintances to see if they had crofts concealed deep in the Highlands, she halted at excited boys' voices carrying from the guest end of the hall.

Surely, after her warning, the tutor wasn't taking them outside?

She trailed the clatter as they apparently took the back service stairs. To her surprise, Arnaud, not Mr. Birdwhistle, followed.

"What is the meaning of this?" she asked, catching up. "Did I not say—"

"Boxing," Davy shouted at her, before rushing down to the ground floor, with Oliver on his heels.

The big Frenchman actually deigned to explain. "You heard him. Davy believes he needs to punch bad men. Quincy has offered to teach them one or two moves suitable for youngers."

Shocked, Thea followed them down. "Quincy's huge! How can he possibly. . ." She could not form the words. How could she trust her little brother to big, grown men who simply did not understand. . . She wanted to rage at him, but she was too confused. Davy would someday be a man. . .

"We shall see. They may tire quickly, but it cannot hurt for them to feel as if they might defend themselves and each other."

Clare might have a word to say about that, but Oliver's aunt wasn't here.

Thea could not imagine Davy harming a fly, but she wondered if she might find someone to teach her to shoot. She didn't think she'd have the slightest compunction about putting lead into Neville. Perhaps the Talbot family name should not be carried on.

After that horrifying thought, she did not protest when she realized where the men had set up a boxing ring—in the tower cellar.

"You are all quite mad," she whispered as Paul Upton lifted the boys down to the cellar level, where he'd apparently removed the makeshift door.

"Quite likely," Arnaud agreed. "But Paul, rightfully, thought it dangerous to explore the tower alone, so we keep him company. Quincy arranges the rest."

The boys disappeared into the filthy, bug-crawling interior. Arnaud dropped into the hole to join them. Thea stood outside, stewing, unable to jump down. Did she even want to try?

Setting aside her billhook, wearing her leather apron filled with smaller tools, Patience stopped to peer into the hole. "We'll need a pretty stone wall to hold up the dirt and some nice steps if we're to use this door. Or do we just leave it to the men?"

"You're asking me?" Thea blinked, realizing she had as much right to decide this question as anyone else. For now. If she stayed. If she didn't. . .

"We probably ought to take a look," Patience continued, with a frown. "See if it's worth saving. I have some men's trousers. Do you think if we wore them and pinned up our hems a little, we might join them?"

Utterly horrified at the notion but unwilling to abandon Davy, Thea followed Patience just to see what she could possibly intend. Surely the daughter of a man of the cloth wouldn't suggest anything immoral.

The curate's sister meant exactly what she said.

Half an hour later, giggling at the sight they presented, Thea followed Patience up the kitchen service stairs wearing trousers and boots under a serviceable old bombazine gown pinned at the knees. She ought to be horrified, but the parson's daughter with the voice of an angel was a very bad influence.

"I can barely walk in these." Thea muffled a laugh as she stumbled over her own feet. "How do men go about like this?"

"Practice." As tall as most men, Patience stomped her too-large boots down the drive carrying a crate to use as a step. "If there is a root cellar we can use, I'm not letting them turn it into a boxing ring."

"Oh, I'm sure they'll be bored in a day or two, but we really should see if it is safe. I don't believe men consider such things the way we do." None of the men in her life did, anyway.

"Because they know they can lift a rafter if it falls on them. So they believe themselves invulnerable. Arrogant stupidity." Sounding a great deal like pragmatic Clare, Patience dropped the crate into the hole, stepped down, and held out her hand to help Thea.

"I suppose that's what sends them off to war, thinking they can dodge bullets." Thea needed to think about anything except rats and spiders and bats.

Inside, she could hear Davy squeal with excitement. Had she ever heard him make that sound before?

She had to adjust her eyes to the meager light once she entered the byre or dovecote or whatever this dungeon once was. The men had hung lanterns from several of the aging timbers that marked storage bins and stalls. In the center of the large circular chamber, they'd scattered a thick layer of straw.

Quincy and the boys had stripped off their coats and shoes. Thea watched warily as the enormous butler showed them how to put up a defensive arm and —kick? Did one kick in boxing?

Patience wandered off, intrigued by the housing for the dovecote and bins that might once have held root vegetables. Thea held her elbows, not daring to move further into the dark filth.

Emerging from a nearby stall, Arnaud watched critically. "I wager that is not what is taught in boxing salons. Our butler must once have been a street fighter."

For no good reason at all, she relaxed a trifle in the company of his solid presence. "They're too small to hurt anyone."

He snorted and cast her a glance. "There speaks a woman. Let us just say that if the lads learn to come out fighting, they have a better chance of escape."

That made some sort of sense, she supposed. "It's a pity women cannot kick to hurt. Slippers and dresses are useless."

"Stamp on toes, gouge eyes, use your knee, carry sewing scissors. . ." He gestured at Mr. Upton coming down stone stairs at the back of the room. "Your curate carries a tool belt for good reason."

The curate wasn't a great deal taller than she, but he was much more muscular. If he swung a hammer, it would hurt. Use her knee? She couldn't imagine how.

Did she dare believe Davy was surrounded by armed, if eccentric, knights who might defend him? She wasn't accustomed to having help. It was an almost dizzying experience after years of fear.

"What is up those stairs?" She changed the subject rather than consider gouging eyes. "A perfumery would be ideal if we could find a place for it."

"Are you planning to stay to find out?" Arnaud asked on a taunting note, before striding toward the curate. The ceiling was tall enough that he need not duck.

Had he realized she'd planned on fleeing? Why would he even care?

Davy landed on his plump bottom and cried out but scrambled up immediately when Oliver offered him a hand. She had to let him learn on his own—and this was not something she could teach him.

If they stayed. . . She needed to know more.

Clenching her fists in her too large gardening gloves, Thea sidled around the circumference of the hard-packed dirt floor. Not encountering anything too dastardly, she approached the curate. "Did you find anything upstairs? Is it safe?"

"I only went up one floor," he replied with a puzzled frown. "There is a perfectly good door into the manor, just what Sophia and Lavender are looking for. But it does not open."

Thea gazed up the dark stairwell. "The tower is older than the manor? And once they built the manor, the earls didn't want anyone entering a ballroom from a byre, so they bricked up the doorway?"

Thea opened up her mind, but The Lady wasn't there. Instead, a child cried.

Instinctively, she turned toward Davy, but he was happily kicking Quincy's shins.

The child was inside her head. She grabbed a stall to prevent collapsing to the filthy ground. Now was not the time to reveal her vaporish weakness.

NINETEEN

ARNAUD: WEDNESDAY AFTERNOON

STANDING IN THE BOXING RING, AIDING QUINCY, ARNAUD WATCHED AS THE MAD heiress turned ghostly pale after speaking with the curate. But little Oliver began running circles around his boots, kicking anywhere he could reach. The boy needed to learn fear and to flee larger opponents, as Davy had. Arnaud leaned over and hauled the lad up by the back of his shirt.

Oliver blinked in surprise, not fear.

"Your aunt will kill me, will she not?" Arnaud asked with a laugh. "But keep kicking if someone does this to you."

Oliver squeezed his elfin face into a thoughtful frown. The quiet lad was more thinker than doer. But just as Arnaud was about to set him down, Oliver lashed out with both feet, aiming below the waist. Only because he had long arms did Arnaud escape being unmanned.

Quincy praised the boy. Before Arnaud could look again, Thea had vanished. He could hear voices emanating from the various stalls. He had no business worrying over her. He returned to learning what he could from Quincy's instruction to the boys.

Perhaps, if he knew how to defend himself properly, he wouldn't have to kill anyone again—as long as no one attacked the boys or women. He'd live with the nightmares if it came to that.

Once the boys tired of the game, Quincy helped them climb up to ground level and followed them out, herding them like a mother duck. The women had departed with the curate earlier.

Which left the tower empty, with no one to notice his cowardice. A large space, filled with friends and laughter, this cellar hadn't haunted him. But alone. . . the darkness closed in. He could feel the heavy weight of stone above, knew if the lantern went out, he'd be abandoned and helpless.

It was time he conquered his unreasonable fear. The family needed to know what was on that top floor—and he was the most expendable member.

Heart pounding, his jaw clenched in irrational dread, he checked the lantern's oil and wick and decided they were sufficient for a brief survey. He raised the light to the doorway of a narrow, stone stairwell circling the tower's circumference. He'd climbed similar ones as a boy in the ruins of an old castle. The stone was more solid than wood, although cupped in the middle from the tread of thousands of feet over the centuries.

He knew in his head that he had nothing to fear but bats or pigeons. If only he could block out the horror of a grim, confining passage. . .

Devil take it! No knife wielding soldier was likely to leap out. He forced himself to take the first step into the narrow passage.

He was large. The stairwell ceiling was low, the stairs, built for smaller men than he. Stooped, he eased up with his back against the outer stones, holding the lantern in front so he could see where he placed his boot. No soldier waited to lock him in—and there were no doors or bars. He had nothing to fear—except himself.

And the deadly silence. He heard nothing of the household through thick stone walls lined with plaster and wood. He might as well be alone in a dungeon. *Breathe.*

Rigid with tension, he reached the next level, the one at gallery level. Gulping air, he stepped into a large, round chamber. It had only one window, high up under the staircase. He'd thought the windows might be on the stairs for illumination. Apparently not.

In the lantern's light, he studied the ornate oak door Paul had mentioned. It opened, but only to bricks. A few strokes of a mallet might break the barrier.

He'd rather find out why the door had been sealed off first. If they knew *when* it had been closed off—they might consult journals and ledgers. He saw no date in the mortar.

The ceiling was open rafters. The shadows were too heavy to tell more.

The enclosed gloom worked on his fears. He forced himself back to the landing and edged up the next flight, to the bedroom level. There was a window in the stairwell this time, thank all that was holy. It faced east and the sun was on the other side of the manor at this hour, but the meager illumination allowed him to see around the bend. His chest still constricted and his heart pounded, but he could move.

He nearly fell into the next chamber and took deep breaths while he studied his surroundings. A large, circular, open space, it had a single window with just enough light to throw dancing shadows on the walls. His imagination conjured flitting ghosts from days gone by. Or soldiers prepared to pounce. . .

He shuddered and forced himself to consider the manor's floor plan. This chamber should connect at the end of the hall containing the loft and the manor's guestrooms. The wall nearest the manor was squared off with panels, as if it ought to have a door into the main house, but this level contained no visible door. He didn't linger.

Continuing upward, he heard noises. . . and froze in the passage. He couldn't identify the rattle but something moved. Black memories of a soldier racing at him with a bayonet. . .

Instinct screamed run or—*kill*. Common sense said ghosts couldn't harm him.

He forced his boots upward. A rush of wings flew over his head, brushing his hair. He nearly leaped backward, down the stairs. Wishing for a banister, he gripped the cold stone walls. The rustle and squeak flew off. *Bats*. He sighed in relief, steadied his cowardly panic, and proceeded onward.

If possible, this flight leading to the attic level was even darker and narrower. He'd hate to take these narrow steps at night.

He flashed his lantern around the next chamber before stepping out, hoping to scare off any more flying creatures. Or scampering ones. The light caught on a heap of. . . fur? What the devil?

He swung the lamplight over a pile of discarded animal heads—hunting trophies, judging by the plaques to which they were attached. Had he given it any thought. . . the manor had once been demoted to hunting lodge. Which earl had flung these monstrosities into the tower?

Better yet, how?

Easing away from the moldering mass of fur and glassy eyes, he lifted the lantern to examine the rest of the chamber. The ceiling probably matched that of the manor's attic in height—not as tall or grand as the public rooms. It might do for servants or a nursery, except, again, there were no walls, just a large open area.

With a door into the attic. . . He found the panel they'd failed to unlock earlier.

That would be how the trophies had been tossed in, before the door was sealed.

The heavy door had no handle. The hinges were rusted iron. He supposed damp might seep through these uncovered stone walls. Unlike the lower floors, this level had no plaster or paneling. No windows. Would the women want to work way up here? He didn't think it had ever been intended for any purpose other than to make the tower high enough for all the countryside to see it.

Arnaud flashed his light up what he assumed to be the final staircase. No wall enclosed this one. The treads were wood, little more than a ladder with a rail leading up to the watch tower and roof. But if it led to a door, the boys might escape this way. They wouldn't be trapped should they find their way in.

Speaking of traps. . . He held the lantern higher but couldn't see the crawl space Davy had found. This chamber had an actual ceiling, which must conceal the crawl space. It might simply be a duct to allow in fresh air or a vent for a chimney.

He'd come this far. . . With the shadows deepening, he approached the wooden stairs. If he fell through, no one could hear his shouts. The tower was little more than a bastille. It only needed prisoners. He shivered and studied the stairs.

They didn't appear as worn as the stone ones, but wood rotted. He applied all his weight on the first step. It held. Taking each one separately, he bounced on the treads. He heard no cracking. The step nearest the ceiling appeared to be loose, but it held his weight.

The top level—Arnaud breathed in the beauty and let his fear fly away. This had no doubt been a later addition or renovation. Windows half the height of the walls circled the round chamber, interspersed with cabinets that must once have gleamed with wax. He could see over the roof to the sun setting on the far side.

The view was spectacular. He could set up a studio here. . . And produce what to sell to whom? And traverse that hideous stairwell every day. . .

He would be as isolated as if he were back in prison. He'd learned to accept the life-affirming chatter of Lavender's ladies. Could he tolerate silence again?

Still, he breathed deeply, enjoying the light and space. The ceiling was vaulted, a collection of rafters supporting the pointed tower roof that could be seen for miles. It would be freezing in here in winter but fine in summer. The window frames were cracked and leaky. Fresh air entered without opening the casements.

He didn't need a lantern to find the exit onto the roof. The heavy wooden panel was locked, of course. They really needed a locksmith. But the boys could open the windows and escape and scream for help, if necessary. Whether anyone would hear them was questionable. He'd need to search for roof access into the manor but he thought he remembered the attic service stairs continuing up.

Definitely best to keep the storage room blocked until they could learn more.

He wished he could fly back down. Instead, he stuffed his fears into the black box where his heart should be and inched his way through the confining gloom back to the byre.

Damn, he needed a brandy. The ladies would definitely not wish to establish a perfumery in here.

As he pulled himself out of the hole to level ground, he heard lowered voices. Patience hadn't tackled the overgrown shrubbery on this side yet. And the manor's bulk cast a shadow well past the hedges to the drive. It must be nearing dinner time. Lavender's birthday celebration. . . He'd been warned they were gathering after dinner. He needed to bathe.

Could Hunt build a bathing room in the tower? There was room for a cistern on the roof.

The furtiveness of the argument caused him to peer cautiously around the bushes. Hadn't they heard him drop the bolt on the byre door?

Two shadows stood under the portico, male and female. He couldn't hear the words, but they appeared to be bickering like husband and wife, or brother and sister. They were definitely not billing and cooing.

Seeing no reason to avoid the side entrance he usually took to his chambers, Arnaud strode from the shadows.

The couple jumped apart. The female ran for the kitchen service door in the rear.

The man waiting to hold the portico door was Herbert, the new footman.

"Good evening, sir, excellent night for a stroll, is it not?"

Hadn't the man spoken in a broad country accent earlier? Disinclined to quiz him, Arnaud passed by without answering, intent on washing and dinner. The tower might be a bastille, but if he could wash and eat, he'd survive.

"Miss Lavender would like to see you," the new footman reported, following him in.

Looking down at his filth, Arnaud grimaced, but it was late. Lavender's ladies would be departing soon, and so would the girl. Reluctantly, he strolled down to the gallery door.

Lavender grinned at his entrance. A pity she wasn't ten years older. She really was quite lovely.

"I have finished your coat, sir!" She glanced at his dishabille and frowned. "But I will not have you try it on looking like that. Take it upstairs and wear it with your best linen. If it needs more adjustment, we can look at it later."

She handed him the frock coat Henri had bought secondhand, and Lavender had cheerfully trimmed and tucked to his size and her specifications. The rich chocolate fabric had contrasting tan lapels to match the brocade waistcoat she'd made for him. The buttons were shiny and new and the pockets mended.

"This will make even Lady Lavinia smile in approval," he assured her.

She grinned impishly. "You need only one of the earl's fabled jeweled pins or one of your own pearls to complete the effect."

Once, he'd owned pearls and stick pins and gold watches. Most had been lost in the war. It would be foolish for a bankrupt artist to wear them, so he hadn't missed them, until now.

But he bowed in appreciation and carried the coat away, nearly running into Thea in the upper corridor. She hovered, as if waiting for him—or for anyone—to listen. He frowned, bowed, and asked, "Is there aught wrong?"

"I think a child died in that tower," she whispered. "I can hear him crying. I think he's warning us to stay out."

TWENTY

PAUL: WEDNESDAY EVENING

PAUL HAD A THOUSAND AND ONE THINGS HE KNEW HE OUGHT TO BE DOING, BUT HE didn't wish to disappoint Lavender by not attending her special occasion. And he didn't often have the opportunity to hear music or dance with a lovely lady. Minerva almost offered a smile in delight when he suggested they join the impromptu reel in the great room after dinner. Hope leaped eternal, especially when he was allowed to hold her waist to spin her around, and her smile broadened, as if she might be enjoying his company.

He was still an impoverished curate, grandson of Irish immigrants, and she was the descendant of nobility, but he let himself dream.

Mr. Birdwhistle and the boys joined in the festivities. A cake was cut and beverages passed around and even the maids enjoyed the occasion. With excited squeals, Lavender opened her gifts from her grandmother and the aunts. The birthday girl now sported a diamond-and-emerald pendant on a ribbon around her throat, beaming as if she'd been given a king's ransom. Paul hoped that meant the rift between the little seamstress and her dowager baroness grandmother was healing.

To everyone's surprise, Arnaud took a seat at the pianoforte with Thea, helping her turn pages and occasionally joining in the harmony, although with his missing finger, he couldn't conquer all the notes. The heiress seemed somewhat subdued and didn't join the dancing. He was grateful that Arnaud had taken it upon himself to calm her.

Thea's fear for her little brother was justified, and one of the reasons Paul needed to be on his way instead of flirting with Minerva.

"Nettie asked me to visit before I leave," he whispered, leading the petite librarian from the dance floor. He couldn't call his stepmother Mrs. Upton as the others did. She'd been Nettie to him since he'd been old enough to toddle. "I don't want to break up Lavender's party. Could you pretend to be showing me something in the library so we might slip away?"

"I'd have to unlock the door." She skirted around the far side of the great hall while the others fell into another reel. "They won't miss us."

"You really aren't invisible, you know," he said in amusement as she led him through the shadows at the side of the room to slip out the open double doors.

When she'd first arrived, Minerva had done her very best to vanish into the woodwork. Now that she'd ordered her trunks sent from home, she wore colors more suited to her fairness. Her diminutive stature might make it easy for her to hide behind others, but she'd never be invisible to him. Her personality was much too strong.

"Lavender is the center of attention, as it should be. We won't be missed," she said dismissively. "I do hope this means she and her grandmother might quit being at loggerheads for a while. If Lady Lavinia would invest some time in her only grandchild, she might direct fashionable customers this way. Lavender's talents shouldn't be limited by our lack of funds and connections." Minerva lifted her skirt hem and followed him down the service stairs to the kitchen.

"No one is about to travel all the way to the back of never for a gown. We need to open an inn, at the extreme least." Paul took her arm at the bottom of the stairs. He was happy for the company.

In the manor's cool cellar, with the stove shut down for the evening, the kitchen staff had taken a break to sample a duplicate birthday cake. Lavender's maternal grandmother cheerfully presided with anecdotes of her granddaughter's childhood. The upstairs/downstairs dichotomy of the manor residents was almost revolutionary. Paul thought he might have to remain in Gravesyde to encourage the mix. Another curate might not be so freethinking—or have a housekeeper for a mother.

Nettie greeted them at the door to her rooms and gestured for them to take seats. "Close the door, will you? I hate to gossip in front of others."

Raising his eyebrows, Paul did as told. His mother detested gossip as much as he did. "What's this about?"

Nettie nodded at Minerva. "I heard about the missing journal, and I've been keeping my eyes and ears open. We've hired a steward, a footman, and two maids in the past week, which is odd in itself. Good servants don't just show up in places like this. The agencies gave up on us long ago."

"I understand Herbert has family in the neighborhood?" Paul took a seat on the sofa beside Minerva, where he might enjoy her proximity.

"If so, he's made no mention of them, and none of my staff know of them. He's not been here long enough for a day off. Perhaps his family is closer to the city. I may be making too much of this."

"Someone stole that book," Minerva insisted. "There is no reason for any member of our family to do so. But I cannot imagine why a footman or maid would be interested."

Too busy with everyday practicalities to give the theft of a useless book much thought, Paul quickly grasped their concern. "You think someone believes the professor knew the key to the earl's codes? And they are looking for the jewels?"

Both Nettie and Minerva tightened their lips grimly. Paul rubbed his brow. "That seems far-fetched. It would point directly to Boston's grandsons. They could have *asked* for the return of the journal."

"Now that we have broken the professor's code, someone may wish to see what's in the journal without letting anyone know?" Minerva grasped her elbows in distress.

"Word has spread through the staff," Nettie added reluctantly. "They know we're hoping to discover more about the earl's codes."

"And besides the staff, we know almost nothing of the grandsons," Minerva fretted. "Mr. Cooper was only seen briefly at the burial. The younger brother has barely ventured inside. Has he even settled into his room yet?"

Nettie shrugged. "I cannot say. I had assumed he had."

"Is the elder still in his grandfather's cottage? I thought Neville Talbot was to let their cottage." At least, Paul had reports that Thea's cousin had packed and left the parsonage. He was planning on returning to his own bed and library tonight.

"Patience said Talbot hired the deacon's wife to cook for him and one other person. Mr. Cooper, perhaps?" Nettie worried at a fraying string on her apron. "It doesn't feel right. Why would a rich lord's heir take up with the grandson of an impoverished scholar? But that is not why I asked you down here."

Paul let his stepmother take her time. Nettie was loyal to her staff, but family came first. She had to balance her priorities.

Minerva poured a little sherry and handed the glass over. "You do not have to tell us anything, but we will almost certainly find out on our own."

Nettie nodded and took a sip of fortification. "It's just. . . I don't like being too critical, and I feel that is what I am doing. Herbert has been a very useful footman, when we can find him. He's cheerful and cooperative and pretends to be eager to learn. But there is something not quite right about. . ."

"We have noticed he is not always where he ought to be," Minerva agreed. "Rather like that Bow Street Runner we had here last month, pretending to be a valet. Herbert always has an excuse for being in the wrong place, and as you say, he's very helpful. I fear, though, he is not really a footman."

Nettie sighed. "My conclusion, also. And part of the problem is that he is often in the vicinity of Eleanor, one of the new maids."

"Courting happens," Paul suggested. "It's to be expected at any age."

He could swear that Nettie blushed.

She hastened to explain. "They do not appear fond of each other. At mealtime, they take opposite ends of the table and often exchange sharp words. But upstairs. . ."

"I've seen them in corners, arguing." Minerva poured a sherry for herself. "We'd better verify their references. *Eleanor* is a rather fancy name for a maid, isn't it? I cannot think of a single one among all the duke's staff. Usually, they refer to themselves as something less lofty, like Nellie. Does she at least know her position?"

"Arrogantly so, I fear." Nettie smoothed her apron and sought words. "If I ask her to dust and sweep a room and try to explain how I wish it to be done, she starts on the task without listening to me. Her attitude appears to be *I know how to do this, leave me alone.* Except, when I inspect later, the task is only half done."

"As if she might be searching the room once you leave?" Paul suggested. "Foolish. It's not as if you and your staff haven't covered every inch of the manor by now."

"Pull rank, Mrs. Upton," Minerva advised. "If she makes you uncomfortable, then we don't need her. She either performs the task to your satisfaction, or we show her the door."

"I hate that. People deserve a chance to learn and grow." Nettie worried at her apron strings again. "But if there is any chance she's a danger to our family. . ."

Paul bolted upright ""Neville! What if this isn't about jewels but Mr. Talbot stealing Davy?"

Minerva gaped. "We have been so concerned about thieves and killers for so long, we have forgotten to see the obvious! Mr. Talbot lingers here for a reason."

"Do I send them packing?" Nettie asked anxiously. "It's not as if we have any evidence of a connection."

"Keep them on the ground floor," Minerva suggested. "Ask Quincy to station his son, and not Herbert, at the portico door where the boys go up and down. Let us keep an eye on the new maid and footman. That's easier than fearing every stranger who comes to the manor."

"We'll need to warn Mr. Birdwhistle and the others." Paul stood and leaned over to hug his stepmother. "Thank you for keeping your wise eye on us. I am not the best person to notice these things."

Frowning, Minerva rose with him. "Thea and I need to decide who shall have entry to the school room. Who carries up their trays and does their cleaning?"

"Betsy," Nettie said with confidence. "She lives in a happy world that knows no suspicion and hasn't a deceptive bone in her body. It may take her twice as long to accomplish any task, but she leaves nothing undone."

"We need more Betsies in this world." Taking Paul's arm, Minerva swept out with him.

Timothy Cooper, the new steward, stood in the dim hallway just outside Nettie's room. He started, bowed briefly, and hurried out the kitchen door to the courtyard.

TWENTY-ONE

THEA: THURSDAY MORNING

IF SHE HAD A PURPOSE, A CHORE TO PERFORM, SHE MIGHT CLEAR OUT THE MEGRIMS and think more clearly, Thea decided the next morning, after a sleepless night. She could do nothing about a crying ghost, after all. She did not even have to listen to it since Arnaud had advised keeping the tower closed until they researched it more thoroughly. She hated to admit that the artist was right.

He'd brushed her off when she'd told him about the phantom cry. Of course, he had. Anyone would. She didn't know why she'd even told him, except that he'd generously helped with Davy learning to defend himself.

And then he'd stayed by her side during the party, giving her time to calm down. But she shouldn't put any meaning into that. He most likely protected Lavender from Thea's hysterics. Still, it was more courteous than she'd expected of him.

To occupy herself, she returned to the withdrawing room. Someone had been ripping off the old wall covering. She suspected Arnaud. He had seemed to enjoy taking out his frustrations on rotten glue and fabric. Destructive sort. . . except his paintings were extremely creative. Perhaps he could paint something suitable for over the mantel.

She doubted if the budget would cover paying him. But if Clare and Hunt were using the library book money to buy furniture. . . Hm, a thought for later.

For now, she needed to recall the bits and pieces she'd taken note of in other rooms, see which ones might work in here. She'd love to have a comfortable family parlor to surprise the newlyweds on their return. They needed more chairs and a sideboard, with clean lines, perhaps, not ornate.

She recalled a delicate old sideboard in the closed off ladies' wing, Queen Anne, she thought. The men would hate it, but she wasn't putting any of that heavy old Jacobean-era firewood in here. She might enjoy the historical significance, but visually, she wanted light. The heavy pieces belonged in the men's wing.

She lifted the linen on the sofa to refresh her memory on the colors. Oddly, one of the cushions appeared to be askew. Had the boys been playing in here?

She pushed it back in place but it stuck. Surely they hadn't broken a brand new sofa? She'd been so very awfully careful. . . Yanking the cover off, she examined the cushion. A rectangular object stuck out. . . A book? She tugged it from the cushions so they slid back properly.

Expecting to find an escapee from the library, she opened the leather-bound volume—and read hand-written gibberish. *The coded journal?*

Excited, Thea nearly bumped into the new maid on her way out of the room. Tall, slender, her reddish hair tucked neatly under a cap, Eleanor curtseyed and fled.

Puzzling over the oddity of a lone maid wandering the hall, Thea continued down the empty main corridor. Breakfast was over. The maids were normally upstairs cleaning bedchambers. Even if they weren't, they'd been trained to travel in pairs. If any were cleaning the ground floor chambers, there should be buckets and mops.

Frowning, she entered the library on the far end of the corridor, where Minerva worked.

The moment the librarian saw the book, she jumped up to grab it almost reverently. "Where did you find this?"

"Behind the cushions of the new sofa—with the new maid hovering just outside. I'm not sure what to think." Thea released it, relieved to be rid of the responsibility.

Minerva hastily flipped through the pages. "There are pages missing. This is bad. I wish I'd been able to read all of it. . ."

"Does this mean someone was able to easily read it and remove pages they didn't want you to decipher?" Thea rubbed her hands anxiously against the apron she wore when working. She'd brought much of her wardrobe with her when she'd fled, but she didn't have the funds to replace anything. She had to be careful.

After removing her sliding scale decoder and notes from a drawer, the petite librarian laid out pages with military precision. "Undoubtedly. But why give the book back? Why not burn it? I used to enjoy a good mystery, but this is seriously irritating."

"Do we need to question the new maid? I can't blame her for anything except being outside the door." Never having had responsibility for servants, Thea wasn't certain what to do.

"We've talked with Mrs. Upton. She's ordered the new maids and footman to stay on the ground floor. It may be upsetting routine." Minerva flipped book pages.

Thea nodded in relief that she needn't question anyone, but that didn't ease her fear. "I'm almost afraid to ask for help in moving furniture. Who can we trust if we have a thief in the manor? I was hoping we were safe here."

She couldn't see how a book thief would be a danger to Davy, but she worried anyway.

"This is Henri's day to stay home. He's helping Paul repair the workshop at the inn. Send someone down to fetch them. Or ask Arnaud." Minerva dived into the journal, apparently making up for lost time.

That was sensible, she supposed. Thea found Quincy and asked him to send a message down to the inn. Heaven forbid that she disturb Arnaud with her petty concerns. He was no doubt painting another Mona Lisa.

At her request, Mrs. Upton unlocked the east wing, and they wandered the mostly empty chambers looking for suitable pieces. Thea had already measured all the paintings. None of them fit the missing space in the vestibule.

Some brilliant countess had favored Chippendale, presumably to match the cabriole legs of earlier Queen Anne pieces. A hundred years or more of use had left the lovely mahogany and cherry scratched and chipped. It appeared much of the original upholstery had been replaced with needlepoint.

Lady Reid, the last viscountess, had created the family tree tapestry in the study. She had been a talented lady who had died much too young. This could be her work.

The Queen Anne sideboard Thea had noticed earlier was really too frail and damaged for family use. They traveled on to the most elegant room in the east wing. Plaster cherubs and bouquets adorned the ceiling. The fireplace was tiled in beautiful greens and blues. A threadbare carpet that may have once featured the same hues covered the center of the wide board floor. Thea itched to restore this room, but Hunt had ordered the wing locked until they could afford more staff.

But right where the frail Queen Anne piece should have been was a sturdy sideboard with traces of gilding on the scrolled legs and carved hutch. Time and usage had worn the gilding and cracked the once lovely veneers.

Thea stood back to examine it. "It won't match, but the men will appreciate it."

"Not if they have to carry it," Nettie said in amusement, testing the weight of the old cabinet. She couldn't budge it.

"Well, it's the only one we've found besides the Queen Anne. They either have a place to store their liquor, or they don't. We can do without it but can they?" Thea began opening the drawers and doors. If there'd ever been any old silver or china in here, it had been removed, leaving only moldering ancient linens.

"And what is this difference between *we* and *they*?" a French-accented voice inquired. Arnaud.

Straightening without looking behind her, Thea placed her hands on her hips and studied the piece. "*We* don't need liquor. *They* usually do. If *they* wish to have a cabinet in the new withdrawing room, *they* will have to find some means of moving it."

"*We* could wait until Hunt and Jack return before moving things all about." Arnaud strode in to examine the piece.

Even in this large chamber, his presence filled the space, consumed all the air. Thea had to back away as he grabbed a corner of the cabinet base and dragged it away from the wall, seemingly effortlessly.

A clatter distracted her. "Did it break? Did something fall off?" She darted back to the wall to look behind the sideboard.

Arnaud did the same, leaning over her, disturbing her equilibrium—not enough to ignore the glitter of gilding.

"Stand back. I can reach it." Arnaud nudged her away as if she were a piece of furniture.

But he was right, she couldn't reach far enough, even had she wanted to battle spiders and cobwebs. She wanted to bop him over his beautiful dark hair and pray at the same time, although she wasn't entirely certain what she was praying about. Except, odd things hidden behind timeless furniture ought to be significant, shouldn't they?

Shoving the sideboard a little further from the wall, Arnaud finally reached the object and hauled it out. A gilded frame could be seen beneath a heavy layer of sticky cobwebs. Nettie produced a cleaning rag from her apron, but wrinkling her nose, she let Arnaud do the wiping. Wrapping her hands in her own apron, Thea watched anxiously. Why would anyone hide a painting?

"Looks like a Reid," Arnaud grunted, holding the portrait so they could see it. "Old, well done, possibly by one of the painters from the gallery portraits."

"Much earlier, I think, judging by the hair style and garments." Thea studied the blond lady with blue eyes holding what appeared to be an ermine muff. "Off the shoulder sleeves, fur trim, heavy boning in the stays to achieve that tiny V-waist. . . 1600s, I'd surmise, but I'm no expert on past fashions. She appears to be dressed rather warmly for indoors." The background showed paneling and a window to the outside.

"That may be this sideboard under the window, with the gilding and veneer still intact. Just imagine, this piece of furniture could be two hundred years old!" Nettie leaned forward to examine the oil more closely. "The lady is wearing a gold necklace with rubies, diamonds, emeralds, and sapphires embedded, hideously vulgar."

"One of the earlier countesses?" Thea examined the oil closer. "I thought our traits were from the male side of the family, but there's the Reid widow's peak and attached ear lobes. Did our traits come from a lady and not the Reids?"

Arnaud did some quick calculating. "Early 1600s, she would be mother of the second earl, wife of the first? I do not believe there is any portrait of them in the gallery."

Thea stepped back and measured the frame with her hands. "I don't have my pattern piece with me. . . but could this be the missing artwork from the vestibule?"

"*Merde.*" Arnaud turned the painting around, held it at arm's length, and immediately began searching the frame.

Boots echoed on the uncarpeted hall and male voices resounded through the empty rooms. Thea darted to the doorway, prepared to defend their find, if necessary. She sighed in relief at sight of Paul and Henri come to help move furniture. "Hurry! We may have found something."

The instant they saw the portrait, Henri unfolded his worn newssheet pattern. Paul removed a tool from his belt.

The pattern fit.

Arnaud took Paul's tool to pry open the cracked and ancient backing.

Thea only discovered she was holding her breath when it escaped in a gasp as the backing fell off—revealing nothing.

Arnaud carefully removed the canvas to examine it, then shook his head. "I may have to clean it to see if there is another code."

No hidden map or letter, no key to treasure. . . Oh well.

He was about to haul it off with him, when Thea recovered enough to shout at the heedless giant, "Wait, carry the sideboard first!"

TWENTY-TWO

ARNAUD: THURSDAY MORNING

By some magical form of osmosis, the entire household loitered around the vestibule as Arnaud carried the newly-discovered portrait down the main corridor.

Leaving Henri and Paul arranging the sideboard in the new withdrawing room, Arnaud sent a servant upstairs to fetch the boys. They'd done much of the measuring and rearranging. They deserved a small break from their routine to admire the results.

Paul and Henri arrived at the same time as Oliver and Davy. The boys perched on the lion statue as their carpenter-curate adjusted the nails in the correct panel on the right hand side of the wide entry, where every visitor might admire it. The garish jewels on the lady's long, slender neck glowed in the transom light, despite centuries of dirt.

"Why would anyone hide such a magnificent portrait?" Thea asked, studying the layout. "It's almost as if the entire array of art is arranged around her."

Arms crossed, Arnaud stood back to observe the arrangement. His gaze was drawn far too often to the real golden lady in her gossamer gown, not the portrait, although Thea's hideous apron ought to be shredded.

Minerva held one of the Wycliffe history books, flipping ancient pages. "If the portrait is from the early 1600s, then it quite probably is Caroline, the first Countess of Wycliffe. She is described as fair and of good family, with a sound dowry. The writer mentions the lady's family had connections to the marauding soldier who destroyed and robbed the priory. He was knighted and his son was made baron. But the baron died while they built the manor. The baron's son became the first earl, the one who probably added to the family fortune as a pirate."

Kings rewarded plundered treasure with titles and estates, nothing new. Arnaud had no interest in history lessons. He wanted to look for a code in the oil. They knew the fourth earl had been the one to inscribe the codes they'd found, because he'd signed the letters the codes led to. Had he hidden the portrait? Why?

A little too aware of Thea's round rump as she leaned in to study the oil, he almost missed her comment.

"Do you think by *family connection*, they mean Lady Caroline's father was a marauding pirate, as well, or one of the first Reid's soldiers?"

"Or all of the above," Minerva suggested. "It's not as if the nobility was large, or even well acquainted with one another at the time. There might even have been family relationships. The family tree in the history only goes back to the parents of each earl, not siblings or in-laws. They liked to keep their fortunes by marrying one another."

The boys studied their maps of the vestibule and the copies of the earl's odd drawings but offered no suggestions.

Realizing they had an audience of servants, fearing one of them might be their book thief, Arnaud removed the portrait. "It needs cleaning."

Abruptly torn from her inspection, Thea glanced around and presumably grasped his concern. "Off you go, boys, Back to your studies." She glared at the staff. "Back to work, all of you."

The new, red-headed maid swished off huffily. The new footman tugged an auburn forelock and sauntered after her. Arnaud gave up on recognizing faces.

"I hate suspecting everyone," Paul muttered as he followed Minerva out. . .

Leaving Arnaud alone with Thea, studying the empty panel. He held the portrait impatiently. "No thunderbolts from on high. The mad earl was just mad."

She shook her head and followed him from the vestibule. "He was a Reid. His madness had purpose. Nearly half a century later, we simply don't understand it."

"Nor do his sister or granddaughters." He gestured at the stairs where the aunts resided above. "Not communicating—"

"The inability to communicate as others do is not a sign of madness. He liked puzzles and he is telling us something." Even a frown looked good with her pretty lips.

Arnaud knew he needed to take himself to the city and a willing woman soon when he started thinking like that. Miss Dorothea Talbot was nothing but trouble, wrapped in pretty ribbons.

And he had nothing to offer a lady. If he'd still been wealthy and titled—he could have handled trouble. As it was, he was worthless. Any parent would firmly agree, including her negligent ones.

A mistress. He needed a mistress, not a wife. With no household of his own, he had only one use for a wife.

Leaving her in the hall, he returned to the gallery. He set the painting on an easel and brought out his cleaning materials while studying the smoke-darkened portrait. He was fairly certain the muddy wine of Lady Caroline's gown should be a much brighter hue. He knew little of English history, but he was fairly confident that scarlet was more popular in earlier eras, even in England.

The codes in the other portraits had been hidden in the darker, shadowed hues, as if the earl had only one tube of paint and barely knew how to use it. This portrait was all light, meant to gleam and glitter like her jewelry—difficult for hiding codes. The Reid ladies definitely took after Lady Caroline, even after all these generations.

Intent on his work, he wasn't aware of the clatter of carriage wheels on the drive outside the medieval windows, until Lavender said *uh-oh* near his shoulder. He glanced up to find her gazing through the bubbled glass panes.

Arnaud wiped his cleaning brush on a cloth and watched as Bosworth, the manor's banker, pulled up in his open carriage. Two other men sat on the seat behind him. Arnaud didn't recognize either, but one wore a clerical collar.

"The outside world approacheth," he muttered.

"Is that a quotation?" Lavender asked, still watching the visitors.

"It is now."

They listened as Quincy answered the door.

"Maybe they'll go away when they learn Hunt isn't here," Lavender suggested.

"And go where? It is nearly noon. They may make Birmingham by tonight if they leave now."

Bosworth's home was in the opposite direction. With a horse, he might make it by nightfall. Not with a carriage.

Quincy appeared in the gallery doorway, a suggestion of puzzlement on his usually impassive brow. Arnaud left Lavender to pounce on the butler. She was taking her new adult duties seriously.

The massive butler shook his balding head and stared right at Arnaud. *Merde.* Not removing his smock, he set aside his brushes and saved Lavender a trip back across the ballroom.

Picking up the visiting cards Quincy offered, Arnaud scowled. "A vicar and a magistrate? One assumes this is about the death of Professor Boston?" He recalled that Walker had written in Hunt's absence.

"They wish to speak with the gentleman of the manor," Quincy said in stiff disapproval.

"And you told them Hunt is not here? Perhaps we could send Oliver or Davy," Arnaud suggested facetiously. "They are the only true Reid males."

The butler didn't even honor that suggestion with a reply.

"Go," Lavender whispered. "We'll send Walker or someone as soon as we find them."

He'd heard Paul and Henri leaving earlier. Arnaud was fairly certain the very white, stiff-necked, rural gentry at the door would not accept an African steward as the man of the manor. There was no one else to greet them but the women, which worked for him but apparently not for Bosworth.

Arnaud had no desire to speak with local dignitaries. One of the benefits of being a bankrupt artist émigré was that he had no responsibilities.

Except to his cousin Hunt, who sheltered and fed him.

With a sigh, Arnaud stripped off his smock. The gallery held an assortment of furniture from its former glory as a ballroom and walking gallery. Some of the idiot statues of Roman gods still littered the niches between the windows. He'd thrown his coat over one of the tattered wing chairs earlier. He yanked it on now.

"The library?" Arnaud suggested, with evil intent in mind. Minerva haunted the library. If she were driven out, she'd head straight for the spyhole they'd discovered in the library's ceiling. Anyone else might spy from the hidden side doors.

Quincy bowed and trotted off.

"You ought to be wearing your new coat," Lavender scolded, brushing dried paint specks off the sleeve of his shabby old one.

"I have no desire to impress them with more than my general uselessness. They would do better to talk to you ladies." He stomped out.

Already in a temper, he wasn't pleased to note that Minerva was nowhere about and the visitors were examining the wall of books over the concealed library door. "Gentlemen? As you've been told, Captain Huntley is not at home."

The middle-aged banker—also a Reid male, although an unacknowledged bastard—made the introductions. "The Reverend Arch, vicar of Bewdley parish, and Abraham Ephraim, Esquire—magistrate from Bewdley. You'll remember Mr. Ephraim was here a month or so ago. Gentlemen, this is Captain Huntley's cousin, the Comte Arnaud Lavigne."

When in doubt, always add a title, even an empty one. Arnaud remained standing. "If this is manor business, then I suggest you speak with the manor's owners or our steward. I am neither."

But a magistrate. . . Arnaud refrained from stomping out, as he'd intended. They needed someone to handle the Boston murder.

"No, no, we simply need to speak with a man. The fairer sex—" The vicar gestured dismissively, eliminating almost the entirety of the manor's population.

The fairer sex, Arnaud mentally snorted. The Reid ladies would have these men tied in knots within minutes. Perhaps that's what they feared.

Interesting thought. . . Thea might turn pale and speak of ghosts. Minerva would produce a mighty tome and read it in the original Latin. . . And they'd terrify men wielding all of society's authority.

"I fail to see how gender matters." Arnaud still refused to sit, forcing them to remain standing. His was the higher title, after all. If he couldn't use it in a fit of spite, what good was it? "Lady Spalding or Lady Lavinia are in a far better position to be useful."

"The matter is delicate," the magistrate said affably.

Tired of avoiding the subject, Arnaud presumptuously leaped to the topic that must have brought them here. "*Death* is not delicate. *Mrs.* Walker examined the professor's body. *Miss* Peniston recognized the significance of his code books. They need to be reassured that the killer will be caught."

Mr. Ephraim held up his soft, white palm. "There is very little we can do about the unfortunate Professor Boston. His death is regrettable, indeed. But it is up to his family to bring the culprit to court."

Good Lord in heaven. . . Arnaud tried not to jump down their throats as he stared at them in incomprehension. "Then why are you here?"

The vicar twisted his top hat. "It is Master David Talbot we have come about, my lord."

Oh hell no was Arnaud's immediate reaction, but before he could fling the trio out a window, a knock intruded. Without waiting for an answer, the door opened, revealing a beaming Patience. Tall, blond, and buxom, their housekeeper's daughter could slay dragons with her irrepressible smile. For a change, she was even wearing muslin instead of her leather gardening apron. "Luncheon is served in the breakfast room, gentlemen."

That's when Arnaud realized he wasn't alone. Minerva had put out a call to arms.

He *almost* grinned.

TWENTY-THREE

THEA: THURSDAY LUNCHEON

"Quincy has promised another boxing lesson," Thea told the boys and their tutor. After listening to the vicar and magistrate at the spyhole, she had dashed up to the schoolroom and was short of breath. "But he only has time while everyone else is having luncheon. He'll carry your meal to the tower. Take the back stairs, please."

Mr. Birdwhistle raised a quizzical eyebrow but no objection as the boys cheered and began stripping off coats and ties.

"We've sent for Paul and Henri to meet you there," she murmured to the tutor, beneath the excited shouts. "They've been working on a bar for the inside of the byre so you can lock out intruders. Neville has sent an army."

Thea's stomach had curdled the moment she'd realized the new arrivals weren't here to help. She didn't have time to take Davy and run. She'd have to send him into hiding, as he had always done. Weeping ghosts or not, the tower seemed safest.

Praying silently, she hustled the boys down the service stairs to where Quincy waited. This far from the central corridor, the occupants of the breakfast room couldn't see or hear them. Thea followed the boys out, simply to verify that Paul and Henri had arrived. They were there, tools and lumber at hand. They opened the tower door to allow butler, tutor, and students inside, then carried their load in, closed the door, and began hammering.

She was so relieved that they trusted her over men of authority that she was almost giddy when she returned to the house. That didn't mean she didn't keep a wary eye out for Neville or any suspicious activity as she hurried toward the breakfast room where the buffet would be laid out. She'd been misled too many times, so it was very hard to trust.

Adam signaled from his post to indicate he was on duty in his father's place. There was no sign of the new maid and footman, although they'd been assigned duties on this floor. Blessedly, she only heard peaceful murmurs.

Arnaud awaited her under the gas lamps by the sweeping marble stairs. A thick lock of chestnut hair hung over his brow, and he frowned more fiercely than a thundercloud, but she'd heard him through the spyhole. He'd refused to act without the *real* owners of the manor—and that included her. This was *her* home. And she thought, maybe, he actually believed in her, even if he did think her mad.

"We need to enlist the aunts," Arnaud said without preamble, holding out his arm for her to take. "Neville's scheming must be presented to these men of authority. And as long as they are here, they can serve as witnesses to the state of Boston's cottage and books. We need them to grasp the possible connection between a dead man and a dead earl's jewels, should we ever find the killer and bring him to court. We will make them forget Davy."

Forget Davy? Was that even possible, to mislead the men of authority that her father sent, as they had often tried to deceive her?

The ungentlemanly gentleman's arm was thick and more muscled than she'd expected. She'd obviously spent too much time with the effete dandies in society's ballrooms.

Reassured by the way he said *we,* she accepted his lead. She hadn't thought the self-involved artist had noticed the existence of the rest of the family.

"How will we do all that?" she asked as she took the stairs at a stride almost more than her skirts allowed.

"First, force them to acknowledge that ladies own Wycliffe Manor and thus, are the law here. That will twist their minds into knots long enough for you to take command."

Thea wasn't certain she could twist *her* mind around to it. He wanted her to do what? Take command? That way led to true madness.

The door to the blue salon was open. The aunts glanced up in curiosity from their luncheon tray as Arnaud knocked and towed Thea in after him.

"Minerva tells us we've been invaded," Lady Spalding said complacently, not waiting to exchange polite greetings. "Have you planned a counter attack?"

"I thought Mr. Walker sent for these gentlemen?" Hunt's mother knew Walker as Hunt's best friend and respected their steward as the captain did. Mrs. Huntley's graying brown curls and lack of any Reid attributes spoke volumes about her actual heritage, as did her son's same dark features. They were Lavignes, not Reids, but the law recognized only marriage lines, not physical traits.

Thea glanced at Arnaud to see if he treated this newly-discovered aunt any differently, but obviously, to him, they were all old ladies. He'd been too long isolated from family. He didn't even bow for them.

"Walker wished their advice on Professor Boston's death. Now that they are here—for whatever reason—we must use them," Arnaud declared. "I am not Hunt. I cannot act as magistrate. But with one available, we need to visit Boston's cottage, question his grandsons and the neighbor. With your aid, we might find more evidence than we have now and have reliable witnesses to call on later, if needed."

"How might we help?" Lady Lavinia, in her seventies and rail-thin, still spoke like a general—or the earl's daughter that she was.

Thea waited for Arnaud to explain, but, to her shock, he nodded for her to direct this next act. He put her in command—because *she* was one of the owners and as responsible as her elders for everyone's safety. She nearly panicked. The aunts had always believed in her, but what could she ask them to do?

What *she* wanted was to drive Neville from Gravesyde with a hatchet and broad sword, but the ladies weren't pirates, like their ancestors. She wasn't that mad.

A magistrate and vicar. . . could be weapons of a sort.

"You have the authority of your titles, wealth, and society. Your words will hold more weight than mine," Thea began tentatively, searching for the right direction. "Our visitors believe gentlemen know better than excitable, feather-headed women and expect men to be more rational and agree with their arguments."

"They simply don't care to listen to us, dear," Lady Spalding said. "I am here because the man I raised from boyhood wants my house for his own purposes—because his plans are more important than mine. They think in practicalities, not sentiment."

"Yes, well, we must show them that in Wycliffe Manor, *people* are more important than their *practicalities*," Thea retorted. "Men are only practical about what concerns their wants and desires. They dismiss our thoughts and opinions because they think us *emotional* when we fret over friends and family. I do not wish to continue being treated as a mindless doll. You need not be either."

It wasn't much of a battle cry. She was unused to rousing troops, after all. But she'd learned a few lessons from Minerva. If the mere daughter of a retired army officer might stand up to a duke, as Minerva had done, then Thea, with all her wealth and position, could stand up to a rural vicar.

PATRICIA RICE

And a marchioness and a baroness, with powerful lords at their command, could terrify a battalion of magistrates and bankers—if only they could be organized to do so. United, they were strong.

"You wish us to demand that they investigate the professor's death before we'll even talk to them about Master Davy?" Mrs. Huntley suggested, showing her son's unruffled grasp of a situation. Apparently, the ladies had informed her of Davy's precarious position.

"Let us drive them out of the manor and their comfortable expectations," Arnaud agreed. "Walker, Henri, and I will stay here to guard the household. Mr. Upton is best suited to convince a vicar of a crime."

"And taking the boy away would be a crime," Lady Lavinia decided. "That is why we brought Dorothea and David here. We will not be deterred." She pushed herself from the sofa and checked her gray pompadour in the mirror over the mantel.

Plump Lady Spalding donned a shawl. The younger Mrs. Huntley shook out her skirts. Armed only with determination, they set out for the breakfast room.

Thea gratefully clung to Arnaud's offered arm a moment longer. She held little hope that they might catch a killer. But if somehow, someway, a household of women could hold her father and cousin at bay. . . Perhaps they might save Davy.

TWENTY-FOUR

ARNAUD: THURSDAY AFTERNOON

ATTEMPTING TO HIDE A SMUG SMIRK AS THE GRAND AUNTS SAILED INTO THE breakfast room in full panoply, Arnaud entered after them, arm-in-arm with Thea. He enjoyed watching heads swivel. Oddly, he enjoyed even more making the heiress giddy with expectation. She squeezed his arm as Lady Lavinia shook her folded fan under the magistrate's nose without waiting for introductions.

The ladies were about to instruct the gentlemen on feminine authority.

He hadn't had this much fun in. . . He couldn't remember when. He was actually *enjoying* himself. What the devil did that say about him? That he appreciated rebellion?

Tall and thin, wearing gray from head to toe, the elderly baroness resembled a preying mantis prepared to bite off heads as she regarded their visitors with a gimlet gaze. "Thank heavens, you are finally here! Where have you been? We could all be murdered in our beds and who would bear witness? You must do something about killers running loose!"

The men stood and the magistrate bowed hurriedly. Perhaps Ephraim had met the aunts when he'd been here last and knew better than to reply before they'd all had their say.

"*Poisoned*," plump Lady Spalding countered dramatically, filling her plate. "We might all be poisoned and dead within an hour without Lady Elsa watching over the kitchen. All those new people. . ." She bit into a stack of cheese on a roll.

"Without my son here, we are all terrified." Mrs. Huntley stepped in front of the startled vicar. "Comte Lavigne, introductions, please."

131

An above average height, portly man with thick graying hair, Reverend Arch seemed nonplussed by the dramatics. He bent over the ladies' hands as Arnaud introduced them. "It's most. . . enlightening. . . to meet the ladies of the manor."

Thea dropped his arm and demurely helped her aunts with their plates. She'd stirred the aunts. He needed to stir the men.

Keeping a straight face, Arnaud explained, "The ladies, they have been near hysterical for fear of their lives and that of their loved ones." Well, they'd kept to their chambers and had drunk tea in comfort without a concern in the world, but a little creativity never hurt.

"A thief, sir, a *thief* stole Mr. Boston's books after we brought them here for safety," Lady Lavinia cried. The elderly baroness was obviously enjoying her role. "We must turn off all the new servants if the thief and Mr. Boston's assailant aren't found! Surely, they are one and the same."

Mrs. Huntley turned on the dapper Ephraim. "You, sir, you act as magistrate in my son's place? He would spare no effort to see that we are safe in our beds. He'd have Boston's cottage searched, his grandsons and neighbors questioned, until we rout the killer. Surely you can do the same?"

The complacent banker had carried a book into the breakfast room and set it on the table while he filled his plate. Accustomed to the drama, he settled at the table to eat and read, unaffected by thieves and killers and not-quite hysterical ladies. Arnaud would have liked to bounce Bosworth off a wall just to shake him up, but admittedly, bankers were singularly useless in this situation.

To his relief, Paul rushed in, still buttoning his clean coat. Arnaud hoped that meant the tower door was safely barred. With a nod in the vicar's direction, he left the curate in charge of his employer.

"Reverend Arch, if we could step outside and speak privately for a moment," Paul suggested, indicating that Arnaud join them in the quieter surroundings of the corridor.

They left the bemused magistrate in the manipulative hands of the ladies.

Arnaud had seen Paul employ his late stepfather's rather useful arm-twisting tactics. He thought he could learn much from the inoffensive cleric. He said nothing, assuming the curate knew how best to persuade a fellow clergyman.

"Sir," Paul began in a tone of anxiety, once away from the theatrics, "Lady Spalding's stepson, the marquess, takes a powerful interest in Wycliffe Manor, as does Lady Elsa's half-brother, Earl Villiers. We have tried to keep the murder and thefts from reaching their ears in hopes of resolving the case ourselves, but without authority, our hands are tied. If the ladies think we are working on the problem, they may refrain from writing their families and demanding soldiers or worse. They have been relying on our promise to bring a magistrate to investigate."

"Lady Elsa?" the vicar asked, processing information he'd surely been told but hadn't quite grasped until now.

Assuming he shouldn't be completely idle, grasping the direction of Paul's argument, Arnaud explained curtly, "Another of the heirs, the wife of *le* Honorable Lt. Jack de Sackville, son of Baron de Sackville. Earl Villiers has been most concerned about his sister's safety, as she is a substantial heiress. One cannot underestimate the power and wealth the ladies of the manor wield."

"And these ladies attend chapel and tithe generously?" The vicar revealed his real interest in the manor.

"They do," Paul assured him. "We are rebuilding the chapel. The congregation has more than doubled since the ladies began attending. The ladies have even volunteered a carriage to fetch elderly parishioners as needed. They have been extremely generous."

Not that tithes from their tiny church were a drop in a wealthy vicar's bucket. Arnaud had no coins to contribute, but he could see church income might be important to the vicar, who paid the curate.

"And what about this disturbed boy, Master David? His father is most concerned that he be placed in an institution where he might receive help." The vicar frowned, having recalled their real purpose here.

Arnaud gritted his teeth and refrained from throttling a man of the cloth. It must be the English air bringing out his latent violent tendencies. He strained to speak without anger. "Master David, he is an *exemplary* student and a most excellent companion of Captain Huntley's nephew. They are the only two true male Reid heirs. There are undercurrents of which you are not aware. To resolve Boston's demise will go a long way toward opening avenues of. . . communication."

Paul took up the banner. "As we understand it, the boy's cousin is currently residing in Boston's cottage. If we visit the crime scene, you will have an opportunity to speak with Mr. Talbot, and ascertain the true situation. It is not beneficial to upset the Reid family over this child."

"How likely are we to resolve murder if we talk to this cousin or visit a dead man's cottage?" the vicar asked grumpily.

"To talk to Mr. Talbot may offer perspective in the boy's case. But I fear the most we hope for in visiting the cottage is to terrify the killer into fleeing. Our main concern, until *le* captain returns, is to pacify the ladies so they do nothing. . . distressing, *n'est ce pas*?" Arnaud let the insinuation dangle. Distressing. . . as in calling a marquess and an earl to attention or cutting off the ladies' largesse.

"Yes, yes, of course, I see what you are saying. We should delay until the captain returns. Thank you, my lord, for explaining the situation. Upton, I'm glad to see a sound man has taken charge of the congregation and will do what is best for the church and community. I shall do what I can to persuade Ephraim not to disturb the peace, so to speak." With a dignified nod, Arch returned to the buffet to finish his interrupted luncheon.

Or persuade the magistrate not to disturb an earl and a marquess, Arnaud thought cynically, following the curate back to the breakfast room, where the ladies were relating tales of horror to the dapper little man of the law. . .

Patting himself on the back for applying diplomacy as well as *practicalities*, Arnaud watched in dismay as Thea abruptly dumped a cup of tea on the banker and cried, "The Lady, The Lady is crying!"

Arnaud had seen the heiress genuinely vaporish while in the throes of her mad obsession with a ghost. This wasn't any faint. Thea was furious.

He was torn between alarm at her fury and laughter at the smug banker's expression.

TWENTY-FIVE

PAUL: THURSDAY AFTERNOON

Despite what were probably Arnaud's good intentions, Paul wasn't at all certain that he appreciated being thrown into the company of a wealthy, aristocratic vicar.

As the son of an itinerant, impoverished curate, Paul had grown up in the shadow of men like this, younger sons of nobles who earned their living through the church but left the actual task of caring for their parish to barely paid underlings.

He supposed, to be fair, he shouldn't judge Arch until he knew him. If he were to keep his position and someday improve it, he needed to impress the man —while persuading his superior to bestir himself for his neglected parishioners.

After the excitement of Thea's inexplicable contretemps with Bosworth, Paul led the magistrate and vicar away from the buffet, to the front vestibule. He'd have to ask what had instigated the attack later. "Shall we take advantage of the lovely day and let your horses rest by strolling over to Boston's cottage? You'll have an opportunity to see what we've done to the chapel and churchyard."

Walker had apparently sent their new grounds steward to go with them. Timothy Cooper reluctantly waited for them on the front steps. Boston's grandson wore a cap, not a hat, and a rough work coat, obviously with no intention of impressing anyone.

At Paul's suggestion, the company followed him down the drive. The magistrate seemed an affable man, interested in his surroundings. The vicar wasn't quite as amenable until Paul pointed out the field the earl had donated to the church.

"Why hasn't it been rented out?" Arch demanded as they crossed the brook into the fallow furrows.

"No men to work it, sir. We have been considering dividing it into garden plots for the few families who subsist here. They could fill their larders and donate the excess to the church." To him, and to the manor, but the vicar thought in terms of his own pockets.

Their new steward studied the field with interest but didn't speak. Ephraim snapped a lingering rose and tucked it into his lapel. "Lovely setting for your chapel."

"The structure isn't large enough to hold a congregation," the vicar commented as they cut through the grounds Patience had worked so hard to restore.

"Once the manor is able to establish ownership of the village, I believe substantial changes can be made to bring in more people." Paul was comfortable saying that since they'd left the banker behind. Bosworth and his bank stood between the manor and repairs.

"Mr. Cooper, did your grandfather attend church, do you know?" The vicar turned his questioning to the dead man's grandson. Paul approved. Even the taciturn steward could not ignore a powerful man of the church.

Tim Cooper shrugged his underfed shoulders. "Reckon he was what they call an agnostic. Didn't believe in preachers. Said he'd worship with the goats and chickens."

"I understand your grandfather was a scholar?" Paul diverted any argument over religion.

"Taught mathematics at the university, yes, sir. A bit peculiar, but harmless." Knowing the terrain, Tim had unconsciously taken the lead of the expedition on the footpath past the church grounds, out of sight of the village.

"So, Mr. Lavigne tells us your grandfather knew codes and ciphers?" The magistrate pushed his top hat down tighter over his thick brownish curls and stepped over a muddy patch. In his soldier's fashionable sideburns, Ephraim assumed the role of gentleman, whether he was one or not.

"Aye, I was told so, but I know nothin' of such things. He liked chess," Cooper added helpfully.

That was probably the most anyone had pried out of the man all week.

"I believe we were told your grandfather used to play chess with the earl when the earl was alive?" Paul added, hoping to feed the company as much information as possible.

"Aye, regular like, I understand. O'course, his lordship was long gone by the time me and Frankie spent our summers here." He shut up abruptly, as if he'd said too much.

"Chess, a most excellent game," the vicar said enthusiastically. "Perhaps we can enjoy a round this evening?"

Cooper said nothing. Ephraim murmured possible agreement. Paul felt it necessary to speak. "There is an old chess set in the parlor. I'll be happy to play. Although I am surprised that there isn't a better set. Did you ever have an opportunity to see the earl's chess pieces, Mr. Timothy?"

"Oncet," he admitted curtly.

They were almost at the cottage. Paul had hoped the magistrate might ask more useful questions, but Ephraim was examining the shaded lane and hedgerow as if they might find a sign saying Killer Here. "What did it look like?"

Cooper shrugged. "Don't rightly remember. Fancy with colors and glittery bits."

Not the ancient pieces Thea had set up in the parlor. Glittery bits? Paul had never seen chess pieces with. . . jewels? Of course, he'd never played with earls. Had Wycliffe given the set away as he'd given away so much of his estate?

"Where is this neighbor with the blunderbuss?" the magistrate asked, trying to discern cottages through the overgrown hedge of trees and shrubs.

"Might I suggest we leave him for last? We should let the occupants of Boston's cottage know we're here first." Hoping to catch them unaware, Paul strode up the kitchen path, past the hen house and goat pen. The animals were still gone. "Mr. Cooper, as their landlord, perhaps you should introduce us?"

No one had actually named the renter. Paul had only heard speculation. He wanted it confirmed.

"Don't rightly know him," Cooper said. "He's a gent my brother knows from university."

"Does your brother know codes and ciphers?" the magistrate asked.

Another shrug. "He does numbers like grandad did. That's all I know."

Hunt was far better at interviewing suspects but was the steward really a suspect? Paul hoped not. Cooper had taken a room in the east wing and could easily find his way into the manor. They'd not taken him into consideration when they'd set up their perimeters. Surely, he had no reason to harm little Davy. Of course, there hadn't been any reason to kill Professor Boston either, that they could determine.

Paul frowned at the drift of a woman's voice from the cottage, but he supposed there was no reason the occupant might not have a maid or cook or even a wife. As Cooper led them around to the front door and used the knocker, more voices— sharp, angry?—rose through the open windows above.

When no one answered, Timothy Cooper shoved open the door. "It's me, Tim Cooper, sir, come to see if all is well." The steward might be taciturn and barely cooperative, but he was not shy. Good thing, since he had to order about a regiment of laborers.

At Cooper's shout, Neville Talbot raced down the enclosed stairs, still tugging on his neckcloth. "You shouldn't barge in like that, Tim."

"You shouldn't be ignoring our knock, then. These gents came all this way to see you." Shoving a forelock from his weathered brow, Cooper stepped aside to reveal the company at the door.

Paul led the way in, studying the cottage's main room, remembering the last time he'd been here, with a dead man sprawled on that worn carpet. He restrained a shudder.

The shovel was no longer by the fire. The books had been returned haphazardly to the shelves.

Buttoning his coat, Neville waited expectantly.

The distinguished vicar rocked back on his heels and regarded Talbot with a frown. "Mr. Cooper, introductions, if you will."

"This here's Mr. Neville Talbot, our lodger," Cooper said grudgingly. "Talbot, this is the Reverend Arch and Mr. Ephraim, Esquire. I reckon you know our curate, Mr. Upton."

Instead of offering gratitude for giving him a bed until he found a place to stay, Talbot ignored Paul to study the other two gentlemen. "I trust you have come about my request to see my young cousin."

"This is where it happened?" Not acknowledging the question, the magistrate wandered over to examine the fireplace. No taller than Paul, just better dressed, he poked around the fireplace instruments. "Where is the shovel? There are still ashes in here."

Thea's cousin wrinkled his brow in bewilderment. "I'll speak to the housekeeper, once I find one."

Uninterested in the bully, Paul turned to the bookshelves. "Last time I was here, these books were scattered across the room. Did the housekeeper you don't have shelve them?"

"My brother and I set the room to rights," Cooper acknowledged.

"Now see here, I demand some explanation," young Mr. Talbot protested when it became apparent his concerns were going unheeded.

The manor ladies had apparently done a fine job of convincing their guests that a murderer was on the loose. Paul bit back a snicker as the vicar joined him at the bookcase. "Eclectic, indeed. I don't see many volumes on ciphers."

"We took the important ones to the manor for safekeeping. There is some question that the professor may have used those books to help the earl code clues to a fortune in his paintings." Paul took down a volume on morals and ethics. It would be nice to have time to read again.

"What is this about, gentlemen?" Talbot demanded, irritated at being ignored. "I am only staying here to assure myself of my cousins' welfare. Once they return home, I will do so also. Have you seen them? I have been denied access."

"You're acquainted with Mr. Cooper's brother?" the magistrate asked, walking the perimeter of the room, testing the door lock. "That is how you knew the cottage was to let?"

Paul could swear he heard someone upstairs. He eased in that direction, pretending to examine books.

"Franklin, yes." Talbot anxiously followed Paul's movements.

"That's his pipe I'm smelling?" Timothy said, unexpectedly, heading for the stairs. "Frankie, you up there? Get yerself down here and talk to these gents. They're here to help find who did for grandad."

A muffled oath drifted down the stairs a moment before the clatter of feet brought Franklin Cooper into the room. "That damned Finkley did for him. Everyone knows that."

Paul noticed a scattering of white dust on the professor's dark coat and sticking plaster on one bruised hand. Without his tall hat and expensive frock coat, Franklin Cooper wasn't quite as distinguished as he had been at the funeral.

He straightened his neckcloth in irritation and glared at the intruders. "What is the meaning of this?"

"They're supposed to be helping me return my cousin to his home," Neville said with increasing annoyance. "Who is Finkley?"

Franklin waved a dismissive hand. "Who are these people, Tim?"

Donning his best clergyman's expression, Paul leapt into the fray. "We met at your grandfather's funeral, Mr. Cooper. I had not realized you were still in the area or I would have had my deacon check to see if you needed anything."

He gestured at the vicar and magistrate. "These gentlemen are here to investigate your grandfather's murder. You say it was Mr. Finkley? Do you have proof of this?"

"He has weapons and threatened grandad all the time," Franklin retorted angrily. "I'm sure he can be arrested for any number of crimes, including theft of our animals."

Paul wanted to see what was happening upstairs, but he supposed it would be inappropriate to slip up there on his own.

To his surprise, the dapper magistrate strode toward the stairs. "Do you mind if we have a look around? Would this Mr. Finkley be visible from the upper windows?"

Paul could almost *feel* the panic as the magistrate vanished up the stairwell. He observed Talbot and the Coopers, but they weren't looking at each other. If there was any conspiracy, it wasn't a cooperative one. Timothy slipped into the kitchen. Talbot looked stricken and confused. Franklin. . .just seemed irritated.

The vicar had found a book on chess and was perusing it, oblivious to men he apparently considered of no use to him.

"I'll keep an eye on him, shall I?" Paul asked of no one, following the magistrate upstairs.

"Wait a minute. . ." Franklin shouted from below.

Paul ignored the shout. Upstairs, half the walls in the back bedchamber had been ripped out.

"Looking for something, wouldn't you say?" the jovial magistrate asked from the front room, poking about in the gap between the timbers. "The shovel is over there, by the way. Covered in plaster and not of much use as evidence, but there are a few suspicious traces of what might be blood on it. Of course, they could have been killing rats."

"Mr. Timothy had planned to bring his bride here. I cannot think he'll be happy to see this, unless he authorized the destruction." Paul surveyed the damage and shook his head. "Someone knows we have Boston's journal. What else did they expect to find?"

"A jeweled chess set?" Ephraim looked under the large bed.

Ah, the dapper magistrate had heard and understood the reference.

"The earl could have given the set to Boston or to anyone, really. Wycliffe gave away most of his estates before he died." Paul opened the professor's wardrobe.

A woman's gown and assorted undergarments hung there now. Paul didn't know a great deal about such things, but the fabric looked fancier than that of most of his parishioners, except for the ladies of the manor.

"These weren't here earlier. Do you suppose Mr. Timothy has already moved in his bride?" Paul gestured at the contents.

Ephraim looked over his shoulder and sniffed. "Not with two other gentlemen staying here. Your steward is up at the manor, isn't he?"

"He is, working dawn to dusk. I thought I heard a woman when we arrived, but there aren't exactly any hiding places." Paul could see through the destroyed wall to the smaller bedroom once used to house the professor's grandsons.

Ephraim trotted to the back chamber and studied the window overlooking the goat pen. "Shrubbery beneath the window. Easy drop." When Paul joined him, he indicated a solid nail in the window frame. "Slip a loop over that, climb down, someone lifts the loop off, and voila, the culprit disappears behind the chicken coop."

"That took practice. Although it's possible, as boys, the Coopers escaped their grandfather's watch by that method." Paul scanned the field behind the cottage, looking for the ramshackle bungalow Arnaud had described as belonging to the drunken neighbor.

"I say, what exactly are you chaps doing?" Neville Talbot stormed into the room. "Why aren't we on our way to the manor to retrieve my infant cousin— who is being held hostage, might I add?"

"Master David—that is his name, in case you've forgotten—is with his tutor and Master Oliver, studying Odysseus, I believe, although he prefers mathematics." Paul shoved past Thea's obnoxious cousin to examine a dresser. "As I understand it, Mr. Talbot, you are the reason he cannot leave the manor. Go away, and he will feel better about playing outside."

"Odysseus? How old is this infant?" Ephraim followed Paul but studied the gaps in the wall and not the furniture.

"Eight. He and Oliver were doing complicated equations even I couldn't follow. They don't talk much but apparently think a lot." Paul couldn't see any other sign of female occupation. "As I understand it, that's not unusual for Reid men."

"Of which Mr. Talbot is not one?" the magistrate suggested.

"No, the Reid ancestry is almost entirely maternal these days, which is why the earl left his estates to women. Neville Talbot is merely the unemployed son of a younger son, seeking to better his position."

Having deliberately insulted Thea's cousin, Paul was prepared when he heard Neville's footstep behind him. He ducked, letting the gentleman's ineffectual fist fly over his head. "You announce your presence," he critiqued mildly.

"I can have you arrested for assault," the magistrate remonstrated. "And I certainly won't recommend that a child be placed in the possession of a man who acts in anger."

While Talbot shouted impotent threats, Paul leaned out the window. "I think that is the neighbor approaching now, and he's wielding the blunderbuss Arnaud warned us about."

TWENTY-SIX

ARNAUD: THURSDAY AFTERNOON

Arnaud watched Thea pace restlessly from gallery window to side door and back. He'd tell her that ripping wallpaper was much more satisfactory for frustration, but he didn't think she'd listen. Besides, she didn't have the strength to unstick centuries-old glue.

Dumping tea on Bosworth apparently hadn't been sufficient to relieve her vexation. The banker should never have called her an hysteric—and The Lady a figment of her overwrought imagination—especially when she was feeling militant. Apparently, mad women could get away with almost anything because people avoided them.

Arnaud had begun to suspect that avoiding Thea and her communication with the spirits led to unpleasantries. He didn't necessarily believe in ghosts, but he was learning that, despite her demure demeanor, she would do whatever it took to make people listen. And occasionally, she had good reason to do so.

He'd have done worse than dump tea had Bosworth informed him that art was a waste of time. Weird, understanding how her brainbox worked.

When Mr. Timothy rode frantically up on a horse not his own, Arnaud set aside his paints and ran as swiftly as Thea. So, he was guilty of watching too.

They dashed out the side door before their new steward could drop his reins.

"Mr. Finkley attacked my brother! The man is quite mad. They've knocked him out and tied him up, but he could come around any moment."

In concern, Thea stepped aside as Arnaud jammed a hat on his head. "Should we send more men?"

"Cart and driver will do. We shall have to haul him back to the dungeon. I doubt he will come willingly." At another thought, he halted. "Have Walker set a few of his men as sentries around the house. Let's not leave the manor vulnerable. Have Adam and Henri guard doors."

Arnaud didn't know where those commands had originated. He must have listened to Hunt a few times too many. Thea's concern turned to terror, but she'd be well guarded. He couldn't manage being a general and a gentleman at the same time.

The lads nearly had the large gelding he preferred saddled by the time he reached the stable. Arnaud signaled for Cooper to follow. "Whose horse is that you are riding?" He knew the company had set out on foot earlier.

The steward regained his saddle. "My brother's, sir. I took the footpath and not the road. It's fine for a gallop."

"Your *brother's*? Is he still around?" Arnaud had thought the fancified Franklin had left town immediately after his grandfather's funeral.

"He knows Mr. Talbot. I assume he stayed to sort through grandad's things. They all belong to him, so I can't say nothing."

Timothy would have to refurnish the cottage if his brother hauled off the fixtures. Perhaps the professor was merely sorting old books.

Galloping down the drive and the footpath, they abandoned conversation. Leaving a vicar and a curate to deal with a madman didn't seem like a wise decision, but Timothy Cooper wasn't a particularly strong man either. Arnaud hoped Franklin Cooper wasn't harmed, and they had the situation under control. He wasn't trusting Thea's noble cousin to do more than watch.

A colorful flash on the other side of the hedgerow, darting in the opposite direction, caught his eye. He supposed villagers might take the lane, but it only led to the manor, as far as he could ascertain. His gut clenched as he wondered who might be entering the manor while he was away.

Most everyone in Gravesyde wore dark colors. Who could it be? Or had Gypsies moved in? Strangers would add a whole new level of concern.

Arnaud didn't know how his cousin dealt with all the potential threats. He'd avoided responsibility all his life for good reason. He was bad at it.

Not that he was much better at taking orders. . .

They turned from the footpath into Boston's yard and rode past the chicken coop. The good curate watched their arrival with relief and waved to indicate the prisoner's location—tied to the goat pen. Arnaud didn't see another soul in sight. Had they frightened off the vicar and magistrate?

Eyeing Finkley warily, he swung down and tied his reins to a post. The old drunk seemed to have passed out. "Where is everyone?"

"Having tea in the kitchen, I believe," Upton said in disgust.

"I was fixing it for the guests when Finkley arrived." Cooper tied up his brother's mount. "Fink was shouting something fierce, so Frankie ran out to confront him. My brother might be book smart, but he's people stupid."

Interesting. The taciturn steward could speak and speak well, when the notion took him. "Did you see what happened?"

Cooper shook his head. "I was looking about for biscuits or anything for the guests. Grandad taught us to do for ourselves and treat callers with respect. Mr. Talbot was too busy throwing fits, and Frankie. . ." He shrugged.

"The vicar and magistrate?" Arnaud asked of Upton. "Still enjoying tea?"

"It's not as if they'd sully their hands by bringing down a common drunk. Cooper apparently placed a punch or two. By the time I arrived, Finkley had passed out, so I removed his weapon." After checking that the angry neighbor was still unconscious, Upton led them toward the kitchen door.

Inside, the vicar and magistrate were bent over a chess set at the table, while Franklin Cooper held a cold rag to his jaw. Where was Thea's reprehensible cousin? The others glanced up at Arnaud's entrance but no one spoke.

"I have a cart coming around to pick up the prisoner and take him back to the manor." The biscuits Cooper had set out looked unappealing, and he'd never learned to like tea, so Arnaud didn't bother taking a seat.

"Good," the magistrate declared, knocking a pawn off the board. "If I might borrow your cart in the morning, I can take him to a proper gaol to await sentencing, although assault is a minor offense. I could add public drunkenness."

"What about murder?" Franklin demanded. "I told you, he killed our grandfather!"

Mr. Ephraim shrugged. "No evidence. Now, if Boston had been shot, it might be a different story. Not many people have firearms."

"Where's Talbot?" Arnaud asked the curate, who led him into the front room while the injured man argued with the magistrate.

"He took off," Upton said worriedly. "Neville Talbot and Franklin Cooper have torn the upstairs apart, evidently looking for something. Mr. Timothy was upset and told him to clear out. His brother said he couldn't do that because the house was his. The blow to his jaw didn't seem to hurt Professor Franklin's loud mouth. Talbot left anyway."

Arnaud cursed under his breath. He wasn't a soldier accustomed to working through all the strategies of defending a battle station. "I don't like Neville being on the loose. You and Timothy must wait here for the cart. I have left Thea and the boys with only Henri and servants in charge. Do you think Neville has a weapon?"

"Not that I'm aware of. Bribery is more his style. Some of our ex-soldiers. . ."

Paul didn't have to finish the sentence. The soldiers had been left with nothing after the war. The manor didn't have the wherewithal to do more than feed and shelter those who accepted the aid, and they were stretching their budget to do that. A spot of gold would be very tempting.

If Neville Talbot had an accomplice inside the manor. . .

Remembering that flash of color, Arnaud raced for his gelding.

TWENTY-SEVEN

THEA: THURSDAY AFTERNOON

"You help no one by pacing the floors, dear," Lady Spalding admonished from her seat on Clare's new sofa.

After luncheon, the ladies had planted themselves in the unfinished withdrawing room as if it were their personal salon.

"Herbert, you missed a spot." Lady Lavinia called to the footman scraping fabric off the walls. "Do be careful. I believe the walls will need to be replastered before painting."

Thea couldn't scream her frustration in front of servants and the aunts. Arnaud had galloped off to join Mr. Upton and now she had no one with whom to share her anxiety. Not that she could put a name to the reason for her pacing. It didn't matter if all the neighbors had murdered all the occupants of the cottage. Where was Neville?

"I appreciate that you helped make the magistrate and vicar do the right thing. Was there something else you wished to share with me?" Thea asked, allowing herself to be distracted by the the presence of the aunts She had expected them to retreat upstairs.

"We were wondering if Lady Reid's journals contained any references to Boston, his grandsons, or Mr. Finkley?" Mrs. Huntley roamed the parlor, examining the paintings that had gathered in here. "They should have all been in Gravesyde at the time of her residence."

"Herbert, be careful with that sideboard! It is quite old. Perhaps it should be moved a little more to the right." Lady Lavinia returned to her needlework. "We'll need a good carpet in here before winter."

The aunts meant to stay through the winter? They'd never have enough coal.

Thea returned her scattered thoughts to the question. "The lady tends to use initials, so it's difficult to remember references to Mr. B or Mr. F or the like. Did you have a particular incident in mind? That might be easier to recall."

"Weren't there some references, at the time of her return after the earl died, about tenants feuding and asking for help?" Lady Spalding pursed her mouth and frowned in thought. "My mother was helpless, of course. But we might try the books from those days."

Anything to keep busy and from going quite mad worrying about what Neville was telling the magistrate. . . Although, she supposed, if the Coopers were engaging in fist fights, there might not be much sensible discussion happening.

Before she could go in search of the volumes from the 1780s, the red-haired maid appeared in the doorway.

"Mr. Adam says as he needs Herbert at the portico entrance." She bobbed a hasty curtsy and rushed off without allowing time for questions. Or even addressing them as *my lady* or *miss*.

Herbert made a hasty bow and his excuses, as if the maid were more important than his employers.

"Well, I never." Lady Lavinia raised her painted eyebrows after the footman departed. "Really, what has become of servants these days?"

Already uneasy, Thea dipped a hasty curtsy. "I'll see about those journals, my ladies."

Mrs. Huntley abandoned her inspection of the oil paintings to join her. "I'll help you, shall I? I've left a few upstairs in the salon."

Thea didn't want Captain Huntley's mother to think her dimwitted, so she didn't remark on her apprehension or her desire to reach out to Lady Reid's spirit. But hurrying down the dim corridor to the front of the manor, she couldn't think clearly enough to summon pleasantries.

"It's been a long while since I've lived in England, and then it was London, so things may have changed, but Herbert and Eleanor are not. . . quite suited to service, perhaps?" Mrs. Huntley asked.

"That's part of my uneasiness, yes." Relieved that she wasn't the only one concerned, Thea wished she could put her vague fears into words.

Adam guarded the locked main entrances. Neville couldn't force his way around their very large footman. The boys were still in the tower, weren't they?

No one would know to find them there. And they had Quincy, Henri, and the tutor with them.

Still, that left the manor containing mostly women. . . It might be time to ask the captain and Jack to return from their honeymoons.

She really was overanxious if she was contemplating asking couples to return from their wedding journeys!

Lady Reid's library of journals was kept in a cabinet in the great room. The two-story chamber was always gloomy, and today, the clouds gathered for a summer storm. Thea lit a lamp from the hall table.

"I know where to find the journals, if you need to check on the boys?" Mrs. Huntley asked, with a hint of sympathy.

Torn, Thea hesitated at the intersection between the gallery and great room. "I. . . might need the journals. . . ." To summon a spirit. She couldn't explain that The Lady's anxiety mirrored her own. Bosworth's insult rankled. "I will just check the side door, first, as a. . . precaution." To what, she could not say. She handed the lamp to Mrs. Huntley.

"I'll start looking for the right dates. Let me know if you need anything." Mrs. Huntley vanished into the cavernous great room, a picture of competence like her son. If anywhere was haunted, the monk's former chapel ought to be. It sat directly over the crypt. Mrs. Huntley didn't appear to have a qualm.

Thea shivered and headed the opposite direction. Adam wasn't at his customary post. She peered into the gallery. Lavender and her ladies were working hard, heads bent over their sewing.

Arnaud hadn't returned.

Hadn't the footman been summoned to help Adam?

She wavered. They might be outside, unloading a wagon. Perhaps the newly-weds had returned. There could be any number of reasons for everyone to be occupied. The manor was immense and the staff was miniscule.

But she couldn't let it go. She needed to see Davy, reassure herself of his safety. People confused him, and he reacted, but that didn't make him any less sane than she. She had simply learned to hide her peculiarities better. It was that realization that had made her so protective of him. He would learn as she had, given time.

She stopped in the gallery to check with Lavender. "No one is in the hall. Did a cart arrive?"

The girl glanced up in surprise. "No, this isn't Henri's market day. Are we expecting visitors?"

A prisoner, perhaps, but Lavender wouldn't be interested.

"I. . ." How did she explain? "I'm just worried, with Arnaud not here and no footman in sight. I'll see if I can find where they're off to."

Lavender frowned. "You're right. With a killer and thief loose. . ." She set down her needle and picked up scissors, her weapon of choice. "I'll go with you."

She was upsetting the adolescent for no good reason, but Thea was oddly comforted by the offer. "Thank you. I know I'm being silly. . ."

Lavender ignored the apology. "It's not so long since we had to chase a mad valet. I've never had so much fun."

Thea rolled her eyes but accepted youthful exuberance as she returned to the hall and the side entrance. "No shouting or shooting. I fear we are in more danger of boredom than killers."

Lavender did not hear the irony. "Oh, I am never bored. I have so many fashion magazines now! I love illustrations. The designs are too frivolous for us, of course, but I am still able to create a current style that doesn't leave us looking like my grandmothers."

Fashion was the last thing Thea worried about. Using her allowance to pay Davy's tutor, she had to make do like everyone else here. It wasn't as if they had balls or operas to attend or morning calls to make.

They stepped outside into a late summer afternoon with threatening clouds in the distance. This side of the house was in shade at this hour. All looked perfectly normal—except for the absence of people.

To her relief, Patience Upton strode up the drive, carrying her gardening tools. With her blond curls in disarray beneath a straw bonnet, wearing a leather carpenter's apron filled with bits and pieces, towering above them like a Viking goddess, she emanated an air of authority and happy confidence that Thea lacked right now.

"Has Mr. Timothy not returned?" their gardener cousin asked. "I have questions about the walnut—" She studied Thea and asked worriedly, "What's wrong?"

"We don't know. Paul and Arnaud went to Mr. Cooper's cottage. Quincy and Henri should be with the boys, I think, but Adam and Herbert have vanished. We thought perhaps they were out here. Or perhaps they've gone to the kitchen for tea." Thea stepped from under the portico to gaze in the direction of the tower door, but the shrubbery around the entrance prevented any sight.

Wearing boots suited for rough ground, Patience followed her glance and diverted in that direction."The door is closed. They left the crate here. I can climb down and look."

There wasn't anyone around to watch, not even the ubiquitous ex-soldiers waiting for small tasks to earn coins. Another anomaly. Thea nodded. "Please. The door is supposed to be bolted from the inside, but Henri should hear you knock."

She eased into the drive so she could watch.

Patience tried the door. It didn't budge. She knocked. No one answered. "Perhaps they can't hear me?"

That was so very not good.

In apparent agreement, Lavender murmured a French curse she'd probably learned from Arnaud.

Patience climbed back out, looking puzzled. "They must have returned to the schoolroom."

And left the door locked from the inside? Thea was almost positive they had not.

TWENTY-EIGHT

ARNAUD: THURSDAY LATE AFTERNOON

Wɪᴛʜ ᴄʟᴏᴜᴅs sᴄᴜᴛᴛʟɪɴɢ ᴏᴠᴇʀʜᴇᴀᴅ ᴀɴᴅ ᴛʜᴇ ᴡɪɴᴅ ɪɴᴄʀᴇᴀsɪɴɢ, Aʀɴᴀᴜᴅ ɢᴀʟʟᴏᴘᴇᴅ up to discover the manor drive had become a war zone. A grim expression on his dark face, Walker commanded a motley group of ex-soldiers circling the house and beating the bushes. Two lads from the stable hacked at the newly installed tower door. He saw no sign of Quincy or Adam, but the women darted about, shouting incomprehensibly.

His non-existent heart sank to his boots.

Patience's worried frown relaxed at his arrival. "Is Paul on his way?"

Arnaud handed off his gelding to one of the younger lads. "Bringing the prisoner in the cart. What's wrong?"

"We don't know. Adam and Herbert have vanished. Quincy says when he went for tea, he left the boys, their tutor, and Henri practicing in the tower. The door is locked, as it should be, but no one is answering. We assumed they'd left, only we can't find them." The curate's generally cheerful sister crinkled her brow again. "We've checked the schoolroom, and now we're searching the manor. Even Bosworth has bestirred himself to look. Henri. . ."

"Will be with the boys," Arnaud said reassuringly, not feeling in the least sure. His brother would protect those lads until *death*. . . Thoughts racing, he sprinted inside the house.

Neville was on the loose, but he was only one man. Had he taken Davy, and the others went after him?

At the end of the hall, demure Thea was shouting directions like a commanding general, all resemblance to the dizzy heiress gone. He breathed in relief. He needed her sensible head right now.

Catching sight of Arnaud, she cried, "Thank all the heavens!"

Before he could reach her, she proved him wrong. She went blank, spun in vague circles, and collapsed in a puddle of muslin.

Emerging from the immense great room, where he'd presumably been searching, the stout banker glanced down and muttered, "Mad. S-said s-so."

Damn the whole lot to hell. Covering the rest of the distance in a few strides, Arnaud scooped her up and carried her toward the parlor, where the aunts dithered. "Find Meera!" He knew better than to panic over a fit of vapors, but he *needed* the damned woman. . .

He laid her out on the threadbare fainting couch, propping a pillow under her head. Thea immediately stirred.

"That's not necessary, dear." Lady Lavinia produced smelling salts from her capacious skirts. "She's simply having one of her spells. She's distraught and doesn't handle the drama well."

Arnaud wanted to rip things apart with his bare hands, if he only knew what to rip. He could start with the mad heiress. "What the devil is happening?"

If Thea was mad, then so must he be. He should leave the damned woman to her vapors and go rip open a tower door. . .

"The boys," Thea murmured, pushing upright. "Where's Neville?"

Right, that was the reason he'd ridden here like a madman. "We don't know. What about the boys?"

"The Lady. . ." She gestured vaguely. "She's horribly distraught. I don't see how Neville could get in if we can't, but. . ."

Arnaud clenched his hands and tried to beat back his ferocious temper. Shaking her wouldn't help. Killing Neville might, should he find him.

Quincy entered, huffing. "Sir, the staff reports. . . I fear the new footman and maid have absconded."

Thea sat up straighter, holding out her hand, demanding to be tugged up. Arnaud did so out of sheer frustration. Madness reigned, and he had lost any control he had briefly assumed.

"Herbert and Eleanor? How do you know? Maybe they're stuck in the tower with every other damned missing person!" Arnaud dragged Thea toward the corridor. He saw no choice. If the tower was the last place the boys had been seen, he'd have to search the bedamned hellhole.

"The man who watches the drive saw them leave, so we checked their rooms. Their clothes are missing." Quincy's usual stoicism was crumbling as he

THE DILEMMA OF A DEAD SCHOLAR

followed them out. His son was missing too. "He says they appear to have taken the footpath you took earlier, across the fields."

The man who watches the drive. . . Quincy's spy so he knew when visitors arrived. Or left.

Paul and officialdom were still at the cottage. . .

Driving the cart, they had to take the longer route through town and wouldn't see any scoundrels on the lane.

Let the pair run off. He needed to search the hell-ridden tower. He couldn't send the old butler to do so.

Arnaud clasped Thea's shoulders and forced her to meet his eyes. Hers were an enormous cerulean blue and he almost drowned in them until he recalled what lay ahead. "I will go into the tower through the roof. Let Walker know. The boys, they have good men with them. Tell your Lady to *fermer la bouche* and calm down and let you think. I need you to take command."

That was an absolutely absurd thing to say, but it seemed to work.

She nodded, dazedly. "I don't know who to trust," she whispered.

"Excellent reaction. Trust no one but your aunts and cousins. And *moi*." He wanted to kiss her awake, so he really was losing his mind. His gray matter probably wasn't worth keeping anyway—not if he had to crawl through that narrow staircase again.

"I. . . I have no one to send with you, sir," Quincy mourned, glancing in distaste at the banker, who was now searching under the hall table.

"We need men guarding the ladies. I'll be fine on the roof." Sunset was hours away at this time of year. Thunderstorms, however. . .

Grabbing a lantern from the selection in the hall, Arnaud took the marble stairs two at a time, avoiding even the narrow servant stairs while he could.

Action, and not thinking, was good, he decided. Pity he couldn't stop thinking.

Pleasant thoughts, then. Thea had felt soft and round beneath his crude hands.

She wouldn't have let him touch her if she hadn't been near hysteria.

That wasn't any better. If he couldn't shut off his brain, then he needed to start thinking *sensibly*. He should have a weapon. He should keep a knife in his boot like Henri. He was far more likely to find a paintbrush.

Which left only his hands as weapons. And the damned lantern. The whole point of narrow tower staircases was to eliminate weapons in close quarters. Pistols hadn't been invented then. How had they fought without light?

He took the damned narrow stairs to the attic but heard no childish voices.

153

Shouldn't the boys be shouting from the roof by now? He'd told them how to open the windows. . . But he hadn't time to hunt for the roof door.

Tightening his jaw, he glared up the narrow ladder leading from the attic to the roof. The rickety rungs were most likely meant for a tiny chimney sweep.

Gritting his teeth, Arnaud climbed the ancient ladder without mishap. At the top, he shoved open the trap door, emerging into fading daylight. He scoured the sky and decided he should have an hour or more before lightning became a problem. The wind was picking up though.

"Oliver! Davy!" he shouted, studying the forest of chimney pots and pigeon roosts for hiding places. "Boys, it is me."

He wended his way past obstructions to the windows of the tower's top floor. Some lady must have used it for a solar at some point. The tower had to have once been accessible. So, what had happened?

Remembering Thea's warning of a child's ghostly cries, he stupidly wondered if some other small boy had tumbled off the roof. Or had a lady fallen down the stairs? Did Thea's lady ghost haunt the tower? Unproductive thoughts.

Where the devil were those boys? They were intelligent lads and knew how to come up here. "David! Your sister is terrified. Quit playing the hide-and-go-seek."

A small towhead finally peered from around a chimney. "He's hiding."

Relief flooded him. The vision of small bones tumbling. . . He took a deep breath to settle his rattled nerves. Good to know the boy could speak when needed.

Setting down his lantern, Arnaud caught Clare's nephew up in his arms, hugging to be certain he was whole and well. "What happened?"

"Bad men. We hid." Oliver wiggled to get down. The boy wasn't affectionate.

He set him down. "Very good. Very smart. Where is Davy?"

The boy tugged him toward the glass room and an open window. "Hurt foot. We know what map means."

Gahhh, too much conflicting information. Sorting through a dozen questions, Arnaud settled on the immediate. "Where did Davy hide? There is no furniture." He refused to lift Oliver back into the tower. "I'll find him. Just tell me where. You must go downstairs to tell all where we are. Warn them of bad men."

Bad men who might still be in the tower? With Davy, Henri, and the tutor? Ominous. Arnaud tried to stop thinking again. Unfortunately, this situation wasn't the mindless brush of paint on canvas that allowed him to push past thought into an emotional outpouring of color. His gray matter had awakened.

Oliver nodded solemnly. "Dead heads, monster."

Dead heads, yes. *Monster*? "Very well, I will find him. Tell Miss Thea he is fine. Ask Walker to send men up here."

"Yes, sir." The boy darted off into the blustery wind.

They needed a boy-sized fish hook if the brat kept going to ground in burrows. How did one hide in a dead head? Or a *monster*?

He was trying very hard not to think why Henri and the tutor weren't with their charges. His younger brother was his lodestone. If he lost confident Henri. . .

Not thinking.

Doing. Thinking and doing had landed him in prison. *Not* thinking and doing had killed him inside.

Ignoring the pain of being ripped apart from the inside out, he picked up the lantern. He found the window Oliver had left open, climbed in, and listened. Nothing. Not even the wind. Not surprising. The tower was solid stone and thick oak.

The gray light through the windows cast shadows but allowed him to quickly search the cabinets, just in case. . . Nothing. Oliver had said Davy hurt his foot. Presumably, he refused to climb more stairs.

Arnaud lit the lantern. Henri and a tutor had to be in the tower somewhere— with a terrified little boy.

The open wooden stairs from the roof room to the attic level weren't too bad. He could see anyone coming up. Of course, with this lantern revealing his presence, they could see him too. But if he meant to search for a small boy among the rotting carcasses and skulls of the trophy room. . .

Fine, thinking *and* doing. He needed weapons for the. . . bad men. He set his boot on the first step.

He'd killed a man once. He'd thought him bad. Only, since then, he'd realized men weren't necessarily bad, just motivated differently. The soldier had wanted to keep Arnaud in prison. Arnaud knew he'd die if he stayed. The soldier had been young and small. Arnaud had been large and half-mad. He had snapped the boy's neck and flung him down stairs—just like the enclosed stairs he'd have to descend to reach the bottom of the tower.

He knew how to do it. He didn't want to. His choices were too limited in that narrow confinement. He feared he'd react the same way if confronted, and he'd have another man's death and a grieving family on his conscience.

Reaching the attic level, he didn't dare call out for fear of drawing the attention of whoever had sent the boys fleeing. Why wasn't anyone up here, searching? Or perhaps they'd given up. He would, too, had he not known Davy's resourcefulness—if one could call it that.

Remembering the vent Davy had crawled into from the attic storage room, he swung the light over what he could see of the chamber from the stairs. The dust had been disturbed, but he saw no construction allowing a small boy entrance. Whatever Davy had crawled into must be behind the wall.

The lantern light caught on shadowed shapes and lumps. Was that a *rhinoceros* head? Disgusting. A monster? Had that been what Oliver meant? The trophy was pretty much down to bare skull. Bad taxidermy.

Now what? *Think.* His boots on the wooden floor would draw attention.

He'd rather fight in the open room than on the confining stairs. Except whoever had chased the boy most likely had weapons and he didn't.

If Davy was safely hidden, shouldn't he find Henri and the tutor first? Instinct warred with logic. Instinct had killed a man. He needed to *think. . .*

Instinct had saved his life.

This wasn't about him. Little boys couldn't save themselves. Neither could their sisters, not easily. Henri and the tutor were grown men. Protect the weak and innocent—

Stepping cautiously around the edge of the room where the wooden floor was less likely to squeak, Arnaud swung his light along the path of the disturbed dust. It led to the enormous skull. The wooden backing had rotted and come loose. Clever boy.

"Davy?" he whispered. "It is I, Arnaud. Your sister sent me. She is worried. May I carry you out?"

Nothing. Had the boy fallen asleep? Or found another hiding place?

Judging by the paths in the dust of decades, the boys had come up the stairs to explore, but someone with much larger feet had followed. The big feet had traipsed across the room, shoving aside the trophies, shouting, possibly? The boys had to have been terrified.

Setting down the lantern so the light hit the plaque, Arnaud pried the rotten wood away from the monster's skull.

Davy lay curled up in a ball inside. Wide, terrified eyes much like Thea's blinked back at him. Recognizing Arnaud, Davy held out his arms.

He felt no relief as he pried the lad loose.

Boots were already pounding up the stairs. He'd been heard.

TWENTY-NINE

PAUL: THURSDAY LATE AFTERNOON

Sitting beside the taciturn steward on the cart bearing their unconscious prisoner, Paul frowned at the activity as they drove up the manor drive. A storm was building. Why wasn't everyone inside, out of the wind?

Holding a rifle, Walker led an army of stable lads with pitchforks and axes, directing them in different directions.

Skirts blowing in the wind, Minerva and Patience carried hammers and a hatchet. Alarmed, Paul shouted for Timothy to halt so he could leap down. He couldn't start to imagine why a librarian needed a hammer. "What are you doing?"

"We believe the boys are locked inside the tower and Henri and Mr. Bird-whistle aren't answering." Skirt whipping in the wind, Minerva glanced at the back of the cart. "Who is that?"

Locked inside? The bolt wasn't working? That might require soldiers, not ladies.

"That's Boston's neighbor, Finkley. There was an altercation with Mr. Franklin. He has accused Finkley of his grandfather's murder." Paul said this for Walker's benefit as Hunt's armed friend approached. "Finkley is drunk, but he's been unconscious for a long time. Perhaps Meera should look at him before we lock him up?"

Walker leaned over the back of the cart, sniffed, and grimaced. "Looks like a nasty bruise. Tim, haul him around the back, will you?" He shouted at a couple of the stable lads to follow the cart.

Relieved of one concern, Paul took up the next. "Did Arnaud warn you that Neville has been ordered to leave the cottage? We don't know where he's gone."

"That why we're arming ourselves." Minerva nodded toward the previously buried tower entrance. "We're afraid he's in there, preventing anyone from leaving."

"That makes utterly no sense. Where's Arnaud?" Removing his good coat and rolling up his sleeves, Paul took the hatchet from his sister. If all they needed was the door opened, that could be arranged.

Setting guards to watching the manor was wise though. Neville could easily be angry enough to be dangerous.

"Arnaud's on the roof, looking for the boys. He showed them how to escape." Patience twisted her hand worriedly now that she held no tool. "Where are Mr. Ephraim and Reverend Arch? Should they be seeing you like that?"

Paul hadn't given his appearance a thought. He merely wanted to save his one good coat. "They're walking back. Send them in the front, if you're worried about appearances." The shrubbery might be neat, but it was still large enough to conceal giants.

"Whoever is in the tower may have weapons," Minerva whispered worriedly. "Perhaps you should leave this to the soldiers?"

Who lingered, waiting for orders, while Walker took the prisoner to the infirmary. Paul shrugged. "I know how to remove the bolt. They can go in shooting later."

While riding over here in the slow cart, he'd had the leisure to consider all the suspects in Boston's death, and he had grown increasingly uneasy. Finkley might have a temper, but Paul doubted he'd venture inside Boston's cottage. He could think of no realistic motive for the old scholar's death beyond the code books, which theoretically led to the manor's jewels. Had someone found a clue that they had not?

Even if they had, locking themselves inside a tower wouldn't help.

But Neville. . . was a desperate man. If he found Davy. . . The tower was a dangerous place where small boys could easily come to a tragic end.

Paul swung down into the hole, gauged the location of the wooden bolt he'd installed, and swung. The temporary frame shattered, exposing a glimpse of the dark interior and the bolt holding the door in place.

Hearing no shouts from inside, he swung again. The bolt took a little longer than the frame. He had to take out a plank of the door before he could reach the solid bar he'd just installed.

Walker returned before Paul had broken through. "Meera says Finkley didn't pass out from drink. He's been struck pretty hard with a blunt instrument."

"Like a shovel?" Paul asked, swinging more angrily at the possibility that the murderer had struck again, right under his nose. "That might eliminate Finkley as a killer."

"Doubt the old man is strong enough, or ever sober enough, to swing a shovel accurately. Might have done so accidentally, I suppose. I understand he has a temper." Walker struggled out of his fancy coat.

Muttering a biblical curse, Paul swung again. The bolt buckled with a loud crack, echoed by thunder in the distance.

Walker leapt down with a crowbar and pried at the remains.

The women cried out in alarm as the door creaked and gaped. Walker and Paul applied their shoulders to it, knocking it inward. They both hastily stepped to either side until assured no one was shooting.

Paul heard his brave Minerva ordering the soldiers to find lamps and follow them in. He couldn't see beyond the shadowy light from the door.

Letting his eyes adjust to the dimness, he scanned the empty byre. Where was everyone? The silence was eerie. Boys didn't know how to be quiet. Henri and the tutor should be greeting them. They couldn't have left through this door. Had they all left through the roof?

Two of the ex-soldiers joined them, carrying lanterns. He stepped further inside and called, "Anyone here?"

At a muffled thump, he held up his hand for silence. Amazingly, everyone froze.

Muted cries—not quite shouts but enough to register—coming from different directions. Paul eased to his left. Walker circled to the right.

Finding a sagging stall door closed, as it hadn't been earlier, Paul tugged it open. Inside, Henri struggled against ropes, kicking the toe of one boot against the rotting wood of the stall sides. The ropes held him to the wall, so he couldn't reach far, but he'd knocked a hole in his fury.

Setting down his lamp, Paul yanked a knife from its sheath and hastily sawed at the rope fastened to the wall. Next, he removed the neckcloth wrapped around Henri's mouth.

"Neville," Henri muttered.

"Davy?" Paul demanded, fear rising.

Henri wriggled around so Paul could more easily reach his bonds. "Upstairs. Most likely hiding."

Please, Lord, let it be so. He couldn't run off to look and abandon Henri.

Rattled, heart pounding, Paul sliced the bond between Henri's wrists and ankles. Henri scrambled up, the frayed pieces of hemp dangling. "As far as I can tell, the bastard ran upstairs, looking for the boys."

"He can't have found them yet or he'd have unbolted the door and fled." Praying he was right, that Neville wasn't wandering the roof, looking for a way down—or to fling Davy off—Paul left Henri tearing at knots.

He returned to the main open area of the byre, working through who they could call on to search. Walker emerged with Mr. Birdwhistle, who was also tearing at ropes, although the tutor seemed to have fewer ties.

"Adam." The tutor nodded toward still another stall.

"How long ago?" Paul opened the third stall. The large footman appeared to be sleeping. Praying, Paul dropped to his knees and felt for a pulse. It seemed strong. The need to run through the tower looking for the boys warred with his need to minister to the helpless and to learn all he could before heading into danger.

"Not long. He's only been out for a little while." Birdwhistle worked on his knots, his tone furious. "It sounded as if they hit Adam hard to bring him down."

The large footman's neckcloth muffled his breathing. Paul removed it and he began to stir.

"They who?" Walker shouted in frustration. "What the devil happened?" He gestured for his soldiers to help Adam up and assist him to Meera's care.

The tutor dropped one of the ropes on his wrist. "Quincy went in for tea. The boys got bored with fighting and decided to explore."

"*Neville,*" Henri spit out, skipping explanations. "They had pistols and swords."

"Who is *they?*" Walker asked again, slicing through the rest of the tutor's bonds.

Paul carried his lamp to the narrow staircase and peered into the darkness. The walls were so thick, he could barely hear the rumble of thunder outside, even with the door open.

Henri joined him, carrying an unlit lamp. "Neville and the new maid and footman. I unbolted the door, thinking Adam had been sent for us. Instead, Herbert held Adam at the point of a pistol. When the lad tried to escape, Herbert knocked him unconscious," Henri continued with chagrin. "The boys were upstairs with their tutor. I kicked over the lantern, but Herbert pulled a knife and handed Neville the pistol. While they trussed me up, Birdwhistle came down to see what was happening, and they got him too."

"The lot of them searched upstairs for a while, then came down arguing. I couldn't tell over what, but they were angry." Birdwhistle removed the last ropes on his ankles. "Then it got quiet and someone slammed the door and bolted it."

"That's when the cursing started," Henri said, almost in amusement. "Once

Neville shut the door, there wasn't any light. The lamp had leaked, and he couldn't light it. So he's upstairs hunting in the dark."

Paul prayed the boys were smarter than Davy's cousin.

THIRTY

ARNAUD AND THEA: THURSDAY LATE
AFTERNOON

THUNDER ROLLED OVERHEAD. WITH NO WINDOW, ARNAUD COULD BARELY SEE DAVY'S pale hands emerging from the monster's skull. He definitely couldn't see whoever was coming up the stairs. "Stay there," he whispered urgently to the boy wiggling out of his hiding place.

The boy froze. Smart lad. Arnaud didn't want him running on the slippery roof in the rain.

The boots stumbled closer. Were the *bad men* drunk?

Covering his lamp, he felt along the wall in complete darkness until he reached the entry to the stairwell. Memories of an unlit dungeon raised his gorge. He shoved the images away—*think, act*—and searched for a door to the stairwell he might block. If there had ever been one, it was gone now.

Instead, he heard footsteps inching closer.

He couldn't see a blamed thing down the pitch-black, curved stairway.

Oliver had said there were bad *men*. More than one. How many more? Had Arnaud been his officer cousin, he would have asked.

A muttered curse as a silhouette passed the one stairwell window. The only way to prevent the intruder from reaching Davy was to enter those stairs again—with no light.

Terror clutched at Arnaud's heart, making him sweat. Damp, mossy walls, an open door, the exultant moment he'd smelled freedom. . . and had the stairs blocked by an armed guard. His hands recoiled at the memory of the pain as the bullet cut through his fingers, of the cold hard metal as he'd grabbed the weapon, the horror of crushing a throat with the barrel, and the bayonet. . .

Behind him, an innocent young boy terrorized by his own family hid in fear. No child should live with that kind of fear. *Think, act. . .*

Arnaud eased down the confining stairwell, until he could equate shadow and sound. He had only his fists as weapons. He reached to grab—

A fistful of neckcloth. The intruder shouted as Arnaud jerked hard, unbalancing him. Briefly, he caught the faint outline of a man in the dim light from the stairwell's window. He'd only seen the wretch once, enough to punch him off the front stairs, but he recognized the poufy hairstyle.

Before Arnaud could throttle him with his own neckcloth, Neville ripped the knot loose, turned, and fled.

Not knowing whether to be relieved or angry, Arnaud stamped back to the attic and snatched up a massive, moth-eaten, lion's head. Climbing down to the bend, he heaved the beast after the man stumbling down the stairs in total darkness. The horrible trophy bounced off walls and stairs, picking up speed. . .

The intruder screamed.

Monsters, indeed.

Wrapping the hood of her cloak closer, Thea stepped onto the blustery wind of the roof. She didn't know which direction to turn. Oliver had tried to explain, but he wasn't very specific.

All she knew was that Davy was trapped and alone with bad men, and Arnaud had gone to find him.

Oliver's tale had Thea dashing for her cloak. That's when Minerva had rushed in, saying the men had battered down the tower door, people were hurt, and the villains were still inside. Which meant Neville—Thea had no doubt that it was lying, conniving, desperate Neville—was still in there. With Davy. And Arnaud.

Davy was her responsibility. She'd promised him he'd be safe. Her parents had said she couldn't. They thought her weak-minded and vaporish but didn't much care. Females didn't control fortunes. They expected her husband to do so. Most men were content with feeble-minded wives if they had money. *Davy* was their concern, because he'd control the estate someday.

Neither she nor Davy was weak-minded—they just weren't *normal*. She knew that. She simply couldn't prove that being *different* didn't mean they were simpletons.

The first splash of rain hit her as she rounded a chimney pot and saw the path to the tower in a flash of lightning. The gray stone loomed dark and ominous against the clouds, but Oliver had escaped up here. Perhaps she was mad to be out in a storm, but she knew she'd find a way in or die trying. She wouldn't be like all the other liars in her brother's life and not keep promises.

She held out a gloved hand to trace it along the tower's wall. The stones emanated ghostly vibrations, but she didn't *have* to pay attention. Listening to the past led to disaster when the danger was in the present.

Glass. Stone. Space. . . An open casement.

Hitching up her skirt, she climbed over the sill. Out of the wind, she could see more clearly. It must be a lovely space in sunshine, but the storm dimmed the light. She could see the stairwell though.

She opened the lid of her lantern a crack, enough to reveal the treads, while straining to listen above the rising storm. The wind howled, rattling old rafters. She tried not to think about bats but pulled her hood tighter.

She eased down the open wooden steps, hoping to see into the room below.

A thud and clatter.

A man's shrieks.

She froze. That didn't sound like Arnaud. Did she run for help? Who would she call on? All the men were in the yard.

Surely the scream would alert the men in the byre.

Both scream and men would terrify Davy. She continued on.

At the bottom of the wooden stairs, her meager light caught on a room of. . . shadowy *monsters*, as Oliver had said.

Shouts. She cast a light along the wall, looking for a way out of this horror chamber. Just as her beam crossed the dark entry to a medieval stairwell, a familiar broad-shouldered figure emerged, brushing off his hands. She nearly fainted in relief.

No fainting allowed.

"Davy?" Feeling safer now, she wanted to call louder, but the name emerged as a terrified whisper.

It was enough to catch Arnaud's ear. He was only a few steps away. At sight of her, he halted to stare. She didn't know why. Perhaps she looked like a ghost.

She opened the lantern. "Davy?"

Arnaud gathered his wits. Rubbing his palms on his trousers, he nodded toward a far wall. "In the monster head." He took her lantern and directed the light toward a most hideous skull half way around the room.

Below, shouts and curses rang out. She caught Arnaud's arm for reassurance. "Is it safe?" she whispered.

"Sounds like a rescue party. Let's hope they'll delay the villain until we pry the lad out." He pressed a warm, reassuring hand over her glove, then strode toward. . . whatever that was.

The hideous collection of deer antlers, dead fish, and moth-eaten vermin really needed to be dropped on a bonfire. She could almost hear animal spirits growling.

Arnaud crouched behind the largest horror. "Davy? The bad man is gone and Thea is here. You can come out now."

A small, chubby hand emerged from the back of the monster head. Arnaud clasped it and let Davy pull himself out.

"You're not small anymore, David Talbot," Thea scolded in terror at seeing his hiding place."You must quit squeezing into such tiny spaces."

He popped out and sat down at Arnaud's feet. His thumb went to his mouth. He took the digit back out and looked at it in disgust.

"That is why food is better than thumbs." Arnaud produced a hard candy from his pocket, then glanced up at Thea. "I do not know what is happening below, but the roof cannot be safe in a storm. Will you be all right if I leave you here a little while?"

"Door," Davy said, complacently sucking his candy. "Unlock it."

"If I were a locksmith and had all day—" Their guardian angel stood and turned the light on the attic door. "Besides, we left a wardrobe there."

Davy fished around on the floor, found some small tool he had no doubt carried with him for just this purpose—because her brother was no fool—and stood.

The furious shouts in the distance escalated but came no closer. Thea held Arnaud's arm and watched in horrified amazement as Davy limped past stuffed heads to the attic door. They'd locked the panel and moved a heavy wardrobe over it so two small boys wouldn't find their way in here.

"Your brother is not insane," Arnaud remarked grimly as Davy pried at the door lock with his tool."He is an engineer."

"Like Captain Huntley?" Thea gasped in surprise as the lock clicked.

Arnaud chuckled at Davy's attempts to open the panel. "There is a latch on top. Someone knew Reid habits."

"How will I ever keep him safe?" she murmured, mostly to herself.

"Teach him to do it himself." Arnaud led her across the room. He reached up and opened the latch. The warped old door still barely budged. "Wardrobe," he reminded them, taking the handle in his big fist and tugging.

Davy inserted his small foot and pushed. Between them, they pried at the edge of the old door until the rusted hinges reluctantly shifted with a terrifying creak. Davy squeezed through the narrow opening. "Door," he said in satisfaction. With another creak, he vanished through the wardrobe's back panel.

"Geminy," Thea muttered, covering her mouth as the oath escaped.

"Who puts doors in wardrobes except criminals?" Arnaud reached through the crack and pushed.

Thea could hear the scrape of wood, but there wasn't any way either of them could squeeze through the opening. The door hinges would need to be removed. "He's safe in the attic?"

"No doubt picking the storage room lock as we speak. Did you want to push through?"

Thea studied the narrow space dubiously. "Only if desperate. I think I'd rather chance the roof."

"My choice, too, except I think we shall have company shortly, and I do not believe either of us will fit into a rhinoceros head."

"Is that what that thing is?" She shuddered. "The Lady seems to have settled down. I think that means—"

"The cavalry has arrived." Returning her hand to his arm, Arnaud led her toward the stairs, opening the lantern so they didn't stumble over stuffed vermin.

Before they reached the stairwell, a man as large as Arnaud stepped out.

Captain Huntley had returned.

THIRTY-ONE

HUNT: LATE THURSDAY AFTERNOON

CAPTAIN ALASTAIR HUNTLEY SURVEYED THE BATTLE GROUNDS OF HIS NEW HOME AND bit back a grin at the expanded territory of a tower. Challenges. He enjoyed challenges. Honeymooning peacefully with his new wife, shopping, exploring a bit of the England he'd never known, had all been very interesting—and a great relief after months of living like a monk. Clare was a quick student in matters of the marital bed.

But a *problem* he could dig into. . . That stirred the mental juices.

With interest, he regarded his eldest French cousin sheltering the dotty heiress who'd only arrived recently at the manor. What he needed now was answers, not romance. "Davy? They said the boy is still in here?"

Arnaud held a lantern up to reveal a partially open door on the far wall. "Our little engineer unlocked the attic storage door, unfastened a hidden door in the wardrobe, and slipped back into the house. I believe it is safe to say he's more than fine. I trust they have his cousin strung up by the heels?"

Hunt raised his eyebrows at the *engineer* designation but he'd question later. "Come down and verify our prisoner's identity. None of us know him. He may have broken a few bones falling down the stairs after being attacked by a lion. I don't suppose you know anything of that?"

The heiress snickered and glanced at Arnaud with appreciation.

The unsociable cousin Hunt knew shrugged and hid what might almost be a satisfied smirk. Had miracles happened while they'd been gone?

"Lions attack," was Arnaud's typical response.

Perhaps Arnaud was finally emerging from the shadows left by war. Or Hunt could be imagining things because he wanted everyone as happy as he was.

"Good thing for lions, then. The wretch was carrying a loaded pistol and a knife. We have him trussed up." Hunt took the steps down two at a time.

Arnaud and his companion descended more slowly. Jaw clutched, his cousin emerged from the narrow stairs, protectively hovering over the heiress as she glared at their trussed prisoner.

"That's the scoundrel," Thea said with assurance. "I forbid Neville entrance to the manor. He is trespassing."

"He is also guilty of assault and attempted murder and a few other crimes as far as I can tell from all the tales flying about." Hunt studied the once-elegant man bound by the wrist but not the foot, because there was a bone sticking out of his leg. The prisoner appeared to have lost consciousness. Or was pretending.

Arnaud glanced around the empty chamber while Walker ordered the patient onto a makeshift stretcher. Talbot groaned. Hunt assumed his normally thoughtful friend wasn't any too happy with the patient and hadn't given any orders to be gentle.

"The walls weren't this damaged when I was here last. Someone has been ripping them out." Arnaud crossed the room to study the damaged plaster and paneling, but there wasn't much to see, as far as Hunt had ascertained. "Looking for treasure?"

"More than likely." Hunt kept an eye on the odd heiress Clare had called Dotty Dottie and who was apparently now known as *Tay-uh.* Her frail muslin smeared with dust, she was spinning in slow circles and wearing a puzzled frown.

Arnaud returned to stand patiently near her. "Was Neville operating on his own? Who told him about the treasure or how to access the tower?"

"Henri and the tutor report that a new maid and footman were involved? I believe they've sent some of the lads out to hunt them down." Hunt headed for the stairs to the byre exit. He'd figure out the attic door another time. "And we now have a banker, magistrate, and vicar at the dinner table because we have another murder? And the killer is in custody?"

"The magistrate and vicar are here because Neville wanted their permission to haul Davy off to an asylum. Bosworth simply provided them an introduction," the normally stoic artist replied in obvious annoyance. "Paul persuaded them to take a look at the crime scene. More than that, they'll have to tell you."

"I need to see the paintings in the vestibule." Thea's voice drifted after Hunt as the pair descended in his wake.

Hunt had learned to accept that women did not think as he did. He wanted to hang a kidnapper and murderer. She wanted to admire paintings. Fine. He clattered down to the byre and examined the space in satisfaction. "I don't know why we didn't open this up earlier."

"Because it's useless, unless you let me knock out a few windows. I might take the whole thing down, if I do." His jaw still set stonily, Arnaud had gone almost pallid as he emerged from the narrow stairwell.

Hunt glimpsed a hint of what lay behind his cousin's taciturnity. If Arnaud had been imprisoned in a wretched dungeon like this for any length of time, he had a right to want to rip down walls.

The storm seemed to be lessening. Thunder followed a flash of lightning at some distance. Hunt shrugged and aimed for his dinner. A few raindrops didn't bother him. "We'll worry about the tower another time. I want all the stories. Let's not allow a real magistrate to escape before we put him to use."

The lady pulled a hood over her head and huddled inside her cloak as Arnaud swung her out of the entry hole. They raced for the portico entrance. Hunt stopped to check that Walker's new steward was positioning some planks in place to cover the opening. "Cooper, I think they called you?"

The thin, stoop-shouldered young man nodded. "Timothy, captain, sir. Mr. Walker said I might learn the position of grounds steward."

"Right. You're working with Miss Upton? Some fellows won't."

"She's a right smart lady, captain, sir. Knows more about them trees than I do." Timothy Cooper climbed out of the hole.

"That's good, then, and I'm not a captain any longer. I'm just Mr. Huntley. Another evening, we'll have you in for dinner. Tonight, you might want to take it anywhere else." Hunt was fairly confident he had a household waiting to pounce on him.

Lacking hat, the steward tugged his forelock. "My brother, sir. . ." he said worriedly. "I should look in on the cottage, see if Finkley did him harm. . ."

"Of course. Check with the kitchen, see if they can prepare a basket of food to take with you. I don't know what's been happening here, but I'm about to find out." Hunt strode after the others.

Quincy opened the door before he could. "My apologies for Adam, captain. He can't never be a boxer because of that jaw of his. One muffler, and he's floored, always been like that."

Hunt translated that as Quincy's very large son would never be a prizefighter like his father because one blow rendered him unconscious. He handed over his hat. "We'll just have to provide him with a truncheon for fighting back. He's a good lad. Hope he's feeling better."

"Yes, sir, he is, sir. The ladies are in the withdrawing room, sir."

Withdrawing room? Hunt wanted to change out of his wet clothes and prepare for dinner but. . . withdrawing room? Was that a new name for the parlor? It wasn't as if the ancient manor sported many modern niceties.

Knowing he could take the backstairs to his new suite in the rear wing, Hunt strode down the corridor, checking the various rooms as he passed. Lights were out everywhere except along this hall and in the dining room, where staff set the table. He'd believe everyone had retired to dress for dinner except he could hear excited voices, one of them his wife's.

He liked having a *wife*. Clare gave him permanence and a loving acceptance he hadn't known he needed.

At the far end of the long corridor, across from the small writing room Clare had taken for her own, he found his family. Tattered wall covering hung in strips. The stiff linen that must have covered Clare's new furniture lay on the floor. No carpet warmed the worn oak planks. He tried to puzzle out what had once been in here, but the company immediately erupted at his entrance.

Clare flung her arms around him, an embrace Hunt normally enjoyed, but he had to concentrate on what she was telling him.

"Meera says Mr. Finkley was hit rather hard with a blunt object, like poor Professor Boston. She fears a killer still stalks the village."

Standing to one side with their new librarian, the curate spoke before Hunt could produce a reply. "Neville Talbot and Franklin Cooper were tearing up Boston's cottage, presumably looking for his journal or more clues to what the deceased knew about the earl. I believe the new maid and footman, the ones who held Adam at the point of a pistol, fled toward the cottage. There is a conspiracy of some sort. They need to be questioned."

"Walker has already sent men after the servants. Surely you haven't driven off our guests already?" Hunt glanced around but the gathering was only family. Arnaud and Thea had taken Davy to the schoolroom. Hunt's mother was down here, but no magistrate.

"We told our guests that we'd hold a reception in the great hall before dinner." His mother beamed at him. Hunt recognized that twinkle in her eye. It was good to see her. He was glad she had traveled all the way from Philadelphia for his wedding. But he recalled all too well her manipulating ways.

"A reception or a trial?" he asked, aware they had crippled a member of the aristocracy and held him prisoner. Although judging by the muffled shouts from the infirmary, Hunt assumed Meera was setting Talbot's bones. The prisoner would most likely pass out before interrogation.

Before anyone answered, Hunt gestured at the tattered walls. "What is going on here?"

"Dear Dorothea thought we'd be more comfortable in this cozy room after dinner, instead of in that huge, drafty parlor." Hunt's Great-Aunt Lavinia lifted her lorgnette to study the nearly empty chamber. "The walls might be painted until an adequate covering is purchased. I believe I have a carpet in my attic that will look well with the new furniture."

"A new room for the new furniture," Clare said with glee. "I love it! With a little polish, that sideboard will look good as new. Has anyone found more chairs? It's a bit sparse in here at the moment."

Most of the company was standing.

They had a killer on the loose, a possible kidnapper in the infirmary, a magistrate and a vicar for dinner, and they were admiring a tattered and empty room. Hunt shook his head. "This is not my territory. You are free to play as you please, but I need to put on dry clothes and greet our guests."

His reminder sent the company scattering. Clare held his arm as they headed for their suite via the back tower stairs. A groan from the infirmary reminded them that Meera was dealing with Dorothea's dastard of a cousin. At a look from Clare, Hunt steered her down to her friend's apartment.

With a large bruise forming on his jaw, their tall footman stood guard at the door. "Should we remove the prisoner to the cellar, sir?" he asked, sounding a little too eager to fling his assailant into the dungeon.

Meera appeared from behind the infirmary curtain, drying her hands on a clean towel. "Mr. Talbot will not be running anywhere. His leg is broken in two places. I've pieced the bone together and splinted it, but if he tries to run, he'll fall on his face and be crippled for life. I've given him laudanum. Besides, they've just carried Mr. Finkley to the dungeon. He's conscious and pitching fits. The two should probably not mix. We'll need a hospital at this rate."

Their apothecary physician appeared ready to deliver her babe at any moment. Clare took her arm and led Meera from her office. "You are over-working yourself. You need to sit down. Walker should be back soon, shouldn't he? We'll have the kitchen send up a tray so you can put your feet up."

Meera was willingly led, but she stopped in front of Hunt. "Mr. Talbot swears he only meant to take Davy to his father, that it was Franklin Cooper who translated his grandfather's code and insisted the tower conceals jewels."

Hunt mentally cursed the damned Reid jewels and wondered if they'd been hidden because they caused this kind of crime.

THIRTY-TWO

THEA: THURSDAY DINNER

THEA'S MAID BRUSHED HER HAIR OUT AS IT DRIED. SHE'D BATHED HASTILY, NOT wishing to appear like a mad hysteric in front of the captain and officialdom. She had to make it clear that Neville must be kept far, far from Davy at all cost. They wouldn't listen unless she appeared calm and sensible, like Clare.

She had a great deal of practice at wearing a pleasant face, but admittedly, she had difficulty controlling violent emotions and ghosts at the same time. And she *really* wanted to kill Neville. Or kick him very hard. Where it would hurt.

Worse yet, The Lady seemed to be encouraging her. The late viscountess had every reason to think poorly of men. Her husband had nearly killed her and *had* killed her unborn child, after all.

Now her head was spinning. Thea took a deep breath to calm herself. She'd been practicing. She could do this.

It helped to know that Hunt and Clare had returned. They'd support her plea to keep Davy. As would Jack and Elsa, but that pair couldn't be counted on to appear for dinner. Now that they were home again, Jack would be eager to see their horses and Elsa, her kitchen. Thea loved that her extended family was eccentric, but she had learned the hard way that, in the face of society, proper conduct was required if one wished to be heard.

With her hair dressed in a neat chignon, dangling curls bobbing at her ears, tiny diamonds in her odd Reid earlobes, and wearing her best silk dinner gown, the one that almost matched the dark blue of her eyes, Thea felt well armored.

She knew how to do this. She simply had to ignore The Lady until she had what she wanted.

When she'd seen Davy in the schoolroom after Meera wrapped his sprained ankle, he'd seemed unperturbed by the day's activities. She'd had to talk him into not exploring the storage attic and tower until it was daylight and others were free to accompany him. He hadn't liked it, but Mr. Birdwhistle had assured her that he'd keep them busy.

Dealing with Davy would never be easy, but with an entire family to help, she might manage—if she needn't worry about Neville.

She met Arnaud—waiting for her?—in the hall. The shabby artist had apparently bathed and shaved his ever-present stubble. His thick chestnut hair was still damp where he'd attempted to brush it into order and out of his face. But without cutting, the locks dangled over his immaculate neckcloth. He'd even knotted the linen properly and wore what appeared to be a pearl stickpin. She knew his family was famous for the pearls they'd collected. His uncle must have left him one of the family's treasures.

He wore a new tailed frockcoat that emphasized his broad shoulders, and she would not look at his evening breeches. His sturdy thighs spoke of hours on horseback, not standing at an easel or sitting in a club. Comte Lavigne was an unusual man.

Still, she found his muscular arm and calm acceptance reassuring. He'd carried her brother up to the schoolroom after Meera had said Davy must stay off his foot for a while. That would be an impossibility, but at least her little brother didn't have to climb all those stairs this evening.

As if reading her thoughts, Arnaud asked, "If I offer to teach the boys to ride, do you think that will keep your brother from trying to crawl all over the tower?"

She almost gasped at the brilliance of that idea. "Oh, Davy will love that! I don't know about Oliver. Will Elsa allow us to use one of her smaller mares?"

"They all need exercise, including the boys. They can't be kept cooped in a schoolroom all day, especially in summer. They have active minds but they also need to be physically active." Downstairs, he stopped outside the entry to the great hall to give her a moment to prepare herself.

Inhaling to steady her nerves and quiet the ghosts, she nodded. "I know you are correct. If we can remove the threat of Neville. . ."

"He's certainly removed for now. He's going nowhere on that leg. Ready?" As if he understood her nervousness, he watched her with concern in his dark eyes.

"Yes, I am fine. Don't let me spin in circles," she whispered as he led her into the towering two-story hall. She hated confiding weakness, but he'd not called her an hysteric earlier. She wanted to trust him. It was just very hard after years of her family's betrayal.

Outside the towering Gothic windows, the storm had diminished to an occasional patter of rain. One of the maids tugged the moth-eaten maroon velvet draperies over the panes to keep out the damp draft. Light from the sconces danced along the walls, but apparently the occasion wasn't grand enough to light the iron chandeliers overhead.

Since they no longer had a spare footman, the maids carried the drink trays again. The company didn't seem particularly concerned by the lack while Henri entertained with his tale of cradle-robbing, treasure-seeking criminals.

Thea almost laughed as Henri blackened Neville's character better than she ever could. "Your brother is a brilliant raconteur. Why isn't he at his tavern this evening?"

Arnaud frowned. "I asked him to tell his story before our guests departed. I didn't expect the tale to become an Odyssey."

She squeezed his arm a little. "You will note that your brother is all talk, and you are the one who threw a lion's head, so do not pout."

"Pout?" He bent his head to study her. The attention thrilled her far more than it ought.

"Pout," she repeated firmly. "Henri is drawing all the attention, while you are the one who actually saved Davy. And Oliver, since you are the one who showed them the roof exit. You don't need the adoration. You need to sell paintings, which your talent will do. Henri has only his story-telling to earn attention and make his living."

He considered that briefly, then nodded. "I tell stories with paintings. Unfortunately, people have to actually *see* them before they can hear what I'm saying."

This, she knew how to do. She hadn't spent years in society learning nothing.

"Let me show you how that is done." She steered him toward Mrs. Huntley, who sat with the aunts while they sipped sherry and listened to Henri's tale.

Bobbing a curtsy, Thea released Arnaud's arm to take a glass for herself. "Mrs. Huntley, did you not say you wished you had a miniature of the captain and his wife to take home with you?"

The captain's mother smiled warmly. "You remembered that! How lovely of you." She eyed Arnaud cautiously. "I did not think you would be much interested in so tiny a matter. Your work is so much more impressive than a portrait."

"Admittedly, I work from my head and not what is before me, but for you, my lady, I would paint both portrait and miniature, if you will accept my nontraditional method. You have raised a gentleman I respect and admire greatly." Arnaud bowed like the gentleman he was trained to be.

"Portraits?" Mrs. Huntley's plump sister, Lady Spalding, glanced away from Henri to study the artist with interest. "You could paint our portraits for the gallery?"

"I believe the comte sells paintings for a living," Thea said with a laugh. We cannot ask him to decorate the walls for free."

Captain Huntley and Clare wandered over to catch this last. "Now that we have a few spare coins from the book auction, it would only be right to invest in good artwork that might be worth a fortune someday," the captain suggested.

"And we'll need new artwork in the withdrawing room, if you do that sort of thing," Clare suggested. "I have looked through the paintings that are gathering in there, but really, fox hunts and dead pheasants aren't suitable. This is no longer a hunting lodge."

Quincy announced dinner before Arnaud could recover sufficiently to reply.

Thea hoped she had helped a little to repay him for what he'd done for Davy. Now, she must twist a magistrate around to her way of thinking.

THIRTY-THREE

PAUL: THURSDAY AFTER DINNER

PAUL THOUGHT DINNER WENT WELL, CONSIDERING ALL THE MANOR OCCUPANTS blatantly badgered the dinner guests in a variety of ways, attempting to convince officialdom that an empty-headed heiress could look after her mad brother. Thea held up well, in his opinion, not displaying any vaporish tendencies.

The altercation, when it came, wasn't at the table. It arrived just as the company was finishing their pudding. A woman's wails and a man's angry shouts echoed down the central corridor. Paul didn't think twice but shoved back his chair and excused himself. The others could wait until a servant summoned them, but he wasn't, and never had been, manor gentry. As the village curate, he had to help his parishioners, both good and bad.

To his surprise, Minerva joined him. "I am feeling exceedingly useless," she whispered. "I have done what little I can to impress our guests that Thea's brother is happy, healthy, and well educated here. The others can do better than I."

Paul resisted his usual urge to hug her. She had not given him that right. Yet. But she was finding small ways to fit into his life, which gave him high hopes.

Neither of them were built large, but in their dinner clothes, he and Minerva represented a more respectable class than the disheveled pair led into the hall. An angry Adam and two ex-soldiers surrounded the pair of missing servants. With their hands tied, they appeared a little less proud than Paul had seen last.

"Miss Eleanor, Mr. Herbert, have either of you come to harm?" he asked.

176

Even as servants, they had always been carefully dressed. Currently, they appeared to have been dragged through a hedgerow.

"Nowhere to run at night. They hid in the hen house," one of the soldiers reported. "They ain't hurt."

"Perhaps they should be taken back to the larger study?" Minerva suggested. "Hunt will wish to question them, and the magistrate, at least, should be there as witness."

"We're free to come and go as we please," the footman Paul knew as Herbert argued. "We're not slaves. You have no right to hold us."

"I have a right to scuttle his nob like he did mine," the usually silent Adam retorted. He nodded at the soldiers to haul the prisoners to the west wing, where they wouldn't disturb the guests at dinner.

Since Adam was well over six feet tall, and the no-longer dapper Herbert a foot less, the former footman could do no more than scowl as the soldiers jerked him back to the new wing.

"Perhaps tie the prisoners to the desk legs so you might enjoy your suppers?" Minerva wickedly proposed, following as they hauled the prisoners into the luxuriously large but sparsely furnished study.

The desk in question was nearly as big as a wardrobe and required an army to move.

"You got no weapons," Adam pointed out worriedly.

"Neither do they." Paul pulled up a leather-padded chair for Minerva. "Send word to the captain that they're here. We'll be fine until he arrives. You might have a pitcher of ale and some sandwiches sent up. We don't wish to mistreat prisoners."

Adam finally left with the soldiers, lured by the call of food.

"It wasn't our idea," Herbert protested, wriggling his bonds. "We're not what you think."

"I assume the court will decide that." Minerva settled into her overlarge chair, one with a tufted back and brass buttons, a relic saved from the rubbish room. "We're simply here to see you don't suffer as poor Henri and Birdwhistle did. You may save your excuses for the magistrate."

"It's not us you should be tying up. It's him." Eleanor jerked her ropes angrily. "You're letting the rat bastard get away."

Paul stiffened. "Who? We have Talbot. There was no one else besides the three of you in the tower, from all reports."

"That's 'cause Frankie lets everyone else do his dirty work. You just ask that brother of his. Get Franklin here, and we'll see who goes before a magistrate!" Herbert shouted.

Franklin? Franklin Cooper. . . their new steward's scholarly brother? They'd sent Timothy back to the cottage with food for his brother after Finkley had hit him. . . Or Franklin had *said* Finkley had hit him.

They hadn't really inquired into the demolition of Boston's garret.

"This isn't good," Paul whispered to Minerva. "Walker should be in his apartment with Meera. Can you run tell him, let him decide what needs to be done?"

Frowning, she nodded agreement and wrapped her small, smooth hand in his rough one, so he might help her wiggle out of the huge chair. She ran off to spread the word. Paul sighed in regret at the loss of her company, but if more villains were on the loose. . . How many villains did it take to make a break for freedom?

"All right, we'll find the Coopers. Would you care to explain your roles in this? I will attempt to mollify the judges, but the captain and the magistrate aren't precisely happy about recent events." Paul wasn't meant to be a barrister, but having grown up on the fine edge of poverty, he understood how people could be pushed to desperate measures. He hoped they might speak more freely to a man of the church.

They sat silent and sullen.

"Well, you've lost any good reference you may have earned by running away, even if we prove Cooper is responsible for your criminal behavior." Paul settled into the large chair and crossed one leg over his knee, making himself comfortable.

"We're not servants. We don't need your references," Eleanor said haughtily. "All we did was try to retrieve what rightfully belonged to Frankie."

Paul frowned. "Professor Boston's books? We would have returned them, if asked. We only took them for safekeeping. Some of them might be valuable." Although he was fairly certain Minerva had taken them to crack the code, but books were always valuable.

"His journal," Herbert said angrily. "You stole his journal!"

"Is that why you tore apart the cottage? You thought it was still there?" Paul asked in astonishment. "And then you came here pretending to be servants so you could steal a book no one can read and that we would have returned, if asked?"

They both fell silent again, although this time, their sullenness lacked their earlier confidence.

"Why did you tear out pages and leave it behind?" He didn't think he was reaching too far to believe this pair was responsible for the earlier theft that had Minerva frantic.

"He made me leave it," Eleanor said begrudgingly, glaring at Herbert. "After we saw what it was, he didn't believe Frankie could read it, so we just gave him the pages he wanted so he'd shut up. We waited for someone here to work it out."

Herbert shrugged. "Kept him from tearing up the walls more leastways. The place might not have been the inheritance he hoped, but it was better than nothing."

"I don't want to live here in the back of never!" Eleanor exclaimed. "We just needed a bit of the ready so we didn't have to scrape by."

Herbert snorted. "He wasn't scraping by until you came along."

The bickering sounded like. . . Paul studied their faces, finding a similarity in their pointed noses and the reddish coloring of their hair. He ought to be accustomed to looking for family resemblances but hadn't really paid attention to this pair until now. "You're related?" he asked.

"She's my sister, I regret to say," Herbert replied with a grimace. "Never should have introduced her to Frankie."

Puzzles pieces clicked. The neighbor had mentioned a tart. . . The maid was inclined to brightly colored clothing. Lavender hadn't made a uniform for her yet. "Mr. Finkley said a woman visited Professor Boston occasionally. Would that be you. . . Pardon, I don't believe I know your last name?"

Herbert shot her a look of scorn. "I'm Hanks. She's Cooper. She's Frankie's wife."

THIRTY-FOUR

ARNAUD: THURSDAY EVENING

AFTER THE DISCUSSION OF FAMILY PORTRAITS, ARNAUD HAD IDEAS AND IMAGES itching for charcoal and canvas. But it was full dark and the sconces in his poor studio had no oil.

For the first time in years, he could see a glimmer of light above the hole he'd dug himself into.

He might emerge as battered and useless as the tower they'd opened, but thanks to his cousin's family, he was still healthy, as the tower wasn't.

Studying the heiress who had showed him a path to freedom, he thought perhaps he might find ways to heal the solitary tower a ghost-loving, vaporish female so obviously needed, even if she didn't fully realize it yet. The heiress, and perhaps her brother, required quiet introspection out of the constant chaos of well-meaning but undiscerning family. Unless, of course, he was as obtuse as everyone else, which was always possible.

One step at a time. After dinner, Thea accepted his arm so he might lead her to the formal parlor. Unlike the unfinished withdrawing room, the parlor had actual chairs, however shabby, to sit on.

Hunt had already departed to consult with Walker about their prisoners. The rest of the family gathered as usual, conversing over tea or coffee. The magistrate and vicar, well filled with good brandy and Lady Elsa's excellent fare, waited expectantly for the evening's entertainment.

Knowing how the village and manor operated, Arnaud didn't expect them to be as highly entertained as he was. Hunt wasn't much on wasting time with card games or musicians. He was impatient to finish business. If their guests were fortunate, the captain would allow them to hold court in the billiard room. They could play games with peoples' lives.

Arnaud wanted Neville Talbot's hide nailed to a wall, but there was more afoot than a conniving ne'er-do-well. While they waited for events, Arnaud bent over Thea's shoulder, inhaling the scent of her floral soap. "Oliver said he knows what the map means. Have the lads spoken to you?"

"No, but I think I've seen what they have. It's a matter of perspective." She sent him a puzzled glance. "Do you wish us to show you tonight?"

"Not in the dark, no. But I believe our recent crimes are related. Keep your eyes open and trust Henri if you see anything untoward." He squeezed her shoulder. She did not protest the familiarity but seemed relieved at the reassurance.

The tightly controlled, seemingly complacent heiress, was a wound-up top who might spin out of control at any moment. In his torpor, he'd been slow to realize.

Paul returned, whispering to the magistrate and vicar, persuading them to abandon the ladies and their after-dinner comforts. Arnaud followed. If he wished the manor to be his home now, he would protect it as Hunt did. He thought, perhaps, he'd found a treasure worth defending.

"They found Franklin Cooper?" Arnaud asked of Paul as they led guests back to the more modern rear wing.

"I understand he and his brother were in the midst of a brawl when Walker's men arrived," Paul murmured. "And our missing servants are bickering like brother and sister because that is what they are."

"Is it not fortunate most of us in the manor are cousins and did not grow up together?" Arnaud knew he and Henri had had their arguments over the years, but they'd been separated by war, so when they were together, their disagreements had been mostly about survival.

"Do you think it matters that even though I grew up with Patience, she's not really my sister? Someone ought to study how families work." The curate actually sounded interested in Arnaud's observation.

He'd not really cared if anyone listened to him in so long, that it was a pleasant discovery to know he could still have a rational conversation. He was a bit rusty, but he might re-learn his social upbringing.

Arnaud chuckled at Paul's observation as they entered the billiard room but didn't comment while Hunt was glaring at the company. Even though his American cousin had been appointed local magistrate, Hunt had no formal training and didn't like presiding over a courtroom.

"You aren't dragging us from the ladies to deal with these reprobates?" Reverend Arch demanded, casting a look of disgust at the cast of characters.

The prisoners were all decidedly worse for wear, although Finkley probably never looked better. Meera had cleaned him up, and the older man merely appeared haggard from lack of drink. The wicked bruise forming beneath his gray stubble didn't help.

The Cooper brothers scowled at each other, while the brother and sister pair sat sullenly, hands tied behind them. They must have tried to run again.

Beside Arnaud, the curate muttered either a prayer or curse at his superior's callous question. Ignoring the vicar, Arnaud lined up chairs, setting them to face the prisoners or witnesses or whatever the farce required.

Hunt already held a billiard mace and was setting up balls on the newly repaired table. "Gentlemen, I appreciate your patience. I know you are eager to ride off in the morning and don't wish to detain you, if you could assist me this evening. I've only just returned from my wedding journey, so this whole complaint is a mystery to me."

Walker and a few of his men stood behind the motley group of prisoners. Arnaud thought it a trifle rude to drink in front of them, but if it would speed the process. . . He crossed the hall to Hunt's study and retrieved the brandy decanter and glasses that had accumulated since they'd opened up this wing.

Mollified, taking the seats Arnaud had set up, the vicar accepted a glass of the excellent vintage, as did the magistrate.

"Cuz, will you or our inimitable curate explain what we know so far?" Hunt sent the billiard balls bouncing into the pockets.

Arnaud knew better than to play against him. He gestured for Paul to tell the tale as far as they knew it. The curate was a preacher, after all. He knew how to use words. While Paul explained, Arnaud studied Franklin Cooper and his brother, Timothy, their skinny steward. He supposed there was some resemblance there, but the older brother appeared more well fed and furious. Timothy merely looked resigned.

Eleanor, the sharp-faced, red-haired maid, had taken a seat on the floor as far from the men as she could. If Herbert was her brother as Paul said, he wasn't watching over her with any concern. Instead, their former footman looked as if he'd take a bite out of Franklin, his purported brother-in-law.

After Paul finished his tale, the magistrate donned spectacles and frowned at the culprits. "So, if I'm understanding correctly, this is little more than theft of a book that was the professor's to start with, plus assault at the behest of the gentleman with the broken leg who cannot be here to defend himself? No jewels were stolen in carrying out this farce?"

The lot remained silent, but Arnaud noted Timothy Cooper twitching uncomfortably. Their steward was not a communicative man and awkward at speaking in the presence of others, as his scholarly brother was not. Taking a seat on the corner of the billiard table, preventing Hunt from taking another shot, Arnaud murmured, "Can we separate the culprits, interrogate them alone? I'd like to hear what Mr. Timothy has to say."

"Excellent thought." Hunt gestured at Walker. "Take all the prisoners into the study and let's hear from this gentleman you hired as steward."

All except Finkley protested, but other than angrily resisting, they stalked across the hall. The professor's drunken neighbor appeared too dazed to be coherent—probably a good thing, Arnaud thought. Belligerent rants grew tiresome.

"Let's hear this story from your perspective, Mr. Cooper," Hunt suggested, taking a seat on the edge of the billiard table with Arnaud and facing the wary steward.

Ephraim, ever the conscientious magistrate, pulled a notebook from his pocket and jotted a few notes while they waited for Timothy Cooper to find his words.

"I don't know why Frankie suddenly got a bee in his bonnet about the books and jewels. I ain't seen him in a pig's years, didn't even know he was buckled, never met this Herbert Hanks until I came to work here." The steward leaned against the wall as if too weary to stand. "To tell the truth, it surprised me that he even showed up for our grandfather's funeral. Don't know how word reached him."

Arnaud was developing a theory about that, but he knew better than to put words in a man's mouth. Brothers didn't stop communicating for no reason. "Why did you lose touch with each other?"

Mr. Timothy looked uncomfortable, shrugging his narrow shoulders. "That was a long time ago, when we was just lads."

"Tell us anyway," the magistrate suggested.

The steward struggled inwardly. "If I tell you, you'll put me out, but we was just kids back then. I like this position here. If I lose it, I'll lose my Abigail and any hope of finding another place."

Paul frowned and turned to Hunt. "Can you promise he'll keep his place if he tells us the truth? Unless, of course, he's actually guilty of one of our recent crimes?"

The magistrate spoke before Hunt could. "Can't convict him of old crimes based on hearsay. Children do foolish things."

Hunt nodded agreement. "Unless you say you murdered someone as a child, I see no reason to hold the past against you."

Timothy shook his head vehemently. "Nothing like that, captain, sir. It was just. . . Grandad fed us stories of the earl and his riches and the jeweled chess set just lying about in an empty castle. That was after the lady died, you see, when we was just lads."

Arnaud did a hasty calculation. The viscountess had died roughly fourteen years ago. Franklin Cooper might be around his age. That would have made them adolescents at the time—of an age to get into all sorts of mischief, as he well knew.

The steward continued. "Frankie wanted to go to university but our da died and grandad offered to help with some kind of scholarship, but he couldn't pay to put him up in rooms. He'd have to work to pay his way. Frankie had notions of rubbing elbows with nobs and thought himself too grand for that."

The jeweled chess set. . . the one no one knew had existed. Arnaud refilled brandy glasses and poured himself one while Timothy gathered his wits.

"One summer, Frankie insisted we explore the manor, said there weren't naught there but an old witch housekeeper and a drunkard. My brother's a few years older, and I was too young and dumb to know better." His lean face twisted into a wry grimace. "We couldn't find a way in, but we watched and waited, and the old lady came out to beat a rug. We slipped in while she wasn't looking."

"Is this really necessary?" the vicar asked. "As Ephraim says, we can't try a man for childhood transgressions."

"If Wycliffe Manor is to revive the village, and increase the church's profits, we need to know our history and restore law and order," Paul admonished. "The captain and his family have been working diligently in an attempt to do so. The church owes them our support."

Arnaud hid his snort as the vicar shut up at the hint of more blunt for his coffers.

At a nod from Hunt, the steward continued his sorry tale.

"The place was awful dark and creepy, like a haunted castle. I just snuck about, hoping for food or dogs to play with. Frankie went straight to the library. I didn't think much of books and didn't think nobody would care when he came out with a sack full."

No one spoke. Seeing no reprieve, Timonthy looked resigned. "When we got back to grandad's place, Frankie insisted we needed to leave the next day. I didn't want to. Grandad had a new nanny about to have kids—" He winced, realizing he was stalling.

"Frankie showed me what he'd stolen. Beat me up when I said I'd tell, promised he did it to make grandad happy. Next day, he was gone."

"The chess set, I assume?" the magistrate asked.

"Yes, sir, so sparkly, even I knew it was costly. I ain't seen him since. No one came looking for it, so I kept my trap shut, but I was afraid to ever come back. I reckon those pieces gave him the fancy life he wanted at university."

"We have only this man's story," the vicar complained. "It always comes down to who you believe."

"Or perhaps how many tell the same story?" Arnaud suggested. "Perhaps we should have the wife next?"

"Take Mr. Timothy to a different room," Hunt ordered. "Let's keep the witnesses separate."

"First, Mr. Timonthy, what do you know of your grandfather's death?" the magistrate asked, peering over his spectacles.

Pulling his shoulders from the wall, the steward looked tired and angry. "That he was a good man and shouldn't have died like that. I knew nothing of his death until I heard it from Abe Bergstein."

"Who is Mr. Bergstein?" the vicar asked as they led the steward away.

"A long-time resident of Gravesyde and a well respected orchardist we consult," Hunt explained. "He lives and works in the city but has family here."

"So we can consult an impartial outsider and verify that part of his story, very good." The magistrate jotted another note.

Arnaud had a dozen more questions he'd like to ask, but they had the worst part of the interview to go.

A jeweled chess set—had that been where the earl's treasure had gone?

So even if the boys and Thea had a key to the earl's map, there would be no gold at the end of the rainbow?

THIRTY-FIVE

HUNT: THURSDAY EVENING

HUNT REGARDED THE RED-HAIRED, HAUGHTY MRS. ELEANOR COOPER WITH DISTASTE as she stalked into the billiard room and shot them all a disdainful glare. They hired her as a *maid*? It was time they reconsidered their hiring practices, if so.

He left her standing. "Mrs. Cooper, wife of Franklin Cooper?" he asked for the sake of those keeping notes.

"For what little that's worth," she said scornfully. "Promised me rose-covered cottages, crystal and silks, and nice company, he did. And what do I get? A filthy flat three floors up where I'm to entertain myself all day!"

"Your husband just inherited a very nice piece of property," Hunt reminded her. "A little effort would result in roses. I like to think the village provides excellent company."

She glowered. "I'm not a farmer's wife. I come from good family. You can't hold me prisoner."

"You aided in the assault of three good men," Ephraim said mildly. "We have witnesses. Were you the woman we were told visited Professor Boston upon occasion?"

She shrugged, letting her fichu open to reveal cleavage. "I like a new gown once in a while. Frankie said I didn't need more, it was more important that he look swell. So I went visiting on my own. The professor was a nice old man, told me those stories about the earl, gave me a little spending money."

Hunt sighed and wished the earl and his wealth to the devil. "Your husband also told you these stories?"

186

"Bastard showed me jewels he claimed came from Wycliffe, said I'd have them when we wed. But all I ever got was this tiny speck." She flashed a thin band with a hint of sparkle in it.

Well, that practically confirmed the theft of the chess set, Hunt thought wearily. "So what caused you to hire on at the manor as a maid?"

"Frankie did," she said indignantly. "Told me his grandfather had an old book that would lead to more jewels. Only, we tore the cottage apart, and there wasn't nothing, no clues, no jewels. So he figured you had the journal, and we needed to be in place to search."

"Why would you think the jewels were in Boston's cottage?" Arnaud asked, sounding truly perplexed.

"Frankie said so." She finally looked a little uncertain. "Said you must have stolen them, and if we hired on at the manor, we'd find the truth. He described that old book we found in the library, so I thought maybe he was right. But Herbie wouldn't let me take it out of the manor. He wanted to find the jewels for ourselves."

They heard essentially the same story when they brought in Herbert Hanks, learning only that he and Franklin Cooper had roomed together at the university, which was how Franklin had ended up marrying Eleanor. The expectations of their youth hadn't turned out quite as they'd. . . expected.

After they sent the defeated footman to join his sister, Hunt wanted to call Franklin Cooper and hear his side of the story. But Arnaud held up his hand and suggested they bring in the old drunk first.

Hunt waited for him to explain, but Arnaud merely crossed his arms. "He is the one who told us about Mrs. Cooper's visits. He is an impartial witness."

Huh. Arnaud was paying attention and had picked up the magistrate's phrases. Hunt would take all the help he could summon. He nodded to Walker to fetch Boston's neighbor. The death of a well-liked old man was more important than a greedy search for nonexistent treasure, and they had yet to solve his murder.

Thinning gray hair straggling to his old-fashioned coat collar, his neckcloth untied and filthy, the old man limped in, blinking blearily. His gaze instantly fell on the brandy glasses. "Could a fella ask for a sip to wet his whistle?"

"Give us the truth, and we shall see what we can do, Mr. Finkley." Arnaud spoke almost gently to the old fellow. "You remember telling me about Boston's visits from the lady in the cart?"

"Reckon I do." He wrinkled his brow in thought. "You said you'd stop the rascals from stealing my blackberries, but they didn't."

"So you came down to the cottage to tell them to stop, correct?" Apparently having established a relationship with the drunkard, Arnaud continued the interrogation.

"They were tearin' up ever'thin'. Made no sense. I just wanted them to leave my property alone." He managed a modicum of dignity in his ire.

"But witnesses say you were waving a shotgun," Hunt said. "What happened then?"

He wrinkled his brow even more, closing his rheumy eyes. "The fancy one with dark hair, he told me it was his property, and he'd do what he wanted with it. I told him them bushes was mine and he hit me. I don't remember more." He rubbed the bruise covering half his face.

"Hit you with what?" the curate asked softly.

Ah, now Hunt understood why they'd insisted on bringing in the unreliable old man.

"Don't rightly know for sure." Finkley fingered his jaw."Warn't his fist. Mighta been a hoe or shovel or some'at. He didn't dare come close 'cause I had my old Bessie." He added the last proudly. "Don't no one mess with Finkley."

Hunt had a suspicion if Old Bessie actually had ammunition, Franklin Cooper would be a dead man by now. Or given the drunk's unsteadiness, perhaps a very lucky one.

"And this was Mr. Franklin Cooper who hit you?" the magistrate asked, apparently differentiating him from the red-blond Herbert and dark blond Timothy.

"Reckon so, the dark one, he was always a mean one. Used to throw rotten apples at me when he was naught but a lad."

"You said you noticed a lady visiting occasionally. Did you often notice visitors to Professor Boston's cottage?" Arnaud asked.

Finkley wrinkled his entire face. "Only if'n I hear 'em."

"Did you hear anyone arrive on Sunday night, the night before Professor Boston died?"

"Well, there was a horse, but I was taking my supper and didn't look."

"Boston didn't own a horse, correct?" Hunt asked.

"No barn to keep it in and ain't no one else out that way to share one," Finkley replied pragmatically. "It ain't far to walk into the village, so why bother?"

Hunt couldn't argue with that, but it did sound as if someone had visited that evening.

After they led Finkley away, the vicar gestured in annoyance. "We can't take the word of a drunkard. And rotten apples don't constitute guilt."

"Our extremely experienced and reliable apothecary says Mr. Finkley was hit by a blunt instrument, just as Professor Boston was. Mr. Finkley may not be reliable, but our physician is." Hunt wanted this matter settled. They still had Thea's cousin to question, and he wasn't looking forward to it.

"The so-called Professor Franklin next?" Walker asked, his dark features impassive but his crossed arms and sarcasm indicating impatience.

Hunt nodded. As Walker departed with one of his men, Hunt smacked another ball into a pocket. "Who wants to question the math teacher? I don't even know where to begin."

"Ask how he heard about his grandfather's death," Arnaud suggested, pacing the room, examining the various games the late viscount and his guests must once have entertained themselves with.

The magistrate nodded approval. "That may throw him off."

Hunt had a notion that Arnaud had a different purpose, but it was as good a place to start as any.

Walker's men hauled the furious gentleman in, ranting. "What is the meaning of this? I am a gentleman and a scholar. You cannot treat me like a common criminal."

"You're being treated no differently than your wife and brother." Walker gestured for his men to release the prisoner.

Hunt agreed with his friend's attitude. He didn't have much use for men who thought themselves better than others. Franklin Cooper had a right to be proud of his education, but that didn't mean he deserved special treatment.

He knew how to use that pride, though. "Good evening, Mr. Cooper, apologies for the inconvenience. If you could answer a few questions, we'll have this matter settled shortly."

The scholar obviously hadn't been hiding in a hen house. With his hands tied, he couldn't straighten his starched neckcloth, but the cut of his clothes was expensive and marred only by the dust from whatever unused room Walker had installed him in. Cooper nodded his dark head as if granting a boon and said nothing. Not a dumb man.

"Since I wasn't here, I need to be filled in on a few details," Hunt continued, bouncing another ball off the bumper and pocketing it. "When did you hear of your grandfather's death?"

That startled the teacher. Score one for Arnaud.

Cooper quickly composed himself. "On Tuesday of this week. I had to ride all day to reach Gravesyde before the funeral."

"You were at the university? Oxford or Cambridge?" Hunt asked casually, lining up the next shot.

"Cambridge," he replied warily.

"Who brought you the message?" Hunt hadn't grown up in England and didn't know travel distances well. But he knew Boston hadn't been found dead until late Monday morning, and that Cambridge was a considerable distance for a postal letter to reach by nightfall. Gossip wouldn't have spread through the village until later on Monday. At very best, any letter would have gone out Monday evening. Overnight delivery might happen in London, not Gravesyde, where there was only one mail carrier a day. That meant either a messenger rode overnight—unlikely—or he was lying.

Cooper shrugged stiffly. "Does it matter? One has ways."

If he couldn't name a messenger, he was lying.

"Where was your wife when you received the news?" Arnaud asked.

Franklin narrowed his eyes. "At home, where she belonged, of course. What are you insinuating? I received word of my grandfather's death and rode in for the funeral. There's no more to it than that."

As Hunt understood it, Herbert Hanks had been hired as footman on Monday, the same day the body had been found. He'd have to find out when they'd hired the maid, but it couldn't have been long after. This was only Thursday and she'd been around long enough to steal a book. Franklin hadn't known his wife was in Gravesyde? That piece didn't fit.

"You are aware, are you not, that your neighbor, Mr. Finkley, watches the road to and from your grandfather's cottage?" Arnaud demanded, apparently taking the part of prosecutor so Hunt could play judge.

Franklin shrugged. "The old sot imagines things."

"And so, he then imagined you hitting him hard enough to render him unconscious?" Arnaud began to pace. With his size, he could be intimidating.

The teacher didn't have the sense to cringe. Yet. "He came after me with a shotgun. Of course I defended myself."

"And your weapon of choice was a shovel?"

Franklin looked a little more wary. "I'm not familiar with farm implements. It was whatever leaned against the fence at the time."

"Unfamiliar with farm implements?" Hunt couldn't resist asking. "Didn't you spend your summers with your grandfather? He never introduced you to rakes and hoes?"

"Look, what has this to do with anything? Our grandfather is dead. I need to return to my teaching position. I don't have time to dally while complete strangers interrogate me."

Hunt turned to the magistrate. "Mr. Ephraim, I am American. Arnaud is French. Perhaps if you question him in British English, he'll understand the seriousness of the situation?"

The twinkle returned to the solicitor's eye. "You are a very astute man, captain." He turned to the prisoner and used his most pompous tones. "Mr. Cooper, did you, or did you not, pay for your education with a jeweled chess set stolen from Wycliffe Manor?"

Hunt thought the scholar might turn purple.

THIRTY-SIX

CLARE: THURSDAY MIDNIGHT

THE BACKWARD HALL CLOCK WAS STRIKING SIX WHEN CLARE'S STALWART HUSBAND quietly slipped into their suite. Clare thought that meant it must be midnight. She needed a watch of her own.

She adored Hunt beyond all reason. He could be cantankerous and authoritative to a fault. He could spend hours taking a cistern apart and preferred his gloomy study to conversing with ladies. But he was a thoughtful lover and husband, a man who did the right thing—once it was brought to his attention. She loved being the woman at his side, directing his inquisitive intelligence.

He started when she stood up in the shadows of their sitting room. Even though he seemed dead on his feet, he welcomed her into his arms. "You shouldn't have waited up."

"I am no less involved in what happens in our home now than I was before," she reminded him."I will politely leave interrogations to the gentlemen, if I must, but only because I expect you to tell me everything later. What happened?"

"Other than the pure torture of prying the truth from murderers and thieves?" He covered her head in kisses while unknotting his neckcloth. "All we learned was that Franklin Cooper sold jewels over the years to pay for a flat and his gambling and drinking. Apparently, the gems had been set in chess pieces that he stole as a youth."

The Reid jewels? Oh, surely not. Clare stayed focused on the immediate. "I thought Neville Talbot was simply renting the Coopers' cottage? How is he involved?" Clare assisted in removing his coat. Her husband had a valet, but she'd sent the old soldier to his room hours ago.

"We had Thea's reprehensible cousin hauled in from the infirmary, but he only knows Franklin Cooper as a fellow carouser from his student days. After Talbot learned his cousins were hidden here, he remembered Cooper came from Gravesyde. He sought him out for advice in positioning servants inside the manor to help him gain entrance—which is how Franklin learned that the manor was open again. They're all in dun territory. Talbot promised a reward if Franklin's wife and brother would hire on as servants and the plot grew from there. I fear our need for servants inadvertently brought about Professor Boston's death."

"Neville Talbot promised to pay the professor's family once he had his hands on little Davy's funds?" Clare asked dubiously.

"One assumes. Thea's cousin vehemently denies knowing anything of Boston's death, and I'm inclined to believe him. He only seems to have his family fortune in mind, to the exclusion of all else—which brought him to Franklin Cooper."

"Who he knew was familiar with Gravesyde." Clare sighed. It almost made sense if they attended the same school and taverns and. . .

Hunt shrugged off the coat. "*Gravesyde* is not a name one easily forgets. Talbot apparently considered it a sign from above that he was meant to attain his goal when Franklin said he knew people here and agreed he could use the blunt." Hunt tossed his coat over a chair and raised his arms so Clare could pull his shirt from the trouser band.

"Which explains how they all descended upon the manor at the same time but does not explain why Professor Boston died or at whose hands. But Cooper *stole* the earl's jewels? Really? They're gone?" She couldn't hide her dismay. The manor and village needed a fortune to be made productive again. Just keeping the mortgage paid, the roof repaired, and rooms heated cost more than they could afford. And to repair the village. . .

It was more of a disappointment than she'd realized. "Can Franklin Cooper be made to give back whatever remains? Will he be sent to assizes now?"

Hunt added his shirt to the chair back and tugged at his tight evening breeches. "Cooper refuses to admit to theft and claims he has nothing. We have enough to hold him, for now, but the evidence is circumstantial. He's in quite a rage. The magistrate says he will haul him to court on the basis of witness testimony, but one witness is his brother and the other, his wife. A good barrister might see him free."

"If we have the wrong man, there's a thief and a murderer out there who will go free. That is wretched news. I suppose we must hope an outsider killed poor Professor Boston and they have left the area so we needn't worry about more deaths?" She hated saying that almost as much as she hated losing a treasure.

"Except. . . Mr. Timothy is an outsider. Do we tell him to leave? Walker says he works well with the men. We haven't exactly had a run of knowledgeable stewards knocking at our door." Hunt struggled with his thoughts as he finished undressing. "I'll have to hold a session in the morning to decide what to do about Thea's cousin and the two miscreants who assaulted Henri, Birdwhistle, and Adam. At this rate, we'll be feeding as many prisoners as servants."

"And here I thought I'd live in luxury and write in peace if I moved into an earl's manor." She wrapped her arms around his neck once he was out of his breeches. "Shall we return to honeymooning?"

Hunt lifted her and carried her to their bedroom. "We can do this part of the honeymoon now. Everything else will wait until morning."

This part was not anything she'd even dreamed of last winter when she'd been desperate to escape London. And she had a quite vivid imagination.

Who needed jewels when she had a man worth more than all the gold in the king's coffers? Tonight, she would not worry about a murderer roaming free.

THIRTY-SEVEN

THEA: FRIDAY MORNING

FRIDAY MORNING, AFTER A STORMY NIGHT, THE SUN SHONE THROUGH THE VESTIBULE transom. With Neville confined to the infirmary and no longer a danger, Thea could breathe again. They finally had an opportunity to explore what the boys had learned in the tower.

With satisfaction, she studied the artwork they'd so carefully assembled on the entry's walls these past weeks. The clue was glaringly obvious once all the pieces were in place. Whoever had hidden the lady's portrait and moved all the rest around. . . really, they should have been shot. She wondered who it might have been. Had the earl had second thoughts about revealing his treasure? Had the late viscountess simply not known better and taken down pieces she wanted elsewhere? She sensed no interest from The Lady and had seen nothing in her journals. They might never know.

The treasure may never have existed, she reminded herself. Or if the jeweled chess set was the extent of it. . . Well, she'd be satisfied solving the puzzle. Well, sort of. A little extra income never hurt, but they'd survive. She was striving very hard to be pragmatic, like her Cousin Clare.

Arnaud finished nailing the oil cloth over the broken transom window and climbed down from the ladder. "If Hunt hasn't shot all the bats inside, I don't know how we'll be rid of them now."

"Unblock the gallery door into the tower, and we'll let them out there," Lavender suggested, waiting impatiently for Davy and Oliver to arrive. "Thea, can't you tell us what this is about?"

Remembering an earlier conversation when they'd all gathered in here, Thea refrained from mentioning the need to be *responsible adults*. They hadn't killed anyone or each other this past week while the newlyweds were gone. Perhaps, they had learned to think for themselves just a little bit more.

"Perspective," Thea replied. Which worked for life as well as paintings, she supposed. "We need to see things from the point of view of others besides ourselves. We become too wrapped up in our own selfish concerns." As she had, regrettably. The manor did not revolve around her and Davy, and she and her brother were not the only eccentrics in the world.

It would take practice simply being herself, not fearing people would call her mad. Taking up adult leadership. . . She might manage, with the support of understanding people.

She tried hard not to watch Arnaud. Fearing all men, she'd ignored his existence until this past week, but now that she was learning to look beyond herself. . . She saw that he had far more depth than she'd expected.

And in her self-centeredness, she'd always considered the aunts as no more than pleasant older ladies. Now, she understood their polite courtesy hid a sharp wiliness. They offered a good example of how to use a barrier of social etiquette to survive social and emotional turmoil.

Happiness had always been elusive, but with Neville currently incapacitated, a heavy weight had lifted from Thea's shoulders. She spun giddily, admiring the meager sunlight dancing through the covered transom. "I do hope we'll be wealthy enough to replace that glass. The entry needs more light to be welcoming and to accentuate the magnificent walls of art and history."

"If you're counting on the earl's treasure, you may be doomed for disappointment. The chess set we shall never see may be the extent of it." Arnaud carried the ladder into the corridor.

She surmised he was building a defense against disappointment. She was learning to look beneath the surface!

Thea knew a good deal more about jewels than anyone else here except Jack, who had stayed in the manor today, just in case they actually found something. "One does not place diamond, emerald, and ruby necklaces in chess pieces. It is simply not done. The earl could not have been that mad. The ones in the chess set may have been small decorative pieces from chains or earrings, at the very most."

She hoped. She knew most of the pendants had been given away, although the necklaces they hung on had not. Still, the gems may have all been stolen or sold. The late viscount had been a sot and a wastrel, rather like Neville, she supposed. And the last earl had apparently been a bit mad.

Or eccentric. She really was in no position to call him mad.

"There are more jewels in those portraits than one could break into dozens of chess sets," Lavender agreed. "Unless, of course, the chess pieces were hollowed out."

"Cooper would be living like a king, if so, unless he didn't find the hidden compartments." After removing the ladder, Arnaud paced the vestibule, presumably looking for what Thea saw. "We are being ridiculous. If the boys don't arrive soon, I shall take a sledgehammer to the gallery wall and open that tower door. Sofia should have her workroom."

He didn't mind opening the dark tower now? Perhaps they *had* come a long way since the awful day they'd found Professor Boston.

By the time the boys slid down the banister of the marble stairs, a small crowd had gathered in the central corridor. Even the aunts had condescended to dress and join them at this early hour. Preparing to haul the prisoners off to court, the magistrate halted in pulling on his driving gloves, and the vicar stopped to frown at the spectacle.

Arnaud helped the boys to climb on the giant lion statue so they could point out the paintings they'd identified.

"The lady," Oliver said. "The one in red."

Thea lovingly stroked the newly discovered portrait. "Minerva has been reading the histories and says the subject is most likely the first Countess of Wycliffe. Tell us what you see, boys."

"Window." Unperturbed by the excitement, Davy dug in his pocket, producing a crumbling biscuit.

Thea pointed at the small window in the background of the portrait. "Does anyone recognize the view?"

Arnaud whistled. He was the only one in here who had been in the tower besides Thea and the boys. "That's the drive as it must have looked how many centuries ago? We need Patience to tell us what kind of trees those were."

"Not apple trees, but I think we can see orchard blossoms further down the hill. Perhaps the monks grew apples too?" Thea stood aside so Arnaud could look closer. She pointed at the landscape hanging on the right side of the portrait, duplicating but enlarging the miniature view behind the lady.

"That's what the orchard once looked like?" Arnaud studied the cloud of blossoms, then glanced back to the window in the portrait. "So this is the view she saw out her window? The paintings are related and that's why they're placed together?"

"But the lady isn't looking out the window." Thea waited for them to make the connection. "The orchard is behind her."

Lavender crowded up to study the portrait. "The walls of the room curve. She's in the *tower*? She's staring at what? The artist? There's nothing there."

"Take it down so we can all see," Lady Spalding cried.

"Remember, perspective," Thea cautioned. "We are trained to see only what's in the frame. But the boys spent weeks measuring paintings and finding exactly where they were placed. And as Arnaud has noticed, their placement was deliberate. Davy, Oliver, what do you see?"

"Pirate," Oliver said in satisfaction. "Maps."

Arnaud uttered a spate of shocked French that Thea loosely translated as *By damn look at that, the squares,* followed by scatology she could not quite follow.

Lavender crowded up, looking puzzled. Unable to resist, Lady Spalding joined them. "Lady Wycliffe is looking at the *pirate*? In the next portrait? How absurd!"

The pirate hung in the square to the left of of the richly garbed countess in her jewels, and she did, indeed, appear to be smiling at him. As he smiled at her.

"The pirate is presumably a portrait from the 1600s, possibly the first earl later in life?" Arnaud suggested. "I am not a student of clothing, just the artwork and paint."

The gentleman in question wore long, black curls, a thin black mustache, layers of white lace, a wine-colored velvet coat, and a plumed hat rested on his knee. Jewels sparkled in his ears, on his fingers, and at his throat. The squares on the wall behind him. . . required having seen the inside of the tower to recognize. Squares within squares, the earl's letters had said, wretched old man. Those hadn't been maps he'd drawn, but panel molding. So many walls of square molding. . .

With any luck, these portraits indicated which squares hid the treasure.

"Stuart finery," Thea confirmed, calling on her studies of the artwork in her grandparents' homes.

"It is possibly in the style of Rembrandt," Arnaud contributed. "I doubt the paintings are valuable as more than history."

Hurrying down the marble stairs, Hunt and Clare joined the magistrate and vicar in the main corridor. They hadn't seen the tower and would not see what the boys did.

"You have found another clue?" Clare asked eagerly.

"Quite possibly." Minerva emerged from the library carrying duplicates of the earlier clues and maps, passing them to anyone who held out a hand. "The earl might not have been as mad as we assumed."

Their guests studied the earl's letters—the vicar with puzzlement and the magistrate with delight.

"You are on a treasure hunt?" Mr. Ephraim concluded. "The thief didn't steal the jewels after all?"

"We can't say until we explore this theory. The earl's letter indicates a *large portrait* in the vestibule hides a clue to jewels. The lady and gentleman are the only portraits. The maps you're holding resemble squares similar to the panel walls in the portrait, and their location is in the tower." Arnaud gestured at the papers they held.

He lifted the boys from the statue. "There are three ways into the tower: through the windows on the roof, behind the wardrobe in the attic, and down the hole to the byre. The tower itself is dark and filthy, although our reprobates did a fine job of dusting cobwebs in their search yesterday. The room in question is the second up from the byre. Boys, which way do you wish to go?"

They aimed for the attic stairs, thank the stars. Thea wasn't much inclined to go through the byre again. She bobbed a curtsy to their guests. "Perhaps you might wish to delay your journey until we discover whether our theory is on the mark?"

"Lady Elsa prepares a fine coffee and her scones are worth dallying over," Clare suggested, as the men hesitated. "And if they find nothing, you may tell the world that Wycliffe's jewels are lost, and scoundrels may find better things to do."

Obviously eager to explore, Hunt almost shoved the guests toward the parlor. "The prisoners haven't been retrieved from the cellar yet. Make yourselves comfortable. This shouldn't take long."

Famous last words, Thea thought as she followed the boys and an excited Lavender. To her surprise, Arnaud fell in beside her. She regretted thinking of him as Skeleton Man. Muscle rippled beneath his ill-fitting attire. He would be needing new clothes soon. A month or two of Elsa's cooking might do that— along with his refusal to sit still, even when painting.

Henri spoke with Hunt, and they departed for the side door, apparently planning on ascending the tower through the byre.

"Jack and Walker are with the prisoners?" she asked worriedly as they hurried up the stairs.

"Franklin and his crew are locked in the crypt. Jack and Walker are escorting them out as we speak. Your cousin won't be going anywhere soon on that leg. I'm not sure what they're doing about Timothy Cooper. Walker wants to keep him as steward, and he doesn't seem to be implicated in anything except showing up for his grandfather's funeral." Arnaud took her arm until they reached the attic stairs. There he released her so she might go first up the narrow passage.

Gentlemen always followed a lady up the stairs, but she had never been so aware that her bottom was almost in his face. Stay with the subject, she reminded herself. "Well, it's quite awful if Franklin Cooper's wife and brother must go to gaol for something he instigated, while he might escape all charges of theft for lack of evidence, but there is no question that Neville and the pair are guilty of assault. I'd like to see them thrashed for terrifying the boys."

Thea flounced into the attic, where Mr. Birdwhistle, Lavender, Davy, and Oliver already awaited them, having raced ahead.

Arnaud produced the key to the storage area. Davy wanted to use the hidden door in the wardrobe, but the men wouldn't fit. Thea held Davy's hand while he bounced in excitement until Arnaud and the tutor shoved the enormous wardrobe aside. The door into the tower still refused to open further.

The boys slid through the narrow opening while Arnaud oiled the hinges. In the light of Mr. Birdwhistle's lamp, shadows danced across the wall. Thea had to close her eyes to shut out The Lady's whispers. She refused to make a spectacle of herself at a moment like this. Perhaps if they cleaned the windows, this area would be brighter, and she'd be less likely to notice the manor's many specters.

She was learning to take charge of her. . . eccentricity.

Using his broad shoulder, Arnaud shoved at the recalcitrant tower door. It squealed rustily and finally gave way. He stepped aside so Thea and Mr. Birdwhistle could follow the boys. She hadn't believed the artist capable of thoughtfulness, but he was proving her wrong in so many ways.

"You have tools for tearing out panels?" she murmured as they passed the awful animal heads and took the stairs down. As a gentleman, Arnaud took the stairs first, in case she tripped over her hem. His pace was guarded, as if he expected miscreants to leap out at them.

"Our culprits left tools scattered everywhere. I think Professor Boston must have provided them with clues we do not know. If he provided the earl's code, he had to have known the secret." Keeping his back to the wall, Arnaud held his lamp high so she could see where she stepped.

"They had our maps, part of the journal, and Boston's tales. They probably thought we'd discovered something when we opened up the tower. It doesn't take much to convince treasure hunters that wealth is at their fingertips." The stone steps were worn and slippery beneath her soft soles, but she steadied herself on the damp wall.

He stopped at the bottom and held out his hand for her to take the last steps. Excited voices indicated the boys had found what they expected. Hunt's deep voice carried over their exclamations, so he was there too.

"Treasure hunters like us?" Arnaud asked wryly.

Thea stepped into the dimly lit round chamber where everyone gathered. "I fear the lure of jewels will create unpleasant chaos, even should we find them."

"I'd concur, except the Reids are not normal," he reminded her, leaving her to work that out as he joined the others in examining the paneled walls of what might once have been a lady's bedchamber and sitting room.

Thea sank into imagining the first countess presiding over her domain from the tower, the tallest structure in the countryside: workmen scurrying about, building her husband's dream of a fortress manor. She sensed love. The countryside in turmoil. Fears for their children. . . Thieves?

A pirate possessing jewels and knowing thieves were on his doorstep. . . would conceal his valuables. Thea felt it in her bones or her instincts or whatever talked to her from the past.

Unafraid of thieves, the more recent earls had displayed their garish jewels to all the world—until the last earl had disposed of—or hidden—them. Had all the Reid jewels belonged to the pirate? His hiding place may already be empty and the earl's still unfound. Except the clues led here. Had the last earl sealed the tower?

Thea watched as the boys excitedly held up the "maps" the earl had left them, holding them over the squares of paneling similar to those in the vestibule. In the flickering light of the lamps, it was difficult to see whether there might once have been paintings hanging between the raised molding of the panels. She thought it possible the lady's and the pirate's portraits may have fit into the squares the men were currently tapping on. Once upon a time, the dusty, faded walnut panels must have gleamed with beeswax.

She could hear the spirits in her head, speaking to her in sensations, not words. She felt the elegance and security of the surroundings, the happiness of a couple reunited after many years apart, the expectations for their future. . . Thea needed to read Minerva's history books. Had they been as happy in their later years, after the manor was complete?

Not if the child's crying ghost meant anything. She shut it out.

"Not hollow but different from the rest," Hunt called, knocking on a panel from his greater height that the boys could not reach.

Henri arrived carrying crates that he stacked against the wall. The boys scrambled up on the precarious stepstools, ready to peer in once Hunt opened the panel.

Lavender squeezed Thea's hand in anticipation. "I don't know if I'm more excited about jewels or the tower," she whispered. "If they'll open the door into the gallery, Sofia can have a perfumery that will draw ladies from the city. And then they'll see my fashions."

PATRICIA RICE

"Where *is* Sofia?" Thea thought the shy French girl might not enjoy the gloomy tower as much as the men did.

"Praying," Lavender said with a laugh. "I'm not sure if it's to God or to her fiancé's ghost. She can be excitable, so it's best if she keeps an eye on my sewing ladies. Look, they have opened the panel!"

Thea was certain everyone held their collective breaths as Davy and Oliver stuck their small hands inside. When they couldn't reach deep enough, Hunt and Arnaud lifted them higher. She nearly fell to her knees in relief as the boys shouted in triumph and pulled out rotting old bags.

No treasure box, just moldering old velvet bags.

The last earl had died only thirty-five years ago. Velvet didn't rot that swiftly. Something wasn't right. Thea held out her hand. "Please, let me touch them before anyone else does."

Davy trustingly laid his treasure on her palm.

She held it in her palm, felt the warmth of her ancestor's love, the depth of her despair, and the tears soaked into the fabric. Nothing on the velvet said mad, scheming old man. "This is a lady's treasure, not an earl's." She handed the bag back to Davy. "We need to see if the histories tell us about the countess."

Solemnly, Oliver held out the bag he held.

Thea squeezed it and sensed only pragmatism and the clink of coins. "Not jewels. Security."

Remarkably, no one looked at her as if she were crazed. That was such a relief that when Arnaud offered his arm in concern, she took it, even though the emotions on the velvet had faded and weren't strong enough to send her reeling.

She feared they were all about to be disappointed.

Hunt set one of Henri's wooden crate in the center of the room, then threw his handkerchief over the dusty top. They held their collective breaths as the boys emptied the contents of their prizes onto the linen. The two French brothers had given what remained of their estates to their uncle in France. They only watched in hopes that their English family might flourish.

Arnaud covered her hand with his big one.

From Davy's bag fell tarnished silver chains with tiny diamonds embedded in molded silver flowers, much like a child might wear, should children wear precious gems. Perhaps in the first earl's time, they did. Necklace, bracelets, all of the finest silverwork—valuable, but not a pirate's jewels. Nor the last earl's.

The other bag contained gold and silver coins—certainly a pirate's ransom, although not the expected gems.

"I don't know whether to be disappointed or delighted," Thea said into the silence.

The boys ran off, content to have solved a puzzle and more interested in exploring.

Arnaud reached his big hand into the concealed opening in the wall, running it around to be certain they'd found everything. He returned with a yellowing letter. "It appears the last earl must have been the one who sealed off the tower."

The earl's familiar hand addressed the letter *To Whom It May Concern.* He had to have had access to place the letter in a pirate's cache. And to know the clues.

"If Wycliffe knew the paintings led to the tower, then he must have been in here at some point," Hunt agreed. When Arnaud tried to hand him the letter, Hunt shook his head. "I don't have my monocle. Let one of the ladies do the honors. It's their family's treasure."

"And insanity," Thea said dryly, taking the paper since Lavender could barely read.

This is your history, she read aloud. *The little girl died in a raid by thieves seeking treasure. Be certain you wish to inherit the curse.*

Another code followed. This time, the map looked like an actual map, except not to any place Thea recognized.

The jewels were still out there? Unfair! Thea wanted to stomp her feet in frustration. But sadly, she saw the earl's point.

She handed the papers to Hunt. "Lord Wycliffe was right, you know. Great wealth *is* a curse. Perhaps we should be satisfied with what we have."

Neville had been after Davy's inheritance. Fortune seekers had sought hers, forcing her to flee society. Franklin Cooper had most likely killed his own grandfather for the secret to this hiding place. They might all be happier without jewels.

In disappointment, Lavender flounced after the boys. Henri took the letter from Hunt to read it for himself.

Before the ghosts could take advantage of her emotional upset and send Thea reeling, Arnaud took her arm and steadied her. She wanted to weep for the lady, for lost expectations, for a world where there was no fairness.

But there was satisfaction in knowledge, and she'd learned quite a bit this past week. Not so long ago, she would have been spinning out of control with all the invisible stimuli in this haunted tower. A week ago, she would never have surmised that Arnaud's presence would be a steadying influence.

At shouts from outside, he abruptly dropped her arm and pulled himself up to look out the high window. The reverberation of gunfire warned all was not well—and the ghosts screamed in cacophony.

THIRTY-EIGHT

ARNAUD: FRIDAY MORNING

At the muffled crack of a gunshot, Hunt and Henri charged down the stairs to the byre.

Conscious of the terrified lady at his elbow, swallowing hard at a responsibility he'd never wanted, Arnaud blocked Thea from the stairs. *"Stay here."*

It had been a long time since he'd felt called upon to defend anyone. But those shouts weren't warring armies. If he couldn't do this, he didn't deserve to live."I'll send the boys to you." They couldn't easily scramble out of the byre on their own.

Sapphire eyes wide with terror, the lady scanned the chamber for a hiding place, but this floor was entirely empty. Still, at his promise to send the boys, she nodded agreement. Her trust terrified and relieved him. He was still a puling coward.

He'd only managed the dreaded stairs earlier by nearly crawling, shoving mental shadows into their cages, using Thea as an excuse to drag his heels.

The need to save those he loved and respected didn't allow dallying this time. Gunfire was for soldiers, not peaceful estates filled with innocents. Pure roiling terror and fury drove him down the frightening passage—not reactions conducive to logical planning. Were the boys safe? If anyone had touched them. . .

He all but closed his eyes to the confined staircase and slid down half the hollowed stones until he hit the ground floor. Swallowing his nausea, he scanned the byre. The boys weren't anywhere to be seen—but they'd been taught defense included hiding if threatened. "Shout if you're in here, lads."

"Pirates?" Davy called.

Arnaud let relief wash over him. "Possibly bad men. Go to Thea upstairs, please. Show her how to escape." That should send them to the safety of other exits. He could hear both of the brilliant little rats scrambling and whispering.

He swung out of the pit that was the byre entrance. Henri was hiding behind the shrubbery, waiting for him. Hunt, with his bad knee, still stood in the hole, prepared to pull himself out. None of them were armed, except with knives.

Arnaud peered from the bushes to scan the situation.

On the drive, the prisoners had been loaded into an open cart. Presumably, the vicar and magistrate meant to ride in the waiting carriage, but they must still be enjoying scones. Walker's ex-soldiers had their hands on their smoking weapons but were stepping back. . .

Because Franklin Cooper, scholar and gentleman, held his wife—with her wrists still bound—by the throat, threatening her with a long blade. Every time the red-haired Eleanor screamed a curse, he jerked her head back to shut her up.

"We need a sharpshooter," Arnaud growled.

"Jack." Henri swiftly assessed the situation. "But too many people around unless he shoots from the tower."

Hunt sat on the edge and lifted his legs over. "Send the boys to find Jack?"

"They are fast, but not fast enough." Arnaud strained to hear the exchange of shouts between Franklin and Walker, who was out of their line of sight. "I doubt there is time to put him in position."

"The rogue is risking everything," Henri whispered. "Why? He cannot possibly believe he'll escape. He might even have gone free if the judge ruled the ancient theft of a chess set can't be tried."

"Only a man in fear for his life will risk living on the run." Arnaud eased out to better hear the shouts. "That is his brother with whom he argues. Henri, send the boys to find Jack, just in case. I shall try to delay." Henri would race up the tower stairs without hesitation. And then his little brother would be safe and not foolishly risking the life he'd been so carefully building here. Arnaud hadn't protected Henri as he ought in the past. He could give it a try now.

Henri dropped back down to the byre entrance and vanished inside.

Hunt frowned. "Wish I had my rifle."

"You have been practice shooting with one eye? That is not a tree or deer out there." Arnaud scoffed. "Besides, your lady wife will not appreciate putting yourself in the way of danger. How attached are you to those coins?"

Hunt pulled the money sack out of his pocket and jingled it. "Not much, but not too attached to that female either. Is she worth it?"

"Killing the red-haired witch will only make him more desperate." Arnaud took the coins with more confidence than he felt.

Hunt was the trained soldier. He was not. But there was little either of them could do while the woman had a knife at her neck. Muttering *c'est la vie*, Arnaud removed a handful of the gold coins and handed them back and kept the sack. "For posterity."

Giving up a fortune ought to be harder, but the grimy metal didn't hold the same reality as a woman's life and more bloodshed. He'd seen far too many innocents die to accept any more wasted blood, if he had any means at all of preventing it. So, maybe he'd been lousy at defending his estate because wealth had never meant anything to him.

People did, apparently. In his paralysis of grief, he hadn't realized that the residents of the manor had given him home and family again.

Staying in the shadow of the overgrown shrubbery, Arnaud eased closer to the argument.

"He was naught but an old man telling tales! Just because he bragged about knowing an earl didn't mean he knew aught about jewels," Timothy Cooper shouted from the stable, sounding near tears. He shook a rifle in his fist but kept it pointed at the sky. "He never had nothing, never wanted nothing but his peas and goats."

Professor Boston knew the earl and had peas and goats. Were they arguing over their grandfather?

"He knew everything and told us nothing!" Franklin shouted back. "And now look where we are. He *knew* where the earl hid the jewels. He helped hide them! He had years to tell us. We could have been living like gentry."

Two mad old men, plotting and playing chess with lives. . . Arnaud could almost respect that.

From his position by the cart, hands still tied behind his back, Herbert Hanks swiveled his head worriedly, trying to watch both brothers at once. He winced every time his sister's neck was jerked. "You'll find another position, Frankie," he shouted. "It's naught to lose your head over. A good solicitor and you'll. . ."

Crouching, Arnaud stayed hidden as Timothy Cooper took a step closer, vehemently shaking his head and almost sobbing. "No, he's shown what he is. I won't let him get away this time. I'll see him hanged first. He *killed* grandad, the only father we ever had. Frankie never appreciated that. He always wanted more. He lost all he stole by gambling, lost his fancy position with the university because he can't pay his debts, he's about to lose his wife, and he decided to do what he always does, take the easy way out."

"Why are you making these accusations now?" Walker asked, reasonably enough.

"Because he's my brother!" their new steward cried. "He's all the family I've got. I don't *want* him to hang. He won't listen to me, so I thought maybe being arrested would make him see sense! He's smarter than I'll ever be, but then he does this. . ." Timothy Cooper was openly weeping now.

"You never had any ambition!" the older brother retorted, bringing the knife to his wife's throat. "Did you think wealth would fall into your hands if you waited long enough?"

Actions spoke louder than words. As far as Arnaud was concerned, Franklin Cooper was confirming his guilt with his attitude as much as his violence. He'd exhibited his propensity for violence with poor old Finkley. Until now, they'd had no proof that he'd done the same with the professor.

Arnaud knew desperation when he saw it. Desperate, angry men did stupid things—like killing harmless old men when they wouldn't turn over their secrets. Still hunkered down to keep his head below the shrubbery, he edged closer.

He could easily snap Franklin's neck, but he didn't wish to kill again, certainly not on the basis of hearsay or jealousy. This was not a courtroom of impartial evidence.

The magistrate and vicar finally emerged from the portico door. They wouldn't be of much use except as witnesses, but if Hunt must send a man to hang, he ought to have what evidence could be found. A confession would be good.

He'd spent too many years lost in the shadows of the hole he'd dug himself into. Time to climb out and be a man again.

Standing, towering head and shoulders above the bushes, Arnaud strode into the sunlight, startling the players in this drama into looking his way. He knew men once turned to him for leadership because of his stature and wealth. He'd failed then, failed miserably. Retreating to his art had seemed the only sensible way to prevent that happening again. But he hadn't been living these past years.

Having all the attention on him was akin to the hot sun hitting him in the face after emerging from darkness—damned uncomfortable. But Wycliffe manor and its residents had offered him a glimmer of hope that he didn't want to lose.

He didn't lack courage. Mostly, he lacked any desire for violence.

With casual insouciance, Arnaud swung the moldering sack of ancient metal as he strode into the open. Franklin's gaze instantly diverted from his weeping brother. Satisfied he had all eyes on him, Arnaud produced a coin from the sack. It was too dull with age to glint in the sun, but it was large and the shape was unmistakable. "Is this what you seek, Professor?"

Franklin appeared almost relieved, releasing some of the tension on his wife's neck."Coins, not jewels? The old man said there were jewels hidden here."

"*Mais oui.*" Arnaud swung the bag. "We followed the earl's clues, coded by your grandfather, and this is all we found—pirate treasure. Did your grandfather call it this?"

"He did," Timothy yelled. "He was just telling tall tales. This fool believed him!"

"There's proof the old man didn't lie," Franklin shouted back, pointing at the coin. "All I need is enough to pay my debts. What good is gold stuck in walls? No one will miss it. What harm is there?"

The prof admittedly had a point. That didn't mean he deserved to keep what he found or that coins were worth killing a good man. Was that sufficient confession?

Arnaud pondered his next move as Franklin backed toward the magistrate's waiting carriage.

"You're a wastrel, Franklin Cooper," his wife cried. "You'd have thrown the blunt away on carousing just as you did before, with me going hungry and homeless. That nice old man was kinder to me than my own husband. *Are you saying you did for him?*"

Ah, nice, leave it to the wife to know how to get a man's goat.

"You weren't homeless," Franklin retorted, not denying her accusation. "We could have lived in luxury if you'd only listened. It was all right there in his journal, just like I said. We'd have been the ones to find it if you'd brought me the book." He waved his knife at one of the ex-soldiers guarding the carriage. "*Give me the weapon.* Anyone coming after us will be shot."

Arnaud nodded at the soldier to do as told. These men had given their all for their country. He wouldn't have them harmed by a cowardly crook. It was his turn to serve.

Now with a rifle as well as a knife, Franklin slit the ropes on his wife's wrists and shoved her into the carriage. "You're so proud of your driving, Nellie, get up there."

Terrified and confused at being set free, she did.

He pointed the rifle at Arnaud. "Hand over the coins and you'll not see us again."

Arnaud eased closer. Without a weapon, he had only one choice. Out of the corner of his eye, he saw Jack and a few of the stable hands saddling up. Henri and the boys hadn't reached him in time, as he'd expected. Damn shame though. Cut from a more soldierly cloth than Arnaud, Hunt was likely to do something stupid like throw himself at the horses from his hiding place.

Franklin had only one shot, but that's all it took to cause devastation. He might eventually be stopped, but the price of losing a life wasn't worth taking a chance. Besides, Lady Elsa would poison them all if anything happened to Jack.

As a boy, Arnaud had been good at boules. He might be missing a finger these days, but he could still hit a target better than Hunt could with his dead eye.

The yard stood silent as Arnaud approached the unemployed scholar—a cold-blooded killer, presumably. He really wanted that confession. "Blood money for killing your grandfather?" he asked, swinging the bag as if he meant to toss it to him.

"He was old and dying," Franklin sneered with more confidence now that escape was within reach. "He could have cleaned out all the valuables in the manor over the years but never had the gumption. No closer. Hand them over."

Arnaud hoped that was sufficient for the magistrate. "*Et voila*, catch."

Before Franklin could react, Arnaud flung the heavy—open—sack of coins as hard as he could—and dropped flat to the ground.

Coins hit the murderous fool full in the face, before scattering over the rocky, rutted drive. Three shots rang out, from different directions.

Franklin screamed and crumbled.

Still lying flat, Arnaud considered the sovereigns and doubloons rolling right under his nose—a pirate's stolen bounty. Was it cursed? If so, all the men shouting and racing to scoop up the gold were in trouble.

Before he could even think to rise, a weeping bundle of sweetness fell on him. "Are you all right? Arnaud? Please, tell me you're all right. That was the stupidest, most courageous. . ."

He was greatly afeared the fool woman wept over his useless hide. He'd conquered a lot of weaknesses lately, but a woman's tears might push him over the edge. Rolling over and up in one move, he caught the mad heiress before she could spin off and go vaporish. "I am fine. You should not be here. Where are the boys?"

He stood, pulling her with him. He ought to be dazed and incoherent just holding the madwoman's warm curves, but he thought she might need him, if only a little bit. As she'd said, he ought to think of others occasionally. Except he wasn't thinking at all as he wrapped her in his arms and half-carried her away from whatever carnage lay in the drive behind them.

"Mr. Birdwhistle has them," she whispered tearfully. "The Lady warned me you were in danger. He had a knife and a rifle!"

"I have been in much worse places. You have not. You should not be here. Now you may have to stand as witness. Go inside and pretend you heard nothing. I know you are not helpless. I know you are not mad. But others do not, and your lout of a cousin will use every word you say as ammunition."

The bold miss kissed his stubbly cheek, and he felt it clear down to his toes. "I'll break his leg again," she promised.

Fighting back a grin at her insanity, Arnaud found Clare and Meera peering from the safety of the kitchen garden and shoved Miss Dorothea Talbot into their arms. "Lock her up for her own good."

Then he turned to watch all the witnesses, including the vicar and magistrate, scrambling for gold coins, while Jack, Walker, and Hunt disarmed a killer, tied him up, and ignored the man's hysterical wife holding the reins to the magistrate's horses.

"Stop *la femelle*, you fools!" he ordered in the same tone as Hunt used to order his men about.

Watching men scramble to grab the reins, he felt good to be in charge again.

THIRTY-NINE

PAUL: FRIDAY NOON

FRIDAY NOON, HAVING ISOLATED HIMSELF IN THE PARSONAGE ALL MORNING, DRAFTING his sermon, then helping one of his widowed parishioners catch a pig, Paul finally left for Wycliffe Manor. Strolling down the dappled path from the parsonage, he wondered if the treasure hunters had discovered the hidden jewels or been disappointed once again. Either way, he'd have his luncheon. He was fair starved.

On the drive, he stepped out of the way as the magistrate's carriage swept past, followed by a bouncing cart bearing the new footman and maid, with their wrists bound. He'd thought the officials should have left by now. They'd barely make it to the city by dark.

Walking farther up the hill so he could see the manor—was that the communal coffin being carried into the stable? *Another* funeral? For whom? Should he panic? Pleasant day shattered, Paul hurried through the side door, handing his hat to Quincy. "Is Miss Peniston in the library?" Minerva would know everything.

"With Mrs. Walker, sir. She's having her baby. The captain and lieutenant are in the stable." Quincy bowed and returned to his post.

A baby! Better news than another death. He said hasty prayers for mother and babe while pondering where to turn next for information.

If Hunt and Jack were in the stable with a coffin. . . He tried counting heads but a loud crash from the gallery diverted him. In the distance, Meera's cries resounded over the intermittent crashes.

Paul wanted nothing to do with delivering babies. He already knew he was incompetent. Both Meera and Minerva were experienced at childbirth. Thankfully, they'd have every maid in the manor at their beck and call. They didn't need him.

But he really didn't wish to join Jack and Hunt in the stable until he learned whose funeral he'd be conducting. Since no one appeared to be grieving. . .

Smashing crashes in the gallery, followed by female cries, begged inspection. Who needed a circus when one had Wycliffe Manor?

Since luncheon didn't appear to be ready, Paul peered into the former ballroom. He could only see a gaggle of females forming a semi-circle around the unused corner near the tower. Holland linens hung from clotheslines, shutting out any view of events on the other side.

He sauntered in, more comfortable now in this immense manor than he had been upon his arrival a few months ago. He greeted the sewing ladies who attended his services. Clare, the new Mrs. Huntley, would be with her friend, Meera, during her lying-in. His sister preferred the garden to indoors, and where she went, Henri followed. So the company was mostly Lavender's ladies.

He was a trifle surprised to see Dorothea Talbot, the prim heiress, lingering by the linen wall, jumping nervously at the crashing. Near her, Lavender and Sofia excitedly bounced on their toes, trying to watch through the linens. Plaster dust filled the air.

Ahhh, Hunt must have given permission to tear out the wall concealing the door into the tower.

Paul disliked asking the ladies about a coffin, but he had other concerns. He waited for a lull in the crashing to whisper to Thea, "Do you have any notion what they've done with Mr. Finkley and Boston's goats?"

Her thin blond eyebrows shot up but she nodded. "Hunt let Mr. Finkley go after the magistrate took his statement. I believe Mr. Timothy took him home so he might retrieve his farm animals. I don't know what arrangement was made to care for them. The cottage is still habitable but not in a condition to be let out until repairs are made."

"The brothers have settled their differences then?" Paul hoped the new steward was inclined to attend church. If Mr. Timothy meant to marry soon, he'd encourage it.

His innocent question unleashed a voluble torrent from all the ladies, one that raised his eyebrows as the horror story unfolded. When they finished, Paul grimaced and said a hasty prayer for lost souls. He hadn't liked Franklin Cooper, but no one deserved to be gunned down like a rabid animal. He'd have to speak with Timothy Cooper about another funeral. How did that poor man feel about losing the last of his family? He needed to summon the community to rally around him.

Did they bury a killer in a sanctified graveyard? Or perhaps in his grandfather's yard. "No one knows whose shot killed Mr. Cooper?"

Lavender shook her head. "Hunt and the magistrate called it self defense and refused to inquire."

Paul kept his opinion to himself. Hunt and the magistrate were pragmatic men more likely to say the shooter had saved the court a lot of trouble.

But a man who killed his own grandfather. . . May God have mercy on Franklin Cooper's soul.

A triumphant grunt followed another crash. Arnaud, indubitably. Knowing he'd hear the full story from Minerva later, Paul lifted the dust curtain and stepped behind it. For some reason, soiling his hands with hard work soothed his troubled thoughts. "Need help hauling away the debris? I can fetch a barrow."

Wiping his broad brow, Arnaud stood back to admire his handiwork. The solid oak door he'd uncovered had once been ornate, carved with the first earl's coat of arms and studded with brass nails. Mortar had splashed on the once fine wood and cracks had formed in the grain. A brass handle had no lock.

"The tower was never meant to be a fortress?" Paul speculated.

"The tower, it was a castle keep those first years. This," he gestured at the door, "was most likely added after the ballroom was completed. Perhaps they used the keep as a powder room for the ladies? Draped it in velvets and filled it with gilded sofas?"

Arnaud stepped over the debris to tug the handle. The brass hinges creaked but didn't move. "Oil," he shouted to the ladies waiting.

The linen instantly tumbled down, and the women swooped in to chatter happily about the entrance to the *perfumery*. Paul went in search of a barrow and oil.

Out in the wide corridor, cries of excitement carried from the rear, erasing any gloom from the morning's tragedy. He might as well exit that way, past the infirmary, since any barrow would most likely be in the garden. If he were in luck, he might catch a glimpse of Minerva.

An infant's loud howl gave evidence that the newborn had healthy lungs. Now *there* was a sound to lift spirits. . . a baptism to remove the pall of still another funeral!

When he arrived at the back of the manor, Clare and Hunt were hugging each other outside the infirmary.

"Girl or boy?" Paul called.

"Boy," Hunt replied. "We need to start thinking in terms of nurseries!"

Instead of cemeteries, Paul approved.

When Minerva emerged cuddling a bundled infant, he completely forgot coffins and graveyards.

There was the future he wanted.

Drawn to the loving scene, he abandoned his quest and hugged Minerva's slender shoulders. Together, they gazed at the tiny new life she cooed over. The babe's round brown face, so much like his mother's, rested peacefully, a tiny thumb already in its mouth.

"Marry me," he whispered in her ear, as he had several times before.

This time, she sent him a fleeting smile and kissed his cheek.

He hoped that meant she was growing used to the idea.

A WEEK LATER

THEA: EVENING

"No, no, a little to the left, please." Thea gestured to indicate where the newly-framed painting ought to hang.

"We'll only have to take it all down after we decide on paint," Arnaud argued, moving the landscape further down the withdrawing room wall.

"I need to keep busy." She nodded approval at the new location, and while he climbed a ladder to put a nail in the picture rail, she sorted through the rest of his paintings. Arnaud's work had a lot to say. Not all of it had sold to the trade market, possibly because there was so much passion here. . . This was true art.

He slipped the painting rope over the nail and climbed down to look over her shoulder at his unframed pieces. He removed the wild and gloomy painting she held of trees bending in a blustery storm.

"You have no need to fear anymore," he reassured her. "Hunt has done all in his power to keep Neville from ever crossing your path again."

Thea understood in her head, but it was hard to contain all the emotions blowing her about, much like the storm in the painting. Had Arnaud once felt like that? "My father is far more likely to listen to gentlemen than to me. I owe the captain and all the officialdom he brought in to reason with him. But once Neville is healed. . ."

"We have affidavits from half a dozen highly respectable people that he is a kidnapper who has assaulted Davy, his tutor, and others. Trust us—he will go to gaol like his accomplices if he comes within ten miles of you. Your father, he has promised to send his nephew to the Continent to learn his business. And you have us." He squeezed her shoulder reassuringly before rummaging in the pile to produce a painting of the orchard in spring sunlight.

Thea acknowledged his comforting grip and let his declaration settle her stormy heart. "I have difficulty trusting," she admitted.

His dark eyes troubled in his masculinely-carved face, he studied her over top of the painting. "I understand. I am trying to learn to trust again, too, but it is difficult."

His reasons were probably far greater than hers, but the way he looked at her had her heart pounding—in excitement or fear, she could not tell. The possibility that she might not have to be alone, that they might someday come to an understanding. . .

"I am rich," she stated flatly. "Or I will be, once I marry and hand my trust over to a husband. That is all men see in me. They smile and flatter and court my money, not me, as I am, with all my faults and foibles."

He winced. "People, in general, are fools. You, perhaps, learned that at a younger age than I. I had to be beaten, robbed of land and title, starved, and flung into *le bastille* before I recognized the inanity of the populace is not about me."

She offered a faint smile and handed him a companion piece to the spring orchard."Maybe a little about you. You are physically and mentally intimidating. People attack what they fear."

"Then, perhaps, you may recognize that they fear what *they* can't see—but *you* can." He took the two pieces and returned to the wall where the first hung.

Thea puzzled that out. "They fear the ghosts only I can see? Or me for seeing them? And you believe I see them? I didn't think anyone did. Everyone believes I'm quite mad."

"You are not any madder than I am." He gestured at the paintings. "Me, I draw things only I see. The orchard does not look like this. Perhaps once, it may have, but I did not paint from what we see with our eyes. The picture is up here." He tapped his skull. "The paintings are what I *want* to see, what I feel, what I fear and love. They are not real."

Thea let his words seep into her heart, where she understood better. "And perhaps. . ." She wasn't a deep thinker, but she tried to follow his thoughts. "When I hear the voices whispering from the past, I am hearing what I feel, in some way? It's possible they're not real, but something I *understand*?"

"Just keep doing what you are doing. You are good at it." He gestured at the room that had been slowly filling with the furnishings she'd collected. "Everyone, they are eager to use this room because these pieces *feel* right in here, because you have given them what they want."

"That's easy," she scoffed. "People are predictable."

"Say as you will, but the room is ready. Henri and I will start work this evening, after he returns with the paint. Jack is helping Paul fix the roof of the workshop. *Et voila*, Paul repairs the chairs so they won't break if we sit on them. Elsa wishes for this room so her staff does not have to traipse so far of an evening. I think even Lavender learns to upholster for you. You make an ugly hunting box into a *home*."

Thea knew that she was happier living in the manor than she had ever been. She hadn't realized others liked it better having her here, not because of her money, but because of what she'd accomplished. It was a notion she'd hold close when doubts assailed her, as they always did.

"Then you'll let me help design your studio in the tower?" she asked, hiding a grin.

He cast her a dark look, but he did not disagree. "The tower needs much work," was all he'd admit.

Davy and Oliver burst in, each waving a gleaming gold piece. "We cleaned them," Davy cried."Mr. Jack says they're pirate doubloons. We can buy a ship!"

Her little brother was talking again, thank all the heavens.

"Then everyone who took one home will have a ship," Thea said dryly. "I think the vicar even gave Paul an increase in his salary after Hunt generously called the coins the vicar walked off with a donation."

"Perhaps, the vicar, he will be more eager to visit us now?" Arnaud suggested.

If their curate meant to marry. . . having a vicar visit would be useful. Thea took the doubloon Davy handed her to admire it. "You've polished it nicely. Don't lose it!"

Davy would some day be worth far more than that coin, but it was good he learned the value of money first. She didn't want him to turn out like Neville.

Hunt and Clare strolled in behind the boys to admire the changes in the new withdrawing room. Oliver actually went up to Hunt to hand him his coin. "With my dinosaur eggs?"

"With your inheritance, excellent thought. Perhaps the value will grow until you need it." Clare hugged her nephew, who instantly pushed away to study the changes in the room.

Clare had once explained that Oliver's father had left him rough gems that he called dinosaur eggs. No one knew their exact value, but she hoped it would give her nephew an education some day.

Oliver was as peculiar as Davy. That they were happy was what mattered,

Thea realized. Now that she need not fret and worry every minute, she could relax and enjoy their company.

"Jack has calculated the value of the coins we managed to keep." Hunt cast Arnaud a look that appeared almost amused. "The ones that vanished from the drive aren't a complete loss. Our ex-soldiers can now afford roofs over their heads, if they so desire. It would be simpler if we can persuade the bank to let them lease cottages. Walker is negotiating to use the manor's maintenance funds to repair the cottages in exchange for lease money. The coins are a significant investment in the village's future."

Thea admired the way Arnaud's broad shoulders hid a large portion of the room's ugly pocked wall as he leaned against it and crossed his arms. More than admiration danced in her insides. The former comte wasn't a flattering, bowing suitor after her wealth. She thought he might be a friend. But someday. . .

"If we use maintenance to fix the cottages, what do we use to feed the growing horde in the manor?" Arnaud asked.

Thea had some notion that they'd been eating off the funds provided for servants, so this was a good question. After starving for so long, Arnaud liked his food.

In time to hear this question, Jack and Elsa arrived, arm in arm, smiling the way newlyweds ought to smile. The lean ex-soldier and his plump Reid-blond wife made a handsome couple.

"Pirate booty is apparently worth a great deal now that war has depleted bank coffers of gold." Jack pulled Elsa down on the sofa beside him and propped his boots on an unadorned wooden boot rest. "I like this room."

His new wife elbowed him. "Thank Thea, then tell them what everyone wants to know."

"Thank you, Thea," Jack parroted obediently. "I'm not sure why but everyone ought to be thanked occasionally."

Arnaud snorted and returned to choosing frames for the paintings. Elsa hit Jack with a pillow and Clare flung another at him.

Bouncing up and down with impatience, Thea might have dared throw a pillow, too, except they were a little short on ammunition. "You're welcome, Jack. Now will you tell us what this is about?"

Seating Clare in a wing chair by the empty grate, Hunt tested a wide armchair. "Thank you, Thea, this is a good, solid piece I don't have to fear will disintegrate under my weight." He turned gravely to Elsa's new husband. "Thank you, Jack, for calculating the value of pirate booty. Now will you explain?"

The former lieutenant and new stable owner waved a casual hand. "Oh, we are no doubt wealthier than all the gems in all the paintings could make us, should they exist and should we ever find them. Our pirate earl apparently provided for future generations the same way the last one tried to do, in his inept way."

Thea leaned against a delicate lady's chair, but in her excitement, she refused to sit. "We are rich? The manor can be repaired as it should? We can have servants?"

"That is my suggestion," Hunt agreed. "Others might differ. We will have to call a meeting of the entire family. Do you think anyone will attend but us if we don't mention money?"

Clare snickered, rightfully so. Most of the earl's widespread, wealthy family had expressed no interest in this isolated, decrepit family estate.

"You gave Davy and Oliver rewards for finding the gold." Thea carefully sounded out her next thought. "Does Arnaud receive one too? If he hadn't explored that grim dark dungeon, we'd never have known how the art reflected the tower."

"The manor has supported me," Arnaud argued, not bothering to look up while fitting a canvas into a frame.

"He gave the coins he found on the drive back to us. Probably saved most of them from the vicar and pried quite a few from everyone else." Hunt grinned. "But, yes, I think we can all agree that Arnaud deserves a reward. Besides, he'll just spend anything we give him on fixing up a studio in the tower, so it's no loss to us."

Arnaud glared at his cousin. "You'll reward me so I'll return the funds as rent on your tower? Fair enough. Just put the coins in the maintenance fund then. I don't need them."

Stupid, dense man. Thea put the back of her hand to her brow and began to slowly circle. "Oh, The Lady is laughing. She says gentlemen without property ought to have dowries like ladies."

"I have property," Arnaud said warily, approaching her in case she fell into a faint. "I have barren vineyards in France. If my uncle is any good, I might even have wine in a decade or so."

"No dowry needed, then." Thea collapsed against him, laughing as he caught her up.

It felt wonderful to laugh again.

"His future income as a famous artist ought to count," Clare added with a grin. "Any lady should approve."

Walker and Meera entered with their newborn just as Arnaud hauled Thea off her feet, probably to shake her from her hysterics. She laughed harder when he abruptly set her down at the infant's wail.

She escaped to admire the tiny bundle with good lungs. "Oh, he's so adorable! May I hold him?"

Meera handed over the bundle and collapsed in the lady's chair Thea had abandoned. "He is exhausting. Anyone may hold him at any time just so I might sit still and think for half a second."

"What are we celebrating?" Walker hovered over his wife's shoulder, keeping an eye on the infant as Thea carried him away.

Clare and Elsa leaped up to admire the struggling bundle in Thea's arms. Tiny tan fists beat the air.

"We are celebrating the future of Wycliffe Manor and Gravesyde Priory," Hunt declared, standing to pound his sleep-deprived friend on the back. "As our curate says, baptisms instead of funerals. Can we make brandy from apples?"

Walker studied him through bleary eyes. "You've been at the brandy already this evening? But if we have the funds Jack claims we have, we can expand and repair the orchards, if you like, hire help."

Before Hunt could explain his plans for the future, Henri and Patience entered, holding hands and looking dazed. Thea gave the infant to Clare and returned to Arnaud's side, catching his hand and squeezing it. She hoped he was prepared for this announcement. He ought to be. Henri had been mooning over the curate's sister ever since she'd arrived. Oddly, joy welled in her that people she was coming to know were finding happiness. She'd kept to herself for so long. . .

She glanced up at Arnaud, who had also been alone too long. He'd actually shaved for dinner this evening.

She thought it was just because she was nearest that he hugged her when Henri announced that he'd been granted permission from Paul and Mrs. Upton to properly court Patience.

The tall, buxom gardener grinned shyly. "By *courting*, he means we'll have banns proclaimed on Sunday."

Arnaud hugged Thea again before crossing the room to shake his brother's hand and kiss Patience's.

Thea laughed at the surprised looks on the company's faces.

They hadn't realized yet that this past week had released the comte from his ghosts, and they now harnessed the passionate whirlwind who had created that brilliant art.

Bemused, Hunt steepled his hands. "Perhaps I shall fix the backward clock now."

WYCLIFFE MANOR ARCHITECTURE

The manor is too extensive to draw on a single page. For those of you who like a mental image: first, picture a three-story, square stone structure with round towers on each corner and two-story Gothic windows in front. This would be the original manor built on the ruins of the priory grounds. There's a crypt below ground, a ground floor with public rooms, a second floor with bed chambers, and a third floor with schoolroom, storage, and servants' quarters. A central corridor traverses both public and bedchamber floors, with rooms to either side. A side hall leading to the portico entrance separates the long gallery and formal parlor.

The newer wings are essentially an entirely different building added on to the back of the old manor. Hallways stretch the width of the manor, between both wings, upstairs and down, ending in two square towers. These towers are basically stairwells and entrances to the wings. The wings are separated by the courtyard gardens stretching the width of the manor.

The ceilings are high and the bats live wherever they can.

GRAVESYDE PRIORY MYSTERIES

The Secrets of Wycliffe Manor
Book #1

Be wary of what you wish for. . .

In Regency England:

The descendant of adventuring—dead—aristo-crats, Clarissa Knightley supplements a modest inheritance by penning gothic novels that cost more than they earn. Upon learning that she has mysteri-ously inherited a share of an earl's estate, she rashly packs up her household. In remote Gravesyde Priory, she hopes to find a safe haven and family who will welcome her and her young nephew.

Instead, she discovers a drunken American army captain, his African servant, and ancient, surly care-takers. Terrified, prepared to flee, Clare is lured to linger by the prospect of secret diaries, hidden jewels, and an increasingly intriguing man. Then a killer strikes.

The crumbling manor's ominous and baffling history offers fascinating fodder for Clare's horror novels—if only she can survive real-life madmen and a spectral murderer who may seek the jewels at any price.

To Buy, Please Visit
https://patriciarice.com/series/gravesyde-priory/

~

The Mystery of the Missing Heiress
Book #2

Wycliffe Manor, a magnet for murder...

On a long-delayed errand to remote Wycliffe Manor, ex-Lieutenant Jack de Sackville stumbles across the murdered body of London dandy, Basil Culpepper, in the hedgerow, a long way from his usual haunts. To Jack's dismay, he discovers the earl's daughter Culpepper ruined hiding in Wycliffe's kitchen.

Disguised as a lowly cook, Lady Elspeth Villiers may have liked to shoot Culpepper for ruining her life, but she dropped out of sight for more immediate reasons than an old scandal—her wealth has become the focus of greedy men. The arrival of Jack, the man she's adored since childhood, along with Culpepper's corpse, mean her hiding place is no longer safe.

But once Lady Elsa reveals herself to the unconventional inhabitants of Wycliffe Manor, they become the protective family she has never known. Outraged to learn the beautiful woman he once loved and lost has become a target of greed, Jack joins the investigation into Culpepper's death.

With a murderer on the loose, the amateur sleuths must unravel a deadly tangle of kidnappers and counterfeiters or the Manor's eccentric inhabitants will be in as much danger as their cook.

To Buy, Please Visit
https://patriciarice.com/series/gravesyde-priory/

~

The Bones in the Orchard
Book #3

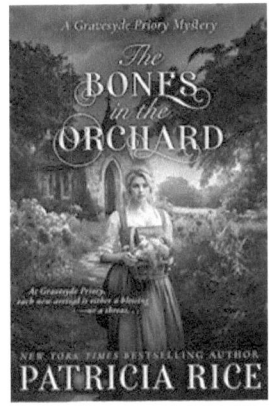

At Gravesyde Priory, each new arrival is either a blessing —or a threat. . .

Wycliffe Manor has been neglected for decades. Its new heirs are determined to create a welcoming home. Yet soon after the latest family moves into the nearby parsonage, bones are uncovered in the orchard. . . and odd strangers arrive.

When her curate father returns his family to Gravesyde for the marriages of the manor's heirs, gawky spinster Patience Upton has high expectations—until her father is murdered. Shock at learning her father had a mysterious past, leads to alarm that the killer may have been after his notebook, which she now possesses.

After the chapel is ransacked and a witness killed, it's clear the murderer isn't done. Desperate to find the truth, Patience accepts the aid of Henri Lavigne, Wycliffe Manor's smooth-talking rake. Intent on saving his new home and family from danger, Henri is drawn to the clergyman's guileless daughter but wonders if she hasn't reason to conceal the killer's identity.

Before there will be any courting, much less marrying, the inhabitants of the manor realize if they want a chance at a future, they must hunt the killer themselves. But are they hunting one murderer. . . or more?

To Buy, Please Visit
https://patriciarice.com/series/gravesyde-priory/

~

**The Question of the Wedding Pearls
Book #4**

Will death ruin the perfect wedding?

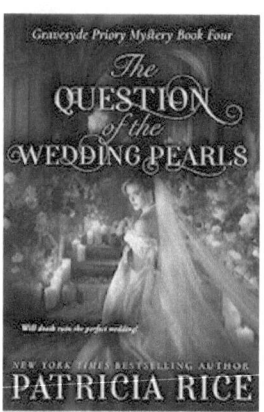

Bestselling author Patricia Rice brings you another haunting country house mystery in Regency England. . .

Spinster and secret novelist Clarissa Knightley and her gruff American engineer, Captain Huntley, along with their friend and cousin, the Honorable Jack de Sackville and Lady Elspeth, are to wed at last! In anticipation of the double wedding, friends and family are gathering at moldering Wycliffe Manor—until a dying stranger is discovered on the neglected grounds.

Despite the tragedy, aristocratic wedding guests, and their retinues, foreign and domestic, continue to arrive, not all by invitation. Compounding the bedlam, tales of missing pearls and ghostly encounters precede a second alarming death. Fearing that a killer lurks inside the manor walls, Clare and Hunt are swept up in a whirlwind of secret bigotries, deceit, and increasing peril. Before their family's joyful plans veer into heartbreak, can they put an end to mayhem and catch a killer?

To Buy, Please Visit
https://patriciarice.com/series/gravesyde-priory/

The Case of the Purloined Pages
Book #5

Death stalks the library. . .Bestselling author Patricia Rice brings you another haunting country house mystery in Regency England. . .

Minerva Peniston, intrepid spinster and booklover, is determined to capture the villain who tried to shoot a duke at a book auction— imperiling her father's position and the only home she's ever known. And now the same wealthy bibliophiles are gathering at Wycliffe Manor. . .

Paul Upton, over-educated and impoverished curate, has volunteered to assist the residents of Wycliffe Manor in preparing for a book auction to save the village and the manor's future. When an intriguing wallflower drags him into aiding her quest to find a potential killer, he agrees for her safety, and to keep trouble from upending the long-awaited nuptials of the manor's owner.

Despite their efforts, Minerva's chatty book-collecting friend is strangled before the auction begins. A killer on the loose threatens to upend both sale and wedding. Paul and Minerva must determine what secrets the garrulous victim revealed. . . and to whom. . . before the murderer strikes again.

With valuable manuscripts at risk and a half dozen more potential victims on hand, only an unlikely white-knight and mousy spinster can save the auction and the wedding. As much as Minerva adores books, even she knows they aren't worth dying for.

To Buy, Please Visit
https://patriciarice.com/series/gravesyde-priory/

ABOUT THE AUTHOR

With several million books in print and *New York Times* and *USA Today's* bestseller lists under her belt, former CPA Patricia Rice is one of romance's hottest authors. Her emotionally-charged contemporary and historical romances have won numerous awards, including the *RT Book Reviews* Reviewers Choice and Career Achievement Awards. Her books have been honored as Romance Writers of America RITA® finalists in the historical, regency and contemporary categories.

A firm believer in happily-ever-after, Patricia Rice is married to her high school sweetheart and has two children. A native of Kentucky and New York, a past resident of North Carolina and Missouri, she currently resides in Southern California, and now does accounting only for herself.

ALSO BY PATRICIA RICE

The World of Magic:

The Unexpected Magic Series

MAGIC IN THE STARS

WHISPER OF MAGIC

THEORY OF MAGIC

AURA OF MAGIC

CHEMISTRY OF MAGIC

NO PERFECT MAGIC

The Magical Malcolms Series

MERELY MAGIC

MUST BE MAGIC

THE TROUBLE WITH MAGIC

THIS MAGIC MOMENT

MUCH ADO ABOUT MAGIC

MAGIC MAN

The California Malcolms Series

THE LURE OF SONG AND MAGIC

TROUBLE WITH AIR AND MAGIC

THE RISK OF LOVE AND MAGIC

Crystal Magic

SAPPHIRE NIGHTS

TOPAZ DREAMS

CRYSTAL VISION

WEDDING GEMS

AZURE SECRETS

AMBER AFFAIRS

MOONSTONE SHADOWS

THE WEDDING GIFT

MAD MARIA'S DAUGHTER

ARTFUL DECEPTIONS

ALL A WOMAN WANTS

Rogues & Desperadoes Series

LORD ROGUE

MOONLIGHT AND MEMORIES

SHELTER FROM THE STORM

WAYWARD ANGEL

DENIM AND LACE

CHEYENNES LADY

Dark Lords and Dangerous Ladies Series

LOVE FOREVER AFTER

SILVER ENCHANTRESS

DEVIL'S LADY

DASH OF ENCHANTMENT

INDIGO MOON

Too Hard to Handle

TEXAS LILY

TEXAS ROSE

TEXAS TIGER

TEXAS MOON

Mystic Isle Series

MYSTIC ISLE

MYSTIC GUARDIAN

MYSTIC RIDER

MYSTIC WARRIOR

Mysteries:

Family Genius Series

EVIL GENIUS

UNDERCOVER GENIUS

CYBER GENIUS

TWIN GENIUS

TWISTED GENIUS

Tales of Love and Mystery

BLUE CLOUDS

GARDEN OF DREAMS

NOBODY'S ANGEL

VOLCANO

CALIFORNIA GIRL

Historical Mysteries

Graneside Priory Series

THE SECRETS OF WYCLIFFE MANOR

THE MYSTERY OF THE MISSING HEIRESS

THE BONES IN THE ORCHARD

THE QUESTION OF THE WEDDING PEARLS

THE CASE OF THE PURLOINED PAGES

THE DILEMMA OF A DEAD SCHOLAR

Urban Fantasies

Writing as Jamie Quaid

Saturn's Daughters

BOYFRIEND FROM HELL

DAMN HIM TO HELL

GIVING HIM HELL

ABOUT BOOK VIEW CAFÉ

Book View Café (BVC) is an author-owned cooperative of professional writers, publishing in a variety of genres including fantasy, romance, mystery, and science fiction — with 90% of the proceeds going to the authors. Since its debut in 2008, BVC has gained a reputation for producing high-quality ebooks. BVC's ebooks are DRM-free and are distributed around the world. The cooperative is now bringing that same quality to its print editions.

BVC authors include New York Times and USA Today bestsellers as well as winners and nominees of many prestigious awards.